About The Author

Della Galton is a novelist, short story writer, and journalist. Writing is her passion. When she is not writing she enjoys walking her dogs in the beautiful Dorset countryside where she lives.

Find out more at dellagalton.co.uk

CW00858240

The Morning After

After

The Life Before

Della Galton

soundhaven books
www.soundhaven.com

Published 2015 in Great Britain,
by soundhaven books (soundhaven.com limited)
http://www.soundhaven.com

Please visit
www.soundhaven.com
for contact details

ISBN: 978-1507730799

British Cataloguing Publication data:
A catalogue record of this book is available from
the British Library

This book is also available as an ebook.
Please visit
www.soundhaven.com
for more details.

*For everyone
who is living with addiction.*

With love.

Chapter One

SJ gave a very deep sigh and glanced once more at the phone. For the last two hours and twenty-two minutes, not that she was counting, the phone had become the focal point of her front room. No, not just her front room – her entire life.

The phone had sat in its cradle on the table by the television. She had sat on the sofa next to it, flicking surreptitious glances at it, while pretending to read Cosmopolitan and occasionally getting up to check that the display was still working in case there was a power cut.

"What if there is a power cut?" she'd said to Penny when they'd done the handover. "I have the plug-in kind of phone – it won't work unless it has power."

"I wouldn't worry – they'll phone back."

"But what if they don't? I thought you said it's a matter of life and death. What if they've spent the last three weeks plucking up the courage to phone the helpline and this is their final desperate plea for help and then no one answers because there's a power cut. What if they die?"

"They might die anyway," Penny pointed out, with unnecessary sharpness, SJ thought, considering she was only trying to get things right. And considering that Penny had actually said – when she'd been trying to persuade SJ to sign up for phone service – that the helpline was a matter of life and death.

"We are the fifth emergency service," she'd said, a mite pompously, SJ had thought. Especially as she hadn't bothered to explain what she meant. Clearly, as everyone knew, police, ambulance and fire were the first three emergency services. But what was the fourth? And why weren't they the fourth?

It was slightly crushing to realise that the Alcoholics Anonymous helpline couldn't be all that important. Not if they were only the fifth.

"What if I miss the phone ringing because I'm out of the room – say I'm in the bathroom?" SJ had asked.

"I thought you said you had a carry-around phone." There was a gleam of triumph in Penny's voice.

"Yes I do, but if there was a power cut I'd be using my back up phone. My in-case-of-emergency, old fashioned, plug-straight-into-the-mains phone, wouldn't I? So I won't be able to carry that around, obviously." SJ sighed patiently and resisted the urge to add, 'so what have you got to say to that then, Miss Goody Two Shoes, know-it-all, pompous Penny?' Which she would have done without hesitation once when someone like Penny wound her up.

But which she couldn't do now because she was no longer *that* person any more. She was no longer judgmental and impatient and prickly – which she'd only ever been because she was lacking in self-esteem obviously. These days, she was serene and calm and peaceful. Serenity was her middle name. She'd considered, in fact, making Serenity her actual middle name by deed poll. Only there didn't seem much point because no one ever asked you what your middle name was anyway. And deed polls were probably expensive.

"Someone might be trying to get through right now while we're talking," Penny said wearily.

"Right. I see. Yes, okay. Point taken."

"Someone might be dying right now. So maybe if I could just put the phone down, SJ? Please – if you're ready to take over. Are you?"

"Of course. Sorry. Um bye."

"Goodbye, SJ."

Penny disconnected. The phone rang almost immediately and SJ was so surprised she dropped the handset. Then when she reached to pick it up she knocked over her cup of calming peppermint tea which was on the glass-topped coffee table between her and the phone. Oh crap. The phone was still ringing. The tea pooled across the glass and began to drip down the wooden leg.

Double crap. What if there was some raging, desperate, suicidal alcoholic on the other end of the phone? What if they were pissed off because they hadn't been able to get through? What if they shouted at her? What if they were an utter maniac? Don't judge, SJ. Deep breaths, in, out, in, out, in, out. Try to stay calm. Serene and calm is where it's at. If you feel serene your voice will be serene. Nothing to it. She punched the green button with a finger, intending to say, 'Yep,' in that ultra-cool voice that ultra-cool receptionists – usually the ones that worked in PR and marketing companies – were fond of using.

What actually came out of her mouth wasn't yep. It was yip. She tried again. "Yip, yep, yip,

3

yap." Oh crap. Now she sounded like the next door neighbour's Jack Russell terrier.

"SJ it's me." Penny's voice held a note of incredulity. "I'm just – er checking that the phone line transferred okay. "Is – everything all right?"

"It's fine. Absolutely fine. Couldn't be better. Sorry, I was practising my – um – my dog whisperer voice. I'm doing evening classes."

"You're doing evening classes in dog whispering!"

"Yep. I mean yip. Yip yip, yap, yippety yip – ha ha! What do you think?"

"Very – er – authentic, but do you suppose you could do it when you're not answering the helpline?"

"Of course. Sure. Sorry."

SJ disconnected and put her head in her hands, before realising belatedly that her elbows were now in a pool of peppermint tea. Fantastic. Why had she ever thought she could do this? She must be mad. She shouldn't have volunteered. She should have contented herself with making tea at meetings or acting as treasurer. Even she couldn't make too much of a hash-up of that. What did she know about giving up drinking anyway? What was she going to say to someone if they did phone up the AA helpline? Oh it's easy – you just swap your vodka for a mug of peppermint tea. Nothing to it. No one was going to believe that, were they? Everyone knew it wasn't easy to give up. Not when you'd been drinking on a daily basis for months, or years, or possibly even decades.

She'd only managed to give up because she'd had an utterly brilliant counsellor who she'd gone to see, week after week after week. And let's face it she probably wouldn't have done that if he hadn't also been utterly gorgeous and if she hadn't also had the most humungous crush on him. Would she have given up drinking at all if she hadn't fallen in love with her counsellor?

Ironically, it was the thought of the utterly gorgeous Kit that snapped her out of the beating herself up mood she'd fallen into. She cleared up the peppermint tea spillage – grabbed her iPad from the kitchen and found her latest To Do list. At the top of the page she wrote:

Things not to say when answering the AA helpline

1. Yip or yap, or yippety yip – or any possible derivative of the word yip.

2. Yep. (Mainly because it was very hard to inject a decent amount of empathy and sympathy and understanding into the word yep. Yes with a question mark would be better – or yeah if you stretched it out a bit or maybe even yo – that was a pretty cool word around youngsters, these days. Except that yo didn't sound very sympathetic either. *Yo dude – you gotta problem with your drinking? Hey that's tough.* And anyway she wasn't exactly young. Forty-two might be the answer to life, the universe and everything – but as an age it was well over the hill. How on earth had she got to forty-two anyway?)

3. *"Hello, this is the Alcoholics Anonymous helpline – how can I help?"*

That would have made the most sense. But unfortunately she couldn't say that in case it was her mother phoning, or her sister, Alison, or her best friend, Tanya. Not that her mother and her sister and Tanya didn't know she was a recovering alcoholic. But there were people in her life, these days, who didn't know. And it wasn't the sort of thing she wanted to advertise when she answered her own phone. That was the trouble – she had no way of telling whether she was answering a call diverted from the helpline or whether it was someone who wanted to speak to her. It was a conundrum.

Although not that much of one because the phone hadn't rung for – what – coming up for three hours now anyway. Soon her phone service shift would be over and she could go back to doing her housework or planning her Poetry and a Pint session. In fact, what the heck, why didn't she do that now? What was she waiting for?

She had barely reached the door when the phone began to ring. SJ stared at it in surprise. She wasn't imagining it, was she? It was ringing? She took a deep breath and strolled back into the room. This time she was going to get it right. She would be pleasant, polite, with a touch of concern. She would be relaxed, calm, the model helpline attendant. She felt her chest swell a little with pride at the thought. This was her chance to make a difference.

She picked up the phone. "Hello, can I help you?" Oh so simple – why hadn't she thought of that before?

"Hello," the girl's voice was tearstained. "Is that the AA?"

"Yes it is."

There was a small silence and SJ wondered if she'd sounded sympathetic enough. Maybe she'd been a bit matter of fact, or even abrupt. She sat back down on the sofa, pressing the phone close to her ear. "Are you okay?" she said softly.

"I don't think I am," said the girl and now she sounded so scared and so vulnerable that SJ forgot all about herself and how she was coming across and she just wanted to say something, anything that would help – even if it was only for a few moments, a few seconds.

"You've done the hardest part," she said. "You've just phoned for help. You've made a phone call that could save your life. I know how hard it is to do that. I did it myself once."

"Did you used to drink a lot then? I mean, really a lot. I don't just mean wine. I mean, well, bottles and bottles of voddie?" The girl's voice grew a little fainter and SJ realised she'd drawn away from the phone. She could hear sounds in the background, the clink of a bottle against a glass and the unmistakable glug of liquid.

"Are you drinking now?"

"No," the girl said. There was a pause and SJ heard her swallowing and the slur in her voice when she spoke again. "No, I'm not drinking. I'm not phoning for myself. I'm phoning about a friend."

"And is your friend able to come to the phone, honey?"

Another pause to swallow. "No – not really. She's er... she's asleep. Maybe when she wakes up."

"Sure," SJ said, knowing there was no friend. "So tell me about you. Are you okay?"

There was another long pause followed by a little beep and SJ realised as she held the phone away from her ear again that the display was blank – that the girl had hung up. She sat back on the sofa feeling terribly sad and also a little sick. So her very first call and she'd done nothing. Nothing at all. Somewhere out there was a very scared, very lonely, very drunk young girl and she – SJ – had been utterly powerless to help her.

Chapter Two

A fine mist of rain hung in the air and the pavements shone wetly in the light of the street lamps as SJ emerged from Camden Road Station. She contemplated jumping into a cab, but that was crazy, the restaurant was only half a mile away. She'd forgotten to pick up an umbrella too and her ultra-cool faux leather jacket had no hood, but Tanya wasn't going to care what her hair looked like. That's if her long suffering friend was even still there – she was already ten minutes late. She hooked her phone out of her bag and sent a text. *Sorry. Be with you in five.*

It was less than five minutes later when she bowled in through the doors of The Oak and the Canary – goodness knows why it was called that – which was her and Tanya's current favourite vegetarian restaurant. Neither of them was actually vegetarian but The Oak was one of those rare places in Camden which did awesome food at rock bottom prices. The atmosphere was amazing and the waiters were uber-cool as well as eye candy if you were on a girlie night out.

Tanya, looking beautiful in a navy and cream Versace jacket, stood up to greet her. "You're soaked."

"No, I'm not. It's not as bad as it looks." She took off the jacket, and shook raindrops over the floor, before hanging it over the back of the chair opposite Tanya. "Sorry I'm late. Bad day."

"It's not a problem. I got you a tonic. Ice and a slice." Tanya smiled her beautiful smile. "How times have changed."

SJ slid into her seat, feeling some of the tension rising out of her and away just at the sight of Tanya. Her friend was like a warm balm, always glamorous, but never too perfect; she was a mixture of slinky elegance and earth mother. The earth mother part had increased since she'd had Bethany but the slinky elegance was still very much in evidence. SJ had often thought that if they were animals Tanya would be a cat – the kind that frequented Egyptian temples – a Pharaoh's cat with the grace of several centuries of royal breeding. Whereas she would be a dog – panting and lollopy and always knocking things over with her tail.

Tanya waved a hand – her green, slightly slanting eyes lit with warmth. "Earth calling SJ – is tonic okay? They didn't have Slimline so I got normal. But if you'd rather a tea?"

"Tonic's fine. Sorry." SJ blinked a few times – and the Egyptian temples faded away into the reality of the glass tables and abstract paintings of The Oak and Canary. It was busy tonight. Tanya had probably got the last table. "It's really good to see you," she said. "Have you ordered?"

"Of course I haven't ordered – but I have decided."

"Let me guess. Butternut squash lasagne. Me too," she said, seeing the acquiescence on Tanya's face. "It's hard to have anything else, isn't it? So how's things? How's Bethany? How's Michael?"

"Bethany's great." Tanya's eyes softened at the mention of her daughter. "I got my first Mother's Day card – look." She reached into her bag and produced a piece of paper which, as far as SJ could see, had a red crayoned circle in the centre of the page, with lines radiating out from it, and beneath, a blue crayoned squiggle mixed with orange. On the top were crayoned, in red and blue, the words. *Hap Mot Da.* A work in progress then, SJ thought. How cute that they let them do that kind of stuff in play school, these days. Her school would have had her sitting at the table until she'd finished – whether you like it or not, Sarah-Jane Carter.

"What do you think?" Tanya's eyes were starry with pride.

"It's fabulous," SJ said. "An unfinished masterpiece – hugely creative."

"It is finished," Tanya said with a puzzled frown. "Look, that's me with my red hair – obviously on a wild day. And she's even got my Gucci chain link belt – and gold sandals – see?"

"Um!" *Really!* SJ leaned closer, spotting suddenly that the missing words weren't missing at all but written in yellow crayon – and not as visible as the darker colours.

"Ah," she said with a sweep of her hand. "Of course. I see it now. I haven't got my glasses on."

"You don't wear glasses."

Luckily at that moment the waitress arrived, and, by the time they'd ordered butternut squash lasagne with a side order of baby leaf salad, feta and olives, and cheesy garlic bread because SJ

11

could never resist that, her imaginary glasses were forgotten.

While they ate, SJ told Tanya about her first attempt at phone service and the girl who had hung up.

"Oh, sweetie," Tanya said, all concern. "That must have been heart breaking. But it isn't your fault. Maybe she just wasn't – what is it you guys say – ready to stop yet?"

"Or maybe I put her off," SJ said. "Because I was rubbish at saying the right thing. Sometimes I think I've learned loads about staying sober and sometimes I think I've learned nothing at all. I mean when I stopped drinking I had Dorothy, didn't I? – and she always knew exactly the right thing to say. She was – is – the wisest person I've ever met."

"It's not the same thing." Tanya's hand slid over SJ's and SJ noticed with a shock that she had a chipped nail. Tanya's nails were her pride and joy. All through her pregnancy, all through the early days of being a mum she'd kept them looking beautiful. *'I might have baby sick on my shoulder but hey my nails look good, don't they?'* had become a bit of a catch phrase. But Tanya clearly wasn't aware of her nails. Tanya had an intense look in her eyes.

"Dorothy had been sober for years and years and years when you met her, SJ. And besides, you had given up by the time you started listening to her – this girl was still pissed."

"She must have been so desperate," SJ said sadly.

"Well, maybe she'll phone again."

"Maybe. Are you going to have dessert – or shall I just order coffee?"

"I'm a bit too full for dessert." Tanya glanced at the menu, her long lashes in profile to SJ and, for no reason that she could put her finger on, SJ felt a flicker of unease. She looked back at Tanya's chipped nail – it was the ring finger on her left hand. Maybe she hadn't noticed it. Maybe SJ should point it out. But for some reason when she opened her mouth instead of saying, 'what happened to your nail?' she said, "So how's Michael anyway? He's not been pestering you to have a little brother or sister for Bethany lately then?"

Tanya blinked a couple of times very quickly and then she looked back towards SJ and SJ saw, to her very great alarm, that Tanya's eyes were full of tears.

"Hey," she said quickly. "What's wrong? Oh crap, Tanya, have I said something out of turn? I'm so sorry."

"You've not said anything out of turn. It's just me." Tanya was unzipping a compartment on the outside of her bag and pulling out a mini pack of tissues. She blew her nose. "Sorry," she said. "I'm probably just being ridiculous and paranoid. In fact, I am. I'm sure I am."

Ridiculous and paranoid weren't words SJ would ever have associated with Tanya. She was level-headed and sensible. She told her this, in the interests of reassuring her, while Tanya got out another tissue and twined it round her fingers until it disintegrated on the table. Then SJ ordered coffee, because the waitress clearly wanted them to either order something else or go, and then she leaned forward and said, "What do you think you're being ridiculous and paranoid about?"

"It's Michael," Tanya said quietly. "I think he's been – well, I think he's been seeing someone."

"Another woman?" SJ couldn't have been more shocked if Tanya had said her husband had decided to take up sumo wrestling. Michael was the gentlest, kindest, most compassionate, most un-womanising man SJ had ever met. "Surely not," she said. "He worships the ground you walk on. You know he does. And since Bethany came along too – well he's got everything he ever wanted, hasn't he?"

Tears were dripping down Tanya's nose now. She swiped at them with the back of her hand. "I wasn't going to do this," she said. "I was so determined not to do this. I shouldn't have started talking about it."

"Yes, you should. That's exactly what you should have done."

"I shouldn't have started talking about it in here. Look, SJ, maybe we should skip the coffee. I feel a fool sitting here bawling my eyes out. Shall we just get the bill?"

"I'll get the bill," SJ said, feeling, for a change, that she was the grown up one. She was the sensible parent and Tanya the child. "You wait there. I'll cancel the coffee too. Then we can go back to mine. If you want, I mean?"

Tanya nodded. Ten minutes later they were outside. It was still raining, but Tanya had an

14

umbrella, which she put up instantly, so they were cocooned against the elements, cocooned together amidst the busy, street lit London pavement, their heads close so that SJ could smell the *Classique* that Tanya always wore and the coconut-shampoo scent of her hair. And it was like this, beneath the security of the umbrella, out of sight and out of hearing of the rest of the world, that Tanya confessed quietly, "I think Michael is having an affair with another man."

Chapter Three

The warmth of SJ's tiny lounge, soft in the glow of the wood-burning stove, which she'd lit when they got in, felt like a sanctuary from the rain spattered darkness of the city. And yet there was a part of her mind that wished they were still sitting in The Oak and Canary – having a good old moan about the vintage clothes shop Tanya had found in Camden where she'd bought a Versace bag that had turned out to be a fake, or about the unofficial blacklist of bad-paying businesses that was being passed around via Facebook between small firms of accountants like the one where Tanya worked. Or even about the drunk girl who had hung up on SJ. Safe, normal, day-to-day problems, which would be done and dusted and forgotten about in a few weeks. SJ would have given a lot to be talking about anything other than the possibility of Michael being an adulterer, Michael, who she had liked and respected and known almost half her life.

She would have given anything not to have had her closest friend sitting on her sofa, gulping out between heartbroken sobs that she thought they really were over this time.

"I can't cope with any more, SJ. I really can't. I coped with him being Lizzie. I thought that was pretty bloody tolerant of me – how many wives would be okay with their husbands dressing up as bloody women? I mean, honestly, how many?" She broke off to take another large gulp of wine from the glass SJ had given her when they'd got

16

in. For the first time in several months SJ wished she could join her. She would have very much liked to have knocked back a bottle or two of good Merlot. To have taken the edge off the hurt and the shock. If she'd been drunk she could maybe even have lightened the mood a little, made some jokes about... about what exactly? Affairs and deceit and betrayals weren't a joking matter, however you looked at them. She of all people knew that.

Wishing the wine didn't smell quite so inviting now she was at such close proximity to it, she sat next to Tanya on the sofa. "Hey, are you absolutely sure that this man, Andy, isn't just a friend? What makes you think that he's anything more? Has Michael actually told you he's having an affair with him?"

Tanya rubbed her forehead, leaving a red mark on her pale skin. "No," she said quietly. "But it's the way they talk to each other, SJ. Or at least the way Michael talks to Andy – I've overheard him on the phone. Oh you know, all soft and flirty and interested. Once or twice I've walked in on Michael and he's been sitting with his feet up on the sofa, utterly relaxed, and laughing. I know it sounds mad."

"It does sound a bit mad," SJ said with a small frown. "To think he's having an affair because of the way he talks and the way he sits on the sofa, I mean."

"It's not just that. I *know* him, SJ. We've been married for bloody eighteen years. I ought to know him." She sounded as though she was going to burst into tears again and SJ stroked her shoulder.

"I know you know him. I'm sorry. I do get it."

"How did *you* know? With Derek, I mean? How did you know he was…?" She paused, tactful even in the midst of her own anguish. How typical of Tanya.

"Carrying on with my sister," SJ finished with a wry little smile. "I found a receipt in his jean pockets – a receipt for a takeaway pizza he said he'd had in town when I'd been away. There were two pizzas on it – and one of them was a Hawaiian, which was Alison's favourite." She gave a little shudder at the memory and Tanya raised her eyebrows.

"And you think that's more rational than me jumping to conclusions from the way Michael speaks to someone?"

SJ smiled. "Point taken. But there was a bit more to it than that. Derek lied to me when I asked him if something had been going on between him and Alison and so did she. That's when I really knew."

"So do you think I should speak to Andy, then?" Tanya finished her wine but made no move to refill her glass. SJ wondered if she should do it for her. But despite the fact she hadn't had a drink for more than four and a half years she still wasn't entirely comfortable about pouring the stuff out for anyone else. Tanya was clearly oblivious to all this. She was frowning now. "Maybe I should, SJ, maybe that's the way forward, but our paths don't really cross. I only ever really met him that one time when we were

18

at Ruby's. I could see then that they got on well, that they were very comfortable with each other, but it wasn't till later that I cottoned on to the fact it was more than that. It wasn't until I realised that they were texting each other regularly."

"And how did you know they were doing that?" SJ slanted a surreptitious glance at the clock above the wood- burning stove. It was ten to eleven. She had an early shift at Mortimer's tomorrow – she was covering for one of the other waitresses. Also, she hadn't quite finished her handouts for Poetry and a Pint tomorrow night, having intended to do them in the morning. She suppressed a yawn. She'd still have time.

"He told me," Tanya said. "Michael's never been one for texting – he's always said it's much easier to phone someone. But suddenly he was texting all the time. He had to tell me something. He told me he was talking to Andy because they were on exactly the same wavelength. Andy has been cross-dressing for years – he's not your average trannie, but he is gay. Michael told me that too." She looked at SJ thoughtfully. "Are you tired? Do you need to go to bed?"

"No. I'm not tired in the least. What about you? Do you have an early start?"

"Only for Bethany." Tanya glanced at her mobile. "Shit, I didn't realise it was so late."

"You're welcome to stop over. That sofa pulls out into a bed. That's why I bought it – so all my friends could still have a drink and not have to drive." It was hard to keep the hint of pride out of her voice. Although, to be fair, she'd never

19

actually used that sofa. Tanya was the only one of her friends who'd ever been in the habit of stopping over and she hadn't done that since she'd had Bethany.

"I can't, SJ. I need to get back. They'll wonder where I am. But thank you for offering. And for listening." She put a hand out and touched SJ's arm. "You're right. I'll find a way to speak to Andy."

"Have you spoken to Michael?"

"Not really, no." Tanya stretched her hands above her head, arching her back like a cat. "He's been pretty busy at work."

"Don't you think you should do that first?" SJ felt a little jolt of shock. Once again she felt as though she was the parent and Tanya the child. "Tanya, seriously, that would be top of my list."

"Okay, I'll do that too."

While Tanya phoned for a cab, SJ took the half-finished bottle of Merlot and her empty glass and her own untouched tonic water – there was only so much tonic you could drink – back into the kitchen and left them on the side. A few moments later, having waved Tanya off, she paused in the doorway of the kitchen to put off the light. She felt too hyped up for sleep. She really should have put the cork back in the Merlot and asked Tanya to take it with her.

Why hadn't she done that? 'So you can put it back in the fridge for the next time she comes,' her internal voice supplied helpfully. *'Yeah right,'* interrupted another not so helpful voice. *'Don't you mean so you can finish it off yourself?'*

"No." SJ said out loud, slightly shocked. "No, I don't."

She was just tired, she told herself. Tired and stressed – and worried about Tanya. She had never seen her friend in such a state. SJ had a feeling that Tanya might be right. Her marriage might be on the rocks – but she was not convinced that Michael was seeing another man. It didn't make any kind of sense at all.

'Who's going to know if you drink it?' drawled the voice. It sounded suspiciously like Alco. Alco – the imaginary demon king of alcohol who had lived in SJ's head and taunted her about her inability to stop drinking. But she hadn't heard his voice for a very long time. She had thought she'd heard the last from Alco. So maybe it was true what she'd heard at AA meetings then. Maybe it didn't matter how long you'd been sober. Maybe there would always be times when the idea of a drink popped into your head. Maybe you stayed vulnerable for the rest of your life.

'Once an alky, always an alky,' crowed the voice. *'Give it up, SJ. You can't win.'*

SJ moved trance-like towards the Merlot. With hands that didn't feel like hers she picked it up. She was breathing very fast and her fingers were shaking. The bottle felt slippery and hot and for a moment she held it in front of her and studied the label. *Louis De Camponac.* 2012. She hadn't bought it – she didn't buy wine any more. It had got left here after her house-warming party, six months ago. She had known that as long as it wasn't open, it wasn't a risk. So she had tucked it at the back of a cupboard, thinking it might come in useful one day.

But it hadn't because Tanya was the only one of her friends, these days, who still drank and she always brought her own and – at SJ's request – took any unfinished bottles away with her again at the end of the evening. It was a measure of how upset she'd been that she hadn't thought to take this one, SJ decided. She yawned. It was now very late and she had to get up very early. What the hell was she doing sitting here looking at a bottle of what – to her – might as well have been poison?

In one swift movement she tipped it down the sink. It swirled around the plug hole like blood, the smell of it made her light-headed, and even when it was gone the ghost of it stained the enamel sweetly pink. She turned on the taps, but she had to run them for a long time to erase the memory.

Chapter Four

Good reasons to phone your sponsor when she is on holiday and supposed to be enjoying herself

1. You spent fifteen minutes staring at an open bottle of Merlot the night before last and wondering whether or not to finish it off.

2. You are worried that you are rubbish at answering the AA helpline and are contemplating giving it up and letting someone saner and better qualified do it.

3. She is a good friend and she's been away a fortnight already and you just fancy speaking to her.

SJ paused from typing her list and put her chin in her hands. She was sure she hadn't spent half as much of her time writing lists before she'd got an iPad – which she'd justified buying for work, but which mostly got used for other stuff, such as following Sherlock Holmes on Twitter. Okay so she knew it wasn't the real Sherlock Holmes but the person tweeting for him was brilliantly funny and in character, and they had 250,000 followers so clearly she wasn't the only one who thought so.

The Photo Booth app was hugely entertaining too. You could manipulate your own reflection through the virtual equivalent of a fairground mirror and take pictures of yourself with puffed up cheeks like a hamster, a massively elongated nose and tiny piggy eyes. Last week she had emailed one of those pictures to her mother for a laugh and her mother had been on the phone ten minutes later in tears.

"Mum it was a joke. Okay, I'm sorry. I didn't mean to worry you."

"Well, you did worry me, Sarah-Jane. I didn't know what to think. Seeing a picture of your face all scrunched up like that – all swollen and distorted and yellow."

"Yellow?" SJ had grabbed her iPad and hunted for the photo with some alarm. "It wasn't yellow. Was it?"

"I think we may have a problem with our monitor," her mother said, sniffing and then pausing to give her nose a good blow. "Now I'm looking at the screen properly, all our emails seem to have a yellowish tinge. Does that sound right to you, Sarah-Jane?"

"Check the cable's plugged in properly," SJ said, but her mother had gone on as if she hadn't heard.

"I thought you must be ill when I saw that photo, or that you'd got yourself into trouble again – you know with all that drinking nonsense."

All that drinking nonsense was as close as her mother ever got to accepting that her daughter was a recovering alcoholic. SJ had tried to explain lots of times about being in recovery since she'd given up, but her parents had never really got it. Which wasn't surprising as they didn't really get her, SJ thought ruefully. She'd always been a misfit. They understood their younger daughter better. Alison had a sensible job, a proper job – she owned a beauty salon – she didn't mess about

24

teaching poetry which neither of her parents understood. She'd also given them grandchildren, which equated to at least a hundred million brownie points. Oh, and she'd stayed married to her first husband, whereas SJ had had the audacity to go through two husbands already. Never mind that her first marriage had broken down as a direct result of Alison. That didn't count.

Not that she was envious of Alison. Yes, she might have been once, but she was over that now. She'd worked through all that. They were practically best friends. Or might have been had Tanya not been her best friend, SJ mused thoughtfully.

She'd had to apologise at least three more times and fix her mother's yellow tinged screen before she'd been forgiven. So maybe the Photo Booth app wasn't quite such an asset as she'd thought. Mind you, it was definitely a whole lot easier writing To Do lists on an iPad because she always lost them when she wrote them on bits of paper.

SJ stared back at her list of 'good reasons for phoning your sponsor on holiday' and decided that any one of them was perfectly valid. Especially as Dorothy had told her when she'd gone that she shouldn't hesitate – even if she just fancied a chat.

SJ dialled the number on her mobile. She wasn't sure exactly where Dorothy was – she was on a ten-week cruise. Keeping her fingers crossed that she wasn't on the other side of the world and that it wasn't the middle of the night she listened to the phone ringing.

"Hello, hen." To SJ's relief Dorothy sounded far too lively to have been roused from her bed. "It's good to hear from you. Is everything okay? How's London?"

"Everything's fine. Absolutely brilliant. Couldn't be better." SJ could have wept with relief just at the sound of Dorothy's familiar lilting voice. "Just phoning for a chat," she added for good measure. "Nothing important."

"SJ it's me you're talking to. So shall we cut to the chase? I don't imagine this wee phone call will be cheap."

"No. Of course. Sorry. Do you want me to go?"

Dorothy sighed. "I do not want you to go, hen, no. I want you to tell me what's going on with you."

"Okay. Where are you?"

"Yangon. It's the former capital of Burma," Dorothy explained patiently.

"Right," SJ said, none the wiser. She told her about Tanya, though not in much detail because it was personal to Tanya, and about the girl on the helpline and then finally, slightly more reluctantly, about the wine.

"And you were surprised to feel like this, I assume?"

"Well, yes. Yes I was actually. I haven't felt like that for a long time. I wanted to drink it, Dorothy. I actually contemplated drinking it."

"Darling, you're an alcoholic. Of course you contemplated drinking it. That's what we do."

"But I've given up all that."

"For today. Yes. That doesn't mean you'll never be tempted again. You were tired. You were upset because of Tanya. You were feeling sad because you didn't help that wee lassie on the helpline. Although, in reality, you don't know that you didn't help her. You may well have helped her. You may be the first person who's ever listened to her. That's huge, SJ."

"She was so pissed I doubt she'll remember talking to me," SJ said, feeling a spark of hope despite herself.

"Well, maybe she will. Maybe she won't. Time will tell. So have you finished beating yourself up now?"

"Yes."

"Good."

"Thank you."

"You're welcome. And, SJ – get yourself to a meeting."

"Okay."

One day, SJ decided, as Dorothy disconnected, she would be like her sponsor. She would be calm and serene and supremely wise in all things. She would be the person you wanted to speak to in a crisis. She would be known for her compassion and selflessness. Hey, maybe it was already starting to happen. After all, Tanya had poured out her heart to her on Tuesday. And she had gone away dry eyed – and quite pissed actually, SJ remembered with a frown. But that wasn't really a problem – Tanya could get as pissed as she liked.

The important thing was that SJ hadn't drunk anything herself.

She had been sage and sensible and sober. A sudden thought struck her. Maybe Dorothy was right. Maybe she had helped that unknown girl far more than she'd realised. Maybe she'd only disconnected because having listened to a few words of wisdom from SJ she had realised she need never get drunk again.

Hmmm. That seemed pretty unlikely. But it was possible. All things were possible. SJ smiled and pulled her legs up on to the sofa. She was so glad she'd phoned Dorothy. That had been exactly the right thing to do. It was only then that SJ realised she hadn't asked Dorothy a single thing about the cruise. Resolving to be less selfish she decided to Google Yangon so that she was fully informed of all its attributes for the next time they spoke. She might even phone Dorothy back. Maybe there was a way she could reverse the charges – could you do that on a mobile abroad? Could they set up Skype even? She had never been a great fan of Skype because of the video bit. Talking on the phone when you felt a bit fed up was one thing – you could put on an act when no one could see you. Being in full view of her sharp-eyed, very perceptive sponsor was quite another.

Besides, despite the fact that Dorothy was more than twenty-five years older than her, she was ultra-glamorous. She always looked as though she'd stepped off of one of the Estee Lauder counters in a posh department store. SJ was not glamorous. So Skype was probably a bad idea.

She Googled Yangon and discovered it was a city in South East Asia. Then, out of curiosity, she looked up the world clock and discovered Yangon was six and a half hours ahead of the UK, which meant that it was – bugger – 3.00 a.m. in the morning there. So she must have woken Dorothy up, after all, and Dorothy had uttered not one single word of protest. She hadn't even yawned. SJ sighed. She guessed she had some way to go before she was anything like Dorothy.

She would go to a meeting tomorrow night, which was Friday, straight after work. She was just about to go and make sure she wasn't missing anything from her teaching bag when the phone rang again. She snatched it up. Maybe it was Dorothy. Maybe Dorothy just couldn't sleep. At least she could apologise and ask Dorothy about Yangon culture – and more interestingly what the food was like there.

"SJ, it's Penny."

"Oh hi, Penny." She felt a little twang of disappointment. Was she about to be dropped from helpline manning duties? Had they decided she was complete rubbish?

"I hope I haven't called at a bad time?"

"No, you haven't. Not at all." It was a pity really – she was sure she would be a million times better next time.

She was about to say, 'look I know we had a few teething problems last time, but that's all they were – teething problems', when Penny said, "I'm doing phone service and I've just had a call from a girl who I think spoke to you the first time she called because it was on Tuesday night."

"Oh," said SJ, her heart beginning to beat very fast. "Was she okay? I didn't upset her, did I? She hung up."

"No, you didn't upset her." There was a smile in Penny's voice. "On the contrary. I think you made quite an impression. She said you were very kind."

SJ could feel warmth stealing through her from her head right down to the tips of her toes. "She really said that?"

"She really said that. And a lot more besides. Anyway, the upshot was that she wants to go to a meeting tomorrow night – if possible. And I was wondering if you could take her. I'd take her myself but I'm already meeting a new lady who's in the opposite direction. Your lady is in Camden. But she's happy to get the train to Hackney."

"Of course I'll take her," SJ breathed. "I'm going to Barney Hall tomorrow night anyway. That's quite a good meeting to start with. I'd love to take her."

"Perfect. You're a star. I'll give you her number. Her name's Didi – short for Carol apparently. She said it was a long story."

When they'd finished speaking SJ gave a little dance around the room. So she wasn't a total failure. She had made a difference to someone's life. It looked as though she was going to finally be able to give something back to the fellowship to which she owed so much. She felt humbled and warm and a little tearful. She might even end up being Didi's sponsor. How cool was that.

Chapter Five

SJ arranged to meet Didi outside Hackney Central, which was walking distance from Barney Hall – short for St Barnabas Church hall – and was convenient for both of them. "If you can get there at 6.30," SJ said. "That'll give us plenty of time to get to the meeting and have a bit of a chat and a cup of tea."

"Sure," Didi had said, but it was now 6.45 and there was still no sign of her. Neither had she sent a text, which she'd said she would do if she got held up at work. Maybe she had changed her mind, SJ thought, as another flurry of people went past: a tall girl in a grey pinstriped suit, a man in a fedora and a couple of teenagers holding hands and chatting animatedly – but on their mobile phones, not to each other. SJ smiled and shook her head. Who said romance was dead!

The air smelled of expensive scent and diesel fumes and coffee from a little stall near the station exit. The hum of the trains was like background music. At a news stand a few yards away, a man was handing out copies of the *Evening Standard*. There was a headline about Sports Relief and below it the word, Easter Bunnies. SJ yawned. The year was flying by at top speed. It would be Easter soon – perhaps it would warm up then.

It was chilly tonight. She probably hadn't put enough on. She was wearing her new black jeans and her black faux leather jacket, the current favourite and, in SJ's view, also the coolest thing in her wardrobe. Cool in both senses of the word.

In view of the fact that she was freezing and the heating didn't always work at Barney Hall, she was also wearing a multi coloured *Per Una* scarf, which ruined the cool image a bit but was gloriously soft and warm, and her calf-length black boots, no heels, because they were incredibly comfortable. They were also a bit scuffed-looking and could have done with a polish. Ah well. Didi probably wouldn't be looking her best either – that's if she ever turned up. SJ remembered how she'd looked when she'd been trying to give up drinking.

She'd been a stone overweight for a start, her hair had been a mess, she'd had zero self-esteem and her confidence had been at an all-time low. Poor Didi probably wasn't in very good shape either. Maybe that was what had happened – maybe Didi had chickened out of meeting SJ because she wasn't comfortable with the way she looked. Bless her.

SJ resolved to smile encouragingly if she ever turned up and to pay her some compliment. Yes that was a good idea. Whatever Didi was wearing she would simply widen her eyes and say, 'great to meet you. Love the jacket.'

She abandoned her post and walked back towards the coffee stall. Perhaps she should have arranged to meet Didi somewhere more specific like outside the Empire, or outside the NatWest. Then an awful thought struck her. There were sort of two exits at Hackney Central. You could go down the steps or you could go down the ramp. She'd used the ramp, but what if Didi had gone down the steps and was actually waiting by the NatWest?

Another train had just offloaded and the place was swarming with people – commuters carrying papers and electronic gizmos, with wires dangling from their ears, a few couples on their way to an early dinner. There were no single women, looking a bit lost and bedraggled.

Slipping into the throng of people SJ hurried round to the NatWest. Crap, she could see a lone woman, slightly dumpy looking with a lime green coat, rearranging the contents of her bag. SJ fixed a smile on her face and marched up behind her.

"Didi," she said, putting all the warmth and brightness into her voice that she could muster. "Hi there. I'm SJ. Great jacket."

The woman glanced up in surprise. Two other things happened simultaneously. SJ's mobile cheerily announced the arrival of an incoming text – cheerily being the operative word as it was currently programmed with *Right Said Fred's, I'm Too Sexy*. (Thanks to her teenage nephew, Kevin, who'd popped round yesterday and thought it was an hilarious wheeze to mess about with her phone when she wasn't looking.)

The other thing that happened was that SJ noticed a tall, glamorous woman had just strolled round the corner and was looking in her direction, with an enquiring expression on her face. The woman, like SJ, was dressed entirely in black, but unlike SJ she looked cool, utterly composed and, well, actually, stunning was a pretty good description.

"I got it in Primark," the woman in the lime green coat was saying as she stroked her oversized material-covered buttons with pride. "Do you like it, dear? I was pleased too. £8.50 reduced from £14. They do it in pillar box red as well." Her face clouded. "But I think they only had size eighteens left. Too big for you. Worth a look though. Do you know where Primark is?"

"Um yes," SJ said, feeling her face flush scarlet. "Thanks." She rooted around for her mobile, which had finally stopped blaring, and her phone confirmed what she already knew. The text was from Didi – and said, *Am waiting at the entrance by the NatWest. Is that right?*

Now SJ glanced up and saw that the woman in black was coming over, although she didn't quite get to them. She stopped a few feet short as if she was apprehensive about getting too close and mouthed, "Are you SJ?"

SJ nodded. Suddenly she felt woefully underdressed. Didi was wearing a long black leather coat and knee-length black boots with stiletto heels – she clearly had no problems walking in them – and they made her tower over SJ, who was five ten in her bare feet. The overall impression of blackness was topped off by her very dark eyes, and very long lashes – they had to be eyelash extensions – and her glossy sheen of black hair, which fanned around her shoulders in a perfect bob.

She did not look like a woman with a drink problem. She looked like a woman who was totally in charge of her life. She looked like a woman who gave orders and didn't hang around to see if they'd been obeyed – because it went without saying. SJ could imagine crowds parting when she strode down the street. Taxis would squeal to a halt for her. Men would fall whimpering at her feet.

She smelled of *Classique* perfume, which was what Tanya always wore, and fleetingly SJ thought that if Tanya ever crossed over to the dark side this was exactly what she would look like.

When she held out her hand SJ noticed she had perfect blood red nails. "I'm Didi," she went on in the same quiet husky voice. And SJ realised that she wasn't shy or nervous – she just didn't need to talk any louder. Because people would strain to hear what she said, even if it meant craning their necks.

SJ had never met anyone with quite so much presence. Mrs Lime Green had stopped babbling and was staring at Didi open mouthed. "Are you that woman off Corrie – the one what used to be in the band?"

"I don't watch television," Didi said, flicking her an amused glance. "Far too busy, I'm afraid."

"Super coat," continued Mrs Lime Green putting out a hand to touch an edge of matt black leather. "Looks pricey. Did you get it in a sale?" She turned back to SJ. "I saw one a bit like it at Primark. I tell you, dear, it's well worth a visit." She clearly felt part of their group and comfortable enough to be in a position to make comments on coats, which was her fault, SJ thought, clearing her

36

throat and deciding it was high time to take charge of the situation.

"Lovely to meet you," she said to Didi, although she'd a feeling Mrs Lime Green thought she was speaking to her. "Sorry about the mix up. We should get going. We'll be late. We can walk from here."

She shot Mrs Lime Green an apologetic smile, but they had barely got clear of her when Didi said, "I thought for one awful moment you'd brought a welcoming committee with you. Did you see those dire shoes? One of the laces was broken and it looked like she'd fixed it with string. And that straw shopping bag! Hideous." Didi narrowed her eyes and glanced at SJ. "I've put my foot in it, haven't I? Do you know her? What was all that nonsense about Primark?"

"No, I don't know her," SJ said, and felt fleetingly ashamed that her first impulse had been to disassociate herself from Mrs Lime Green and not to defend her and that her second had been to glance down at her own scuffed boots and hope Didi hadn't noticed them. "Maybe she was broke," she added. "She didn't look like she had two pennies to rub together."

"A straw bag lady. Maybe." Didi linked her arm through SJ's and leaned close in an over-familiar fashion. "So what are they like the people that go to AA? Are there lots of freaks and weirdoes?"

"No," SJ said, feeling slightly distracted because in that moment when Didi's mouth was close to her face she had smelled alcohol. Or at least she thought she had. "They're mostly normal men and woman just like us," she added, steering Didi towards a pedestrian crossing. "We need to go over here. It's not far. Is it hard to walk in those boots?"

"I'm used to it. I wear them for work." She smirked as though at some private joke, or perhaps she'd been right about the alcohol, SJ thought, and she was a lot drunker than she'd first appeared – which paradoxically made her feel less in awe of Didi than she had a few moments before. Kit had taught her that people wore all sorts of masks. Things were rarely what they seemed on the surface. Kit himself had been wearing the ultimate mask. SJ had learned that once her counsellor had become more than a counsellor – once he'd become a friend and then a lover. She felt a little ache in her throat at the memory of Kit. And about how things had worked out for them. But she knew she would never regret meeting him – he had saved her life – and one of the most important things he had taught her was not to make snap judgments.

"Here we are," SJ said a couple of minutes later, steering Didi, whose arm was still linked in hers, towards a gap between two buildings. "This is the back entrance." She stopped midway along the alley and looked at Didi's face properly.

She was extraordinarily pretty – and Mrs Lime Green had been right – she did look a bit like Kym Marsh who'd once been in Hear'Say and was currently on Corrie. But for the first time SJ could see the doubts in her eyes, the slightly dilated pupils, the tiny broken veins – not quite concealed with make-up – around her nose, and SJ felt a pang of something that was a cross between empathy and recognition. And she knew suddenly that Didi was nowhere near as confident as she was making out.

"Are you okay?" she asked softly.

Didi nodded. "I can't think of a single thing I'd rather be doing on a Friday night." She gave a brittle little laugh, which to SJ's ultra-sensitive ears sounded distinctly hollow, and added, "Yippee ki-yay."

A curious thing to say, SJ thought, as they walked up to the heavy wooden door and she pushed it open.

Chapter Six

SJ had a feeling Didi would have stood out wherever she was, but here she was as conspicuous as a Harrods bag at a car boot sale. A few heads turned as they went into the room, mostly men's, and SJ wished Dorothy was here with her poise and easy glamour and quiet wisdom. Barney Hall was a small meeting, they rarely got a turn-out of more than twenty – it was held in a cosy little church hall, with wooden floors and whitewashed walls. Well, it was cosy when the ancient fan heater was working, which it didn't feel like it was today. The room smelled of cold overlaid with damp, and draughts skittered around the eaves.

She had chosen the back entrance on purpose, because the front one was usually obstructed by a sleeping bag or two belonging to the local homeless population. The front door lay in a deep recess and was sheltered from the weather. Fairly often the front door residents came to the meeting – not because they wanted to listen to anything anyone said, SJ presumed, as more often than not they fell asleep, but because they knew they wouldn't get kicked out, and there was free coffee and tea and usually yummy homemade cake as well. Barney Hall had been SJ's regular group since she'd been living in Hackney and most of the faces were familiar, but today she couldn't see anyone she knew well. Bugger.

Didi stood just inside the entrance, a little way apart from the bare painted wall and scanned the room, her eyes widening with interest. "So this is what Alcoholics Anonymous looks like," she said, surveying the table littered with leaflets at the front and the circle of orange plastic chairs facing it, some of which were occupied with people chatting and laughing and drinking coffee. "I was convinced it would be full of old men in scruffy macs without any teeth."

"Who've come straight from their park benches, clutching their bottles of meths," SJ said dryly and Didi gave her a sharp look.

"Yes, yes, I suppose so." She had the grace to blush. "It's part of the stereotype, isn't it." She looked around the little room, her gaze assessing. "Most people really do look quite normal."

"They are," SJ said firmly, wanting Didi to see the best of this fellowship in which she'd had so little faith when she'd been introduced, but which she now cared passionately about. "In lots of ways they're better than normal. I've made some brilliant friends. Real friends, I mean, since I've been coming here."

She wished she could see some of them now, but there weren't many women here today. And then, oh crap, she saw Half Pint Hughie come through the front door. SJ watched as he paused to undo the top few buttons of his faded grey mac. He unwound a scarf the same colour from his long scrawny neck, round and round and round as if removing a bandage. He'd always reminded SJ of a tortoise with his leathery skin and beady eyes and he was harmless enough, but he did like to get up close and personal with the ladies.

41

She wondered if she could get Didi into the kitchen before he reached them. But past experience told her that wouldn't work. Half Pint Hughie wasn't going to be deflected from trying to get a kiss from the prettiest woman in the room – especially as she was a newbie and this might be the only chance he got.

"So what happens in meetings?" Didi was asking. "Is that the same as how it's portrayed in the movies? Does a man in brown corduroy trousers and a roll neck sweater stand up and tell everyone his tragic tale of life in the gutter?"

"There's a bit more to it than that," SJ said, noticing with a little start that a man in a roll neck sweater was talking to the secretary, and, oh my goodness, he was quite possibly wearing brown corduroy trousers too. She gulped, but was instantly distracted by the fact that Half Pint Hughie was heading their way. He dodged people and chairs and was closing in fast on Didi's left shoulder.

And then he was there. "Good evening, ladies." His voice was nothing like his appearance. His voice had the depth and beauty of Richard Burton's, but he had a strong Northern Ireland accent. Didi turned round in interest and was confronted by a man in a mac. Clearly surprised, she glanced over his shoulder, as though expecting to see someone else, a more likely partner for the voice. But then he spoke again. "Your first meeting, is it?" He patted her arm. "I'm Half Pint Hughie. I've been coming here for twenty-six years, so I have. Walking through those doors was the best thing I ever did." He smiled, treating them to a vivid close up of his dark pink gums – he had no teeth at all. He had told SJ once that he was so afraid of dentists as a boy he'd had every tooth removed when he hit twenty-five and he'd never missed them. She wasn't sure whether to believe him or not. All she could think of right now was to get Didi away from him before she decided that the stereotype was, in fact, pretty much spot on, and made a run for it.

"Good to see you, Hughie," SJ said, smiling at him and then deftly turning her face as he puckered up and zoomed in for a full frontal smacker, thus ensuring his lips landed on her cheek instead. It was a kiss dodging manoeuvre she had perfected across the years. For men everywhere who clearly thought women just loved the touchy feely approach and would grab any opportunity for a swift grope. "We're just about to get a coffee, aren't we?"

Didi nodded. Her face was expressionless. Hughie took a step towards her and then to SJ's surprise he paused, cleared his throat, rocked back on his heels and didn't try to kiss Didi after all. It was as though there was some sort of an invisible shield around her. SJ was surprised. He wasn't known for his respect of personal space. But then Didi was quite imposing.

"It's lovely to meet you," she said graciously. "I'm quite sure we will meet again. Did you say something about a coffee, SJ?"

As they headed towards the hatch that led through to the tiny church kitchen, SJ caught her gaze and Didi winked.

"There's always one," SJ could feel her face burning, but Didi seemed more amused than put off.

"Sure," she said. "I suppose the clichés have to come from somewhere. Why's he called Half Pint Hughie?"

"Because he only ever drank half pints," SJ said. "He thought if he didn't drink pints he couldn't be an alcoholic. Only in the end he was drinking half pints of Jim Beam, which blew that one out of the window."

Anxious to move on she said, "There are people from all different walks of life here. We've got teachers, doctors, solicitors, policemen and women – nannies." She waved a hand, aware that she was gabbling and also that she sounded a bit pompous. Somehow it was almost as nerve-racking taking Didi to her first meeting as it had been coming to a first meeting herself. She felt personally responsible. As though whether AA made a good impression was entirely down to her. Which was stupid, she knew. "What did you say you did for a living again?"

"I work in the entertainments industry," Didi said with a little smile.

"Oh really, do you mean you're an actor?" SJ wasn't surprised. With Didi's looks and presence, she was probably very successful too. And acting, like many other creative jobs, writers, artists, painters, attracted its fair share of drinkers.

"I do a little acting – yes." She broke off because another man was heading their way. SJ followed her gaze and groaned inwardly. That was all she needed.

"Who's this?" Didi asked in a stage whisper.

"That's Number Ten Tim."

"And is that a drinking reference too? Did he down ten bottles of rum a night? He certainly looks like he could." Her eyes were wide with interest and SJ smiled. Tim, who looked like a younger, taller version of Denzel Washington, was at least six foot four of solid muscle and drop dead gorgeous. Today he was wearing a suit – he was a city banker and had clearly come straight from work.

"You'll find out in a minute. Hi, Tim. Can I introduce Didi – it's her first meeting."

"Hello, sweetheart – good to meet you." Tim, who was one of the few men in the room tall enough for Didi to look up to, proffered a hand. When Didi responded he lifted her delicate pale hand, which contrasted sharply with the giant blackness of his, and kissed the back of it.

Didi certainly seemed to have a dramatic effect on men. SJ had never seen Tim do anything like that before.

"I love your scent," he said. "When I'm in Number Ten I'm going to make it compulsory that all women wear scent. The world would be a much better place if all women wore scent."

"How about men?" Didi asked with a hint of challenge in her voice.

"What have you been up to today?" SJ interrupted, feeling as though she was intruding on a private flirtation, but wanting to save Didi from any more of Tim's terrible chat up lines. "Good day in the office?"

"I haven't been in the office much. I had a meeting in Dartford. I was sitting on the M25 for an hour both ways. Totally stationary. No accidents, no roadworks, just the sheer volume of traffic. When I'm in Number Ten I shall make the M25 a toll road. You'll have to pay in advance to get on it. That'll cut down the number of unnecessary journeys. And I shall make a law that no one can travel by car alone. Everyone will have to travel in twos. When I'm in Number Ten I shall revolutionise the roads in this country. Journey times will halve. I'll make it compulsory that everyone has a satnav with live traffic updates so there will be no more congestion. When I'm in Number Ten I shall…"

"Sorry to cut you off, Tim," SJ broke in, aware that Didi's eyes had started to glaze over. "But there's someone I want Didi to meet." She'd just spotted Penny in the kitchen.

"It's the woman you spoke to on the helpline," she told a slightly bemused Didi, as she steered her in Penny's direction. "Sorry about Number Ten Tim – he can go on a bit. When the meeting starts someone – usually someone who has been sober a while – tells you how they did it. That's called a share."

She shut up, aware that Didi wasn't listening anyway. She was scanning the room – perhaps she was afraid she'd see someone she knew.

"Hello, love." Penny, who was on the edge of a small group of women, gave them a beaming smile, which caused dimples to appear in her cheeks and her eyes to shine with warmth. "Now there's no need to worry. Everyone's a lot more normal than you think. I was amazed at my first meeting. I'd fully expected the place to be brimming with oddballs."

Didi acknowledged this with the slightest lift of one eyebrow.

"Not that there aren't a few," Penny continued. "But they're mostly men." There was a ripple of laughter.

A few other women joined their group – Alana had brought her new baby in a buggy and everyone cooed over her, and Alana, who'd only managed to give up drinking when she was four months into her pregnancy, swelled visibly with pride.

"I was so scared there'd be something wrong with Hermione," she said. "But I still couldn't stop. I wouldn't have been able to do it at all without you lot." Her voice dropped almost to a whisper. "But she's okay. She's so beautiful."

Didi was looking at Alana thoughtfully. SJ could see she was taking all this in. Hopefully Half Pint Hughie and Number Ten Tim hadn't put her off too much. The meeting was due to start in ten minutes but for a while they sipped coffees and nibbled chocolate biscuits. The chatter was general, and they could have been a group of women anywhere. SJ began to relax. Didi's eyes weren't as glassy as they had been earlier. So if she had been drinking she was starting to sober up. It was going to be okay. Didi was not going to think everyone who came to AA was mad. She would get that they were just a normal bunch of people – the kind of women you would meet anywhere with ordinary jobs and normal interests like fashion and films and going out. Totally normal, just minus the alcohol.

SJ wondered what Didi did in the acting industry. Maybe she did television. Maybe Mrs Lime Green had recognised her – not because she looked like Kym Marsh, but because she was actually on television. Or even in films. After all, there were heaps of programmes that SJ didn't watch. Hadn't Didi said she didn't watch television though? Yes, but that didn't mean she wasn't on it. Dozens of actors didn't like watching themselves on telly – it probably felt odd. Maybe she and Didi would become friends. Maybe she would help Didi give up drinking and Didi would be eternally grateful to her – rather like she was with Dorothy. Not that she wanted or needed Didi's gratitude, of course. She would help her unconditionally – just as she had been helped unconditionally by older wiser members of AA. But it would be quite cool if Didi was a famous actor.

SJ drifted off into a little fantasy in which Didi was introducing her to Ant and Dec and saying, "This is the girl I told you about. The one who saved my life. I owe her absolutely everything." Whereupon Didi's eyes would mist a little and SJ would shake her head and say, "No, really, you don't owe me a thing. It's what our fellowship's about. It's what we do." There would be some suitably stirring music going on in the background and everyone around them, even Ant and Dec, would be wiping their eyes.

SJ became aware suddenly that Penny was saying her name. "SJ…SJ, love…" and by the sound of her voice she'd been trying to get her attention for a while.

She gave Penny her most benevolent smile, still half stuck in fantasy land. "Sorry, Penny, I was miles away." Penny was probably going to ask her about doing more phone service, or perhaps there was another newbie who Penny thought SJ might be a good influence on – after her success with Didi. "How can I help?" she said and then for no good reason except that she wanted Penny to know she was really keen on being of assistance she added, "Your wish is my command."

Penny seemed slightly startled to be faced with such enthusiasm. "Well, actually I was just going to ask you a favour – it's on behalf of a friend of mine who's having a problem with her dog."

Suddenly SJ knew what was coming, but it was too late to wriggle out of it. Due to the fact it had taken a while for Penny to attract her attention, the entire group, including Didi, was now looking at her expectantly.

In fact, it seemed to SJ's hyper-sensitive ears that the entire room had paused from their individual conversations to eavesdrop. She was tempted to put her hands over her ears and run for the exit. But that would have probably given Didi the wrong impression so she decided she'd have to brazen it out.

"Are you still doing that dog whisperer course you told me about?" Penny went on with casual disregard for SJ's feelings. SJ couldn't think why she'd ever thought Penny was a kindly, sensitive and empathetic lady. "The one where you learn to speak dog language. Where you actually learn to yip like a dog." She leaned forward expectantly. As did everyone else. As did the room itself.

"Mmm," SJ said, nodding sagely and trying to look as though it was perfectly normal to be learning to yip like a dog. She was aware that Didi's eyebrows had shot up a few millimetres and that she – like everyone else – was waiting, with eager anticipation, for her answer.

Chapter Seven

"So what did you say?" Tanya asked, biting her lip. To SJ's consternation she was clearly finding this whole thing very amusing. "What did you do?"

They were at Kew Gardens, sitting on the patio outside one of the cafes overlooking an avenue of pink trees. Blossom scattered the grass like so much confetti. Birds were singing. The sounds of cutlery scraping plates and the muted voices of the other diners surrounded them. The air smelled of Thai vegetable curry and fried burgers and spring freshness. It had to be one of the most peaceful places on earth, SJ thought, glancing at Bethany who had just finished eating chips with tomato ketchup. Most of the ketchup was now smeared around the lower half of her face.

"I think I turned it around," she said, watching Tanya get out her baby wipes and begin to clean her reluctant daughter's face.

Tanya gave up the pretence of a straight face and she smiled properly now. "Of course you did. Can you keep still, Bethany, please?"

"Hurting, Mummy." She wriggled away. "See ducks?"

"Yes, darling, in a minute. Well?" She looked back expectantly at SJ. "What did you say?"

"That I didn't think I'd be that much help. That actually I was thinking of giving up the dog whispering course. Because I didn't have a dog any more – and actually it brought back sad memories of Ash."

51

"Ah," Tanya said, and her face sobered. "So what did they say to that?"

"Well, that started people off talking about dogs they'd lost. And how much they loved their own dogs and that dogs were part of the family and all that."

"Nice recovery."

"I guess," SJ said, realising with a shock that she was close to tears. "Why am I such an idiot, Tan? Why do I get myself into these stupid situations in the first place?" She wasn't sure whether it was the beauty of their surroundings that was making her ache, or the memory of Ash who had died peacefully in his sleep a year ago, or the fact that she always seemed to end up in the kind of crazy situations that Tanya would have gracefully sidestepped. She plucked a paper napkin from the table and folded it into a tight square. "I wish I was more like you. Sane and sensible and totally in charge of my life."

Tanya gave a sound that was somewhere between a snort and a burst of laughter. "I'm nowhere near as together as you think. Not at the moment anyway." She turned her green gaze on SJ. "You are sane and sensible. And you are NOT an idiot. You're the loveliest person I know. Stop beating yourself up."

"Sorry."

"Stop apologising."

"Sor… I mean…right. No apologising. What do you mean you're not very together at the moment?"

Tanya flashed her a look. There was a flicker of hurt in her eyes and SJ could have kicked herself. Of course Tanya wasn't very together. Not right now. Why on earth would you be together when you thought your husband was having an affair? She still couldn't get her head around that. She glanced at Tanya's hands. Her nail varnish was perfect again. Pink today and unchipped. There was a small spot of tomato ketchup on her coat sleeve. SJ swallowed. She wanted to ask about Michael. But it wasn't so easy to just come out with it. Especially when you had a toddler with you – a toddler who needed endless attention. When would be a tactful moment? She opened her mouth.

"Mummy, ducks, puleeze."

"Yes, darling." Tanya shot SJ a look as though she had read her thoughts and understood them. "We can chat on the way."

They got up and Tanya began to pack up Bethany's things and transfer them to various pockets in the buggy. "How can a two and a half year-old need so much stuff?" she grumbled.

SJ smiled. "You need one of those little cases on wheels."

"This is it," Tanya said, releasing the buggy's brake and pushing it along the tarmac path. Bethany began to run along ahead of them on the grass. She had her mother's red hair but it was a paler version, a kind of strawberry blond, and it was a lot more wayward than Tanya's had ever been. Red glints caught in the sunshine. She was wearing a pale blue tee shirt, which had a smudge of something brown on the front, and denim shorts and a gorgeous little denim jacket. Clearly Tanya had given up putting her in pretty dresses. She looked exactly like the tomboy she was.

"Do we actually know where the ducks are?" SJ asked. "This place is a lot bigger than I thought it was."

"According to the map," Tanya said, spreading it out across the handle of the buggy as they walked, there's a lake over to our left. Was there anything you particularly wanted to see? I wouldn't mind seeing the carnivorous plants – they have some quite big Venus flytraps here, I think."

"Do they?" SJ breathed in a lungful of clean fresh air. "They sound good." She hesitated. "I'd quite like to see the Palm House – that's the closest I'm going to get to anywhere hot and tropical, this year."

Tanya nodded sympathetically. "Yes, we've had to pull our belts in too. What with me cutting my hours."

"I didn't realise you had cut your hours. I thought Michael was being a househusband."

Tanya frowned. "Yes, that was the plan. But it kind of happened naturally after Bethany was born. I lost a couple of my regular clients – a lot of small businesses have gone to the wall. The only thing they need accountants for is to file for bankruptcy. Sad isn't it."

"Yes." SJ was having trouble finding the right words to ask about Michael. *'So did you discover Michael wasn't having an affair, after all?'* sounded too dismissive, and as if it had never been a real problem at all, when clearly Tanya had been desperately worried about it last time they'd spoken.

Also, it felt different when they had Bethany with them. The dynamics were different. They were a family group, they weren't two gossipy friends. Although they were the same age SJ had always felt slightly less grown up than Tanya, and now that Tanya was a mother the feeling had been amplified.

Maybe she should let Tanya raise the subject. Yes, that was a good idea. If she was still worried about it she would say something, wouldn't she?

They were approaching the banks of the lake – on the far side the Palm House rose up like some great glass palace. Its domed roofs and huge arched windows reflecting the sun like a giant multifaceted diamond.

"Wow," SJ said. "Isn't it stunning?"

"Don't go near the edge," Tanya warned as Bethany spotted a swan and four cygnets drifting through the dark water.

"Ducks," she shouted in excitement. "Feed ducks."

"I should have brought bread," SJ said in frustration. "I had half a loaf in the bread bin going stale."

"We have bread," Tanya said, smiling at her and producing a plastic tub from one of the buggy's numerous pockets.

Of course Tanya had bread. SJ felt some of the tension drain away from her. Of course Michael wasn't having an affair. Especially not with a man, which she definitely did not want to think about. Everything was the same as it had always been. Their conversation beneath the heat of Tanya's umbrella, on London's darkly, rain spattered streets, seemed a million miles from today's sun. So did the one in her flat when, let's face it, Tanya had drunk too much wine. Which was enough to get anyone paranoid. The status quo was just as it had always been – everything was fine. Everything was good.

Bethany was standing on a part of the bank where it sloped down to the water's edge in a tiny shallow beach. She scooped out handfuls of breadcrumbs and scattered them out on the lake in flamboyant handfuls to the swan, who dipped her head elegantly to receive them. SJ wondered if Tanya had actually put the bread through the processor or whether it had formed crumbs naturally.

"I got Michael a bread maker for Christmas," Tanya said, as if she had read SJ's mind. "He makes loads of bread but we don't always get through it so I've taken to bread-crumbing the ends of loaves and freezing them. In case I ever learn to cook properly and need breadcrumbs. In the meantime it comes in very handy for the ducks."

Her voice was soft now, cooler, as though a shadow had passed over it and then she added. "I asked Michael, you know, if he was having an affair."

"You did?" SJ chewed the inside of her lip. "What did he say?"

There was a pause which funnelled between them. Then Tanya turned to look at her. "He said that he wasn't. Which was what I expected him to say. He's hardly going to admit it, is he? Men never do."

"Maybe he was telling the truth." Tanya looked so sad. This was all wrong. She and Michael had gone through so much. The tragic loss of Maddie their first baby who hadn't quite reached full term – that had been awful. Then the shock of his cross-dressing, Tanya rarely mentioned that, these days, but SJ assumed it was still a fixture of their marriage. They had survived all of that. And now they finally had the little girl they had always wanted. They should be enjoying their life now. They shouldn't have the shadow of adultery hanging over them.

"He was adamant that he loved me," Tanya said with a sigh. "I believe him – that's not really up for debate, but the whole time we were talking there was this niggling little voice in my gut telling me that something was wrong."

"An instinct," SJ said, nodding. "Yes, I know that one. Did you mention Andy?"

Tanya shook her head. "I didn't feel I could. Michael kept looking at me and saying, 'I don't know what you want me to say, lovely – I can't confess to something I haven't done.'"

"Well that does sound very promising," SJ said. "It does sound like he's being honest with you."

"I know." Tanya's eyes sparkled with unshed tears, just as Bethany threw out the last of her bread and turned around with a purposeful expression on her face. "SJ, do you think it's possible for your instincts to be wrong? Do you think it's possible that I'm imagining the whole thing?"

Once, SJ would have answered that question immediately with an emphatic no. Instincts were always right. You should always trust them. It was one of those universally accepted truths. But since she had stopped drinking she was no longer so sure about things that she'd once accepted as universally accepted truths.

Her instincts had been wrong on several things over the last few years. One of the biggest had been the fact that she and Kit were soulmates; that they would have a future together, go the distance. Her instincts had told her that if you had seen the darker side of someone, if they had told you their darkest secrets and you had told them yours, then the only way was up, into the light. Together.

She had been so sure that once they were no longer counsellor and client, once they no longer had a professional connection, they would be able to step into the arena of friends. And when they'd taken that first step, she had been so sure that the raging sparks of lust between them would turn into passion. And then that the passion would turn into something bigger. Something like love.

Actually, she'd been right about the passion bit. The first time they'd made love was not something she was likely to forget because it had also been the last time. It had happened at Kit's flat.

Chapter Eight

It was a Wednesday night in January, just over three years ago. They had just been to the Hackney Empire to watch a comedy duo SJ had never heard of, but who Kit had clearly found hilarious.

He was still smiling as they went outside into the frosty air. "This is the bit where I ask you back for coffee," he said, sounding oddly vulnerable. "As I think I might have mentioned, I don't live in a palace."

"And as I think I might have mentioned," she said, leaning into the roughness of his denim jacket. "I don't need a palace or a castle or a knight in shining armour. I don't need pretty wrappings, Kit."

That was the understatement of the year, considering they were both in recovery – his love affair had been with cocaine.

"I know." His voice husked a little over the words. His eyes were smoky on hers. "Then follow me."

She felt safe beside Kit. She thought she would have felt safe anywhere with him. It wasn't just his craggy lived-in face, or his muscular strength – he worked out regularly – but the way he carried himself: the streetwise edge of hardness in his walk. SJ had never thought of herself as middle class but that was exactly how she felt when she was beside Kit.

He lived in a 1960s tower block beside a kids' play park, which, at this time of night, was frequented by groups of youths, swigging from cans and exchanging packages in the shadows. Lately, every time SJ saw a man with a can in his hand, she had wanted to run up to him and say, 'You don't have to do this. There's a better way.' But so far common sense had stopped her.

Anyway, they probably weren't all alcoholics. They could probably stop any time they wanted. Dorothy had told her often that not every man on a park bench swigging a can of Special Brew was an alcoholic, any more than every woman who sipped a tulip of champagne at a cocktail bar wasn't.

"Welcome to Chez Oakley," Kit said, when they finally reached the sixth floor, via the stairs because the lift was broken. He unlocked the door of his flat and gestured her to go ahead of him.

SJ stared around her in fascination while she tried to stop panting (not very cool – she really should get fitter). It was nicer than she'd expected, given the outside. A white carpeted hallway which had several doors leading off it, one of them to a lounge, which smelled faintly of lemons, she discovered, when Kit led her into it. It had wooden floors and was square with a brown leather, box-shaped sofa against one wall.

It was a man's room, SJ decided. The main purpose of it was clearly to watch the supersized flat screen television. Over the mantelpiece was a picture of a semi-naked woman, draped in a burgundy robe and looking back over one shoulder. On the wall next to the television was a book case. While Kit made the promised coffee, SJ checked it out.

There was a biography entitled, *Life on the Street*, a *Where to Find* pamphlet of all the NA meetings in London and a dried out money plant.

Losing interest, she abandoned the bookcase and followed the sounds of coffee-making into the kitchen.

"Would you prefer chamomile tea?" Kit said, glancing up as she came in. "I've got some somewhere. It's a bit on the late side for caffeine. It might stop you sleeping."

"I'm hoping it won't be caffeine that stops me sleeping," she hedged, putting her arms around him from behind and laying her head against his shoulder. She felt him tense ever so slightly. "Are you nervous?"

He stopped messing about with the mugs and swivelled round to face her. "I am a bit." His eyes were dark. "Aren't you?"

"I guess I am," she said. "First times – first times for anything, I mean. They're always…"

"Yeah, they're always…"

They stared at each other. And SJ felt a thousand things: excitement; love; relief that they'd finally got here. They'd been seeing each other or dating or whatever it was called these days, for a few weeks but they had never done more than kiss. She still lived at Dorothy's house in Bermondsey – she wouldn't have felt comfortable asking him to stay the night there – and Kit had been curiously reluctant to bring her here.

Maybe because of its less than salubrious location. She had never really questioned why. Maybe because it was still early days for them in relationship terms. But this was it. Tonight was the night. The stars were all aligned.

As if reading her thoughts Kit cupped her face in his and kissed her. And the kiss was everything she loved about Kit. Warm, gentle, unhurried. He explored her mouth in exactly the same way he'd explored her mind. She responded in the same way she had responded to that – a little uncertainly at first, but swiftly gaining in confidence as the ache of longing grew in her. An ache of longing that was finally, finally going to be fulfilled. They had been building up to this point for such a long time.

They'd known each other forever, first as counsellor and client, then as friends, their relationship slowly growing, brick by brick into something solid and real and good. He knew all her secrets, every dark cranny of her mind and she knew a lot of his too – they had seen the very worst of each other. And now SJ knew they were about to see the very best.

This was their time. Only theirs. She slipped a hand beneath his shirt, felt the warmth of his chest and then undid the top two buttons so she could kiss his bare skin. Kit smiled as he watched her undo the rest so she could take off the shirt completely.

When she began to unbutton his jeans he said, "Let's go to the bedroom." His voice was husky. "More comfortable."

63

They were both undressed by the time they got to the door, discarding clothes like old sweet wrappers between one room and the next.

Well, SJ had actually kept on her pants (new silky black ones bought especially) – and her matching bra – but that had more to do with the fact it was quite tight and tricky to unclip.

She was curiously shy now they were so close to seeing each other fully. They sat on the edge of the bed. Kit hadn't put on the light so the room was full of shadows and the faint smell of *Paco Rabanne* aftershave and overlaying that the more pungent and more exciting smell of man.

"Are you keeping this on?" he asked, trailing a finger across her cupped left breast.

"I don't think so."

She unclipped it for him, aware of the sound of his breath, the warmth of his skin, the heat of his gaze. He kissed her mouth again and then he leaned across and kissed both her breasts in turn, lingering just long enough to arouse. She watched the top of his head, and felt torn apart with love. It was such a vulnerable, tender moment. Her whole body was on fire with lust. It had been too long since she'd felt like this. Way too long.

Finally he resurfaced, but only for long enough to push her gently on to her back and to position himself above her – skin against skin.

"So here we are." His eyes gleamed in the dim light. "What shall we do now?"

"I've got a few ideas," SJ said.

Much later, when she awoke in the night, there was a tiny part of her that was afraid it had all been a wonderful dream. A tiny part of her that was afraid she would open her eyes and find she was in her own bed at Dorothy's. Alone.

But then she had heard his breathing and seen the dark curve of his head and the unfamiliar contours of his bedroom. And she'd remembered little snippets of their love-making.

The heat of his mouth, the solid, lithe weight of him, the expression on his face, almost of pain, as he'd climaxed. She'd hugged it all to her, a little parcel of joy that she could unwrap to warm up future moments. Their love-making had been just as perfect as she'd always suspected it might be. They were in tune with each other. Totally in alignment. Matched.

The next time she woke up it was to daylight streaming in the windows and the smell of toast. Bless him, he must be making them breakfast. Or maybe he was getting up his strength for seconds. SJ was very much hoping he was a morning man.

There was a white towelling robe on the back of the bedroom door. It was scratchy, but it smelled of him. Smiling, SJ tugged it down and hugged it around herself. She padded silently back out to the kitchen. The room was empty but, as she stood in the doorway, four pieces of toast pinged up from a chunky black toaster. Maybe he'd gone to the bathroom. Unusually for a flat, there were two. One of which also housed a shower and a huge triangular shaped bath. He'd shown her last night.

"You can fit two in there," he'd said. "We could try it out tomorrow – if you fancy it?"

"Sounds like fun."

The toilet door was closed – he was clearly in there. But as she went past the bathroom door, which was ajar, she heard movement. So maybe he wasn't.

"Hi," she said, pushing it open fully.

For a moment she wasn't quite sure what she was seeing. It was like part of a play, a little tableau set in ice. Kit was kneeling by the toilet, in profile to her. His dark head was bent over something shiny on the closed toilet lid. A mirror. Then there were his eyes as he looked up at her. Eyes full of shock and guilt.

"Fuck."

SJ wasn't sure which of them said it. Maybe both of them. She was too busy backing out of the door. Kit was getting up too – an ungainly scramble to his feet. He wasn't fully dressed – barefoot and just in jeans. His tanned, muscular torso was bare. That gorgeous body that had pressed against hers last night. That gorgeous body that he had just pumped full of chemicals. What chemicals? She didn't know anything about drugs – not the kind of drugs you snorted off mirrors. Her heart was slamming about with shock.

"The strongest thing I ever put into my body these days is caffeine." She could hear him saying it. He'd told her that so many times.

It was a lie. It had all been bullshit. What else had he lied about?

"SJ. Wait." He was behind her in the hall. "Wait."

Where did he think she was going? She was only wearing his dressing gown and she certainly wasn't leaving in that. She sped back into the bedroom, one hand over her mouth. She felt sick. But she needed to get dressed. She was too vulnerable without clothes.

Her jeggings and top were folded up on the chair. He must have picked them up from where she'd discarded them. He must have done that before he'd gone for his fix. Before he'd gone to make toast. Her heart turned over with pain.

She felt his hand on her shoulder. "I'm so sorry. I'm so sorry you had to see that. Shit, I thought you were asleep."

"Clearly." She hardly recognised her own voice. How could you get so much venom and pain into a single word? "And I suppose you're going to tell me it's not how it looks? That you weren't just snorting some bloody crap up your nose." She swung round, brushing off his hand in the process. "Well, are you?"

He shook his head. "Of course not." His eyes glittered. Somehow they were both bleak and bright. Was that the cocaine? It had to be cocaine. What else could it be? Not that it really mattered what it had been.

Something had died in her when she'd seen him there kneeling – kneeling at the altar of his erstwhile lover. Because Kit had always represented recovery to her. He had been there at the start of hers, telling her that she could do it. That it was worth it. That *she* was worth it. That he would help her. For a very long time Kit had been all that was tender and good and wholesome in her life – okay so she knew he had a past, but it was years behind him. He'd said it was years. She'd blotted out the images of what he might have been like as an addict.

"SJ, can we talk?"

"I'd like to get dressed first."

"Sure. Of course." He put up his hands, backing away from her. Backing out of his own bedroom, his head lowered in defeat.

Chapter Nine

Five minutes later they sat in the lounge. Light streamed through the slatted blinds of the window and striped the wooden floor. They were both fully dressed now. Both sombre-faced. He was on one end of the box-shaped sofa and she was on the other. He had offered her coffee. But she hadn't wanted coffee. And the toast had gone untouched into the bin.

"I had a relapse," he said slowly. "A few months back."

"Why? What happened?"

"Complacency." His voice was low. "The truth is, SJ, I don't really know. I was at a party. Someone shoved it in front of me. It was the stupidest, stupidest thing. A moment of madness."

"Why didn't you tell me?"

He gave a half shrug. "I'm not sure. Shame, I guess. And I thought I could handle it. I thought I could stop again."

"But you couldn't?"

"Not properly, no."

"Were you on it last night?"

There was the slightest pause and then he nodded. She wasn't sure why that hurt so much. That he'd been off his face the first time they'd made love. A first time that would never come again.

He read her eyes. "It's not the same as booze. It doesn't dull the senses...I was...I..." He stuttered to a halt. "I took it last night because I was worried that I may not be able to…you know…"

"Right," SJ said. "Right." And what a stupid word that was too, because none of it was right. The joy of the previous evening suddenly all tainted and soiled.

He went on softly, "And then, this morning I had to… Shit. I'm so sorry."

New pain washed through her. "Kit - if I ask you something, will you tell me the truth?"

He rubbed his forehead. "Yeah. Sure." His voice was full of irony as if the words, 'for what it's worth' hung in the air. And she thought, I know him so well. I know every nuance of his tone, his face, his gestures. And yet I didn't know this. How is that possible?

She braced herself. "Were you ever taking it when we were talking - you know, during our sessions? When you were counselling me?" She didn't know why this was so important, but it was. She didn't want the whole of the past to be a lie. Even if the present had crumbled to dust - at least the past could stay perfect.

"No," he said. "I wasn't. I promise you." He paused. He bowed his head, blinked a few times and then looked up straight into her eyes and she saw a deep shame there. "I was still working at S.A.A.D. though, when I had the relapse. That's why I left. I couldn't have carried on counselling people when I was taking the shit myself. I'm not that much of a hypocrite."

SJ nodded, aware in the gap, of the small sounds in the room: the clicking of a radiator behind them; the muted throb of someone's radio in another flat; the drum of rain on the windows. She hadn't realised it was raining.

"So S.A.A.D. didn't really close down?"

"It did actually. They did run out of funding. But that wasn't why I left."

"You can stop again though, can't you?" Now the first thumps of shock had worn off, she didn't feel quite so bad. It didn't feel so terminal. Okay, so he'd lied to her, but it wasn't irretrievable. He was being honest now, wasn't he? They were talking now. And she knew what it was like, the call of addiction. She had been there herself. It ate you up. It got into your soul and obsessed you. All that had really happened was that he'd shown himself to be flawed and therefore human – like everyone else. People had relapses in AA all the time. It didn't mean they couldn't come back. Start all over again.

"I'm not sure if I can stop, SJ, no." He picked at a stray thread of denim on his jeans. "I've been in treatment again since I relapsed. It didn't work. It's much harder than it was first time round. It's like the stuff's got into my bones."

"I could help you," she said, glancing at him and horrified to see that he was slowly shaking his head.

"That's very sweet of you, but I don't think you can."

"Why can't I? I've been there."

"Not with my friend, Charlie, you haven't. I don't know who it was that said cocaine is one of the most dangerous drugs known to man. But

71

they knew what they were talking about. Survival rates are very low once you've developed a full blown addiction." His voice was very quiet, very calm, as if he was talking about someone else.

"Kit, at least let me try. I can be there for you. I can help. I'm in love with you." Bugger, had she said that out loud? She chewed the inside of her mouth. It was true, though. She had been in love with him for a very long time. Or at least she had been in love with the person she'd thought him to be. Maybe that wasn't the same thing.

He was frowning – although he was still looking at her in that considering way he had done so often, as though he was weighing up what to say. Not wanting to say the wrong thing. And suddenly she realised that just because it was true for her, it didn't mean it was true for him. She felt a dark pain where her heart should be and she wished she could take back what she'd just said. Or at least tell him to ignore it.

She didn't think she could bear to hear him tell her she was kidding herself. That she'd fallen in love with an image she'd had of him. Not the real flesh and blood person that he was.

He shifted on the settee. "Only you could say that after what you just saw. But the truth is – shit…" He rubbed distractedly at the side of his nose and she wondered if it hurt. "It's not happening, SJ. It's not safe for you to be around me. Don't you remember what I told you? What they're no doubt still telling you at every AA meeting. Stick with the winners. Stay close to the people who are strong. There's a very good reason for that. It's called survival." He leaned forward then, his eyes were very serious.

In that moment he reminded her of the old Kit. The Kit who had bullied and harangued her, who had forced her to be honest with herself week after week. Her throat ached with grief. Please God let this all be some awful nightmare. Please let her still be asleep in his bed. Please let it be that the next time she woke up he would be beside her. There would be no smell of toast, no bathroom door ajar, just a future with the two of them going to silly comedy clubs and eating ice cream and doing very normal stuff.

"I'm not dragging you down with me," he added. "Like I said, I'm not that much of a hypocrite. I mean it," he said, as she shifted along the settee to get a little closer to him. "I know I should have told you before. I certainly didn't mean you to find out like you did this morning. I am truly sorry about that."

"So you expect me to just walk out on you?"

"Yeah, I'm afraid I do."

"But I won't know how you are?"

"If I crack it, I'll phone you."

"Do you promise?"

"Yeah, I promise."

He had made her go soon after that. He had walked her down the grimy stairs to the front entrance. The whole place had seemed more squalid in daylight. A place full of graffiti and damp patches. There was a broken kiddie's bicycle on one of the landings, alongside an empty syringe. SJ wished she hadn't seen it. Vicious little pictures of Kit with a syringe in his arm kept popping up to the surface of her mind. Not that she thought cocaine addicts used a syringe – did they? But he was a junkie, nonetheless.

She had known he'd done all that – but when she'd thought it was way back in the past it hadn't seemed so awful. It hadn't seemed so bloody real. It hadn't touched her like it had done today.

They had parted in sadness once before – long ago she had stood up in the little counselling room at S.A.A.D. and she had told Kit that she didn't need any more appointments – that she thought she could cope on her own. Even though the prospect of never seeing him again had filled her with grief.

She felt that same ache as they stood outside the front door of the block of flats, but it was much worse because she had engaged with him on so many levels. She could still feel the effects of his body on hers. She had the awful feeling that once she left she would never see him again. But, just as before, there had still been nothing she could do about it except to leave.

He hadn't called her, although he had texted just to say how sorry he was. SJ had left it two days and then she'd gone back. Kit hadn't answered his bell so she'd rung the others one by one until someone had buzzed her through the main door.

When she'd got up to his flat there had been no answer. Convinced he must know it was her, she'd banged on the door until his neighbour in the flat opposite had come out and glared at her.

"No sense in banging, lady – he's gone away."

"What do you mean gone away?"

"I mean as in buggered off, scarpered, skipped town. He ain't in that bloody flat – I can tell you that for nothing. Tosser owed me a fiver too!"

"Do you know where he's gone?" SJ tried to suppress her rising panic. She'd been so sure he'd be here – that they'd have another chance to sort things out.

"No bloody idea at all." The door had slammed with a finality that shook the frame.

SJ had stood there a while, waiting for her heart to settle. Then she'd phoned him, knowing even before it happened that his number would be unobtainable.

A month later he had phoned from a landline that he said wasn't his to tell her he was going back into treatment again. "Please don't try and contact me," he had finished. "I mean it, SJ. I need to be alone."

Feeling her heart break with pain she had wished him luck. She would have done more but Dorothy had stopped her. "He's told you how he wants things to be," she'd said. "So take him at his word, SJ. He's right, you know."

SJ probably wouldn't have taken this advice, wise though it was, but around the same time she discovered quite by chance that Kit and she had a mutual friend.

Ebby was a Rastafarian who came to AA meetings sporadically because he was also a member of Narcotics Anonymous. "Never could make up my darned mind about which lady I was lusting after most – never mind which addiction," he'd joked to SJ a few times. "Man, there's just too many tempting gigs out there to choose from."

But Ebby, despite his flippancy and his wild appearance, was rock solid in his sobriety and very kind.

"Kit and me, we go back years." He touched SJ's arm as he spoke. "I'm gonna keep an eye on that boy – don't you worry."

"Could you let me know that he's okay? You know, how he gets on." SJ had tried to keep her voice as flippant as Ebby's, but without much success. And she knew she hadn't fooled Ebby for a second.

"Sure thing, sister." His eyes had been soft. "You can count on your friend, Ebby."

And SJ, knowing that she could count on him, had left it at that. She hadn't seen Kit since that day, which was more than three years ago. He was still alive. Thanks to Ebby, she knew that much. He also still lived somewhere in Hackney, Ebby had made it clear that was as much as Kit wanted her to know and SJ hadn't pushed him. In time, the pain had shifted slowly into a more peaceful acceptance of the situation. She didn't hate Kit. She couldn't. She did, after all, owe him her life. And if Kit ever did want to contact her, well he knew where she was, didn't he?

Chapter Ten

Four things NOT to say to a newbie at their first AA meeting

1. Most people in AA are absolutely normal.

2. The person sharing their story is always wise and sane. (Hmmm, not when they're having a bad day.)

3. Going to meetings is one of the highlights of my life. (Makes you look like a saddo if it isn't a good one – see number 2.)

4. I'm doing a dog whisperer course.

You should definitely never say number 4. SJ paused mid list. Not if you wanted the poor, unsuspecting newbie to think that you were actually one of the sane ones. Was she sane? She still wasn't convinced despite Tanya's pep talk at Kew Gardens. Once again, they had mostly talked about her problems, not Tanya's.

"You've had a lot going on in your life the last few years," Tanya had said, putting her hand gently over SJ's as they sat on a bench overlooking the lake. "You've had a marriage break up – that's a toughie – you've started a new career. And there was Kit, wasn't there? " Tanya knew all about Kit and what had happened.

SJ hadn't meant to tell her. She hadn't wanted Tanya to judge. And let's be honest, it was a difficult situation not to judge. "I caught my boyfriend snorting coke in the loo – but he's not a bad person." She didn't want to see the look of disappointment in Tanya's eyes. It had been hard enough for her to bear the break up. But she'd had to say something and in the end the truth had been best.

Tanya hadn't judged. "I don't know why you thought I would," she'd said in mock reproof. "Hey – you're talking to the woman who caught her husband trying on her bra – remember?"

SJ had smiled despite herself. "True."

"These are all major life changes." Tanya had said. "And you gave up drinking. And you haven't been tempted to start again. You're awesome."

"I have been tempted to start again," SJ felt it was only fair to point this out. "Don't worry. I haven't done it," she said hastily when Tanya looked shocked. Maybe she wouldn't mention the Merlot incident. "Anyway, you've had major life changes too. All Michael's stuff. And Bethany – having children's a major change."

"Ain't that the truth," Tanya said, and they both looked at Bethany, who had dug a hole in the grass with a stick, and was currently filling it up with water collected from the lake in the bread container.

"Is she allowed to do that?"

"It's keeping her quiet," Tanya said with a wan little smile. "SJ, I wouldn't worry about that new woman. What does it matter what she thinks? She doesn't know you. You probably won't hear from her again, will you?"

"Probably not. Although I hope I do," SJ said, realising with a little start that she meant it.

Maybe she wasn't quite as selfish and horrible as she thought. Maybe there was hope for her yet.

Tanya looked surprised. "You do? I thought she was quite snobby and bitchy."

Crap – had she really said that? She sighed. Note to self – do not make snap judgements about people and then tell everyone. "Well, she was a bit snobby, I suppose. And she wasn't very nice about the woman in the green coat, but underneath it all – well, to be honest I think she was very scared."

SJ had actually texted Didi a couple of times since the meeting, but hadn't got a reply and in the end she had left it. Dorothy's words echoed in her head when she was tempted to do it again. 'We're not ambulance chasers, SJ. If they want our help let them come to us. It's hard enough when they do want our help. No point in forcing it on them when they don't.'

Then to her surprise, the day after she and Tanya had been to Kew Gardens, Didi did, in fact, text back. The text was in block capitals.

THANKS FOR TAKING ME TO THE MEETING. COULD WE CHAT?

She'd wondered why Didi hadn't just phoned her. Maybe she was low on credit or something, she hadn't mentioned the other texts SJ had sent either, but SJ decided to give her the benefit of the doubt and called.

The upshot of this conversation was that they were meeting this afternoon, between SJ's waitressing shift at Mortimer's and her Poetry and a Pint class. "Would it be terribly inconvenient for you to come to mine?" Didi had asked. "Only I'm seeing a client at three and another one at five, which doesn't give me a great deal of time in between, especially if one of them is late or early – I'd be eternally grateful."

SJ had agreed, even though she'd felt a little bit irked. Didi wasn't the only one who was busy and it was she, after all, who was helping Didi, and not the other way round. Stop it, she berated herself as she put on some lippy in the cloakrooms at the bistro before she left, and sprayed on Miss Dior from a handbag size bottle Tanya had given her for her birthday. She wished she was less selfish. After all, people in AA had helped her freely and unconditionally when she'd wanted to give up drinking. No one had ever said no to anything she'd asked – not that she'd ever demanded they come to her house, actually. She wouldn't have had the nerve. Didi hadn't demanded, SJ reminded herself, she had asked very politely. It wasn't Didi's fault if her voice had an imperious quality to it.

Anyway, it would be interesting to see where Didi lived. The address in Barnsbury looked posh when she'd Googled it. Didi must be a pretty successful actress. Odd that she didn't have any credit on her phone.

It was even posher in real life. It was a three-storey town house with Juliet balconies at the windows of the top two floors and its own driveway. SJ doubted you'd get much change from a million. Blinking, she rang the bell.

For several seconds no one came. SJ was about to text when the front door opened. Didi looked every bit as imposing in her own home as she did out of it. Possibly because she was all in black again, a dress this time, which showed off her gorgeously slender figure, accompanied by the same black, immensely high stiletto boots. SJ realised suddenly that she was holding in her stomach in a vain attempt to compete. Or maybe she was just holding her breath.

"Darling, thank you so much for coming." Didi air kissed her cheeks. "Welcome to my home."

Strange thing to say, but then maybe she'd have done the 'gracious hostess' thing a bit more herself if she'd lived somewhere as fabulous as this, SJ thought, as she followed Didi through a spacious, mirrored hallway, which smelled of lilies, although she couldn't see any.

The kitchen, also vast, was amazingly light and airy, especially considering that it was mostly red. Even the things that were usually white in a kitchen like the fridge and the dishwasher were red. The worktops and the oven were a sparkly black granite.

"Can I offer you a coffee?" Didi asked, picking up a jug from a percolator and gesturing to a row of stools alongside the breakfast bar in the middle of the room. "Do sit down."

"What an amazing kitchen," SJ said, noticing that Didi perfectly matched it. Her finger nails were painted the exact same colour red as everything else.

"Do you like it?" Didi beamed. "Thank you. I had it done when I moved in."

"Where did you find the fridge? I didn't even know they made them that colour."

"Special order. I don't like white."

"Boring," said SJ.

"Absolutely." Didi put an oversized green cup and saucer in front of her, along with a bowl of brown sugar cubes. "You're clearly a woman of impeccable taste. A woman after my own heart. But then, I knew that the moment we met."

"You did?" SJ wondered if she had forgotten the dog whisperer incident. Thinking about it Didi had been quite drunk so maybe she had. Phew. She'd been worrying unnecessarily all this time. "Would it be possible to have some milk?"

"Sorry, no." Didi perched on the stool next to her. "I'm afraid I don't have any. I don't like white."

SJ wasn't totally sure she'd heard right. She frowned. Didi twirled a gold sovereign ring on her middle finger and after a little pause she said, "I have what I suppose you would call a white phobia – I don't like anything white. White food, white implements, white clothes, white furniture, not even white cars – in fact, especially not white cars. They always look like they haven't been painted yet, don't you think?"

"Um – yes. Well, I guess they do. I've never really thought about it." For a moment SJ thought Didi might be winding her up. In a minute she would laugh and say, 'had you going there, didn't

I? Of course I have milk' and leap to her feet to get it.

She didn't.

SJ hesitated. "Doesn't that make it difficult for you – the food part, I mean?"

"Not at all. I just don't eat white food. No milk, no cream, no white sugar, no white meat, no white bread, no pasta, no potatoes. It's perfectly healthy. And I can eat wholemeal bread and pasta, of course."

"Is it to do with allergies?" SJ asked, anxious to find a rational explanation.

"No. I just don't like the colour white. It started when I was very small. I had to go into hospital and the bed had a white blanket. I screamed until they changed it, apparently. I don't remember."

"Maybe it was just the fear of hospitals," SJ ventured, thinking that this was one of the strangest conversations she had ever had and not sure how to go about changing the subject without seeming rude. Involuntarily, she glanced down at her own outfit. Because she'd come straight from the bistro she was wearing a white blouse and a dark skirt – which was kind of the unofficial uniform. She tugged her jacket around her in a vain attempt to cover up the blouse.

Didi gave a brittle little laugh as she followed her gaze. "Oh, don't worry. I can't control what other people wear – obviously. But I can control my own environment. So I do. Absolutely."

"Right," SJ said, thinking that when it came to control it was high time she got some semblance of it back over this conversation. "Anyway, I'm sure you didn't ask me here to talk about that." She smiled her warmest smile. "How are things with you? How's the drinking?"

A shadow passed across Didi's face – no more than a flicker but SJ's hypersensitive emotional radar picked it up. She softened her voice. "Have you been drinking today, honey?"

She hadn't smelled any alcohol but that didn't necessarily mean anything.

After a moment Didi shook her head, her glossy black bob catching the light which streamed in through the glass back doors. "I don't drink when I have clients – well not when I see them in the day. Or for short periods. It's much more difficult when they're staying over."

"Yes," SJ said, wondering again just exactly what Didi did. She couldn't think of any acting jobs where you had clients that stayed over. Not that she knew anything whatsoever about acting. Despite the glamour and the posh voice and the amazing house, there was something extremely vulnerable about Didi. Layered between the white phobia discussion and Didi's brittle laughter and the way she had of twiddling her gold sovereign ring, SJ sensed a huge amount of pain. The pain of having a secret that no one else knew about, the fear of discovery, the worry that even though things looked good on the outside, on the inside you were falling apart.

"When I was drinking," SJ began softly, "I got so good at hiding it – even from myself – that I don't think I even knew it was a problem until it was too late. It's denial, isn't it? We don't want to admit we can't stop. We don't want to admit we're different to everyone else. But we are. Alcoholism's a disease, Didi. And it's not just about how much we drink."

She hadn't meant to say that last bit. It was a conclusion she'd only recently come to, and one she'd only discussed with a few other recovering alcoholics, but she could see she'd got Didi's attention. So she carried on.

"People who are alcoholics tend to have other things in common. We can be a bit obsessive, we tend to be complete perfectionists, we never do anything by halves – we take everything to extremes. We're extreme people. Like say…" She hunted around for an example of extremism in her own life, which wasn't hard to find. "Take the other day – I went shopping and I bought four pairs of shoes – one pair just wasn't enough."

"I usually buy at least eight pairs," Didi said with a slight lift of her eyebrow. "You might just as well, mightn't you – if you see ones you like."

"Yes," SJ said, thinking that she probably wouldn't have stopped at four if she was as well off as Didi seemed to be. "Okay – bad example. Say I was doing some DIY in the house. Painting a radiator, maybe, well, I wouldn't just stop at one. I mean I wouldn't stop because I was tired. I'd keep going until I'd done every radiator in the house. Even if it meant staying up all night."

"I don't really do very much decorating."

"No, well – okay, have you ever been to a gym?"

Didi nodded. "I have a membership at Islington."

"How many times do you go in a week?"

"Once or twice."

SJ frowned. Didi didn't seem to be fitting her definition of an extremist at all; she was proving to be far too moderate. "Running then – have you ever done that?"

Didi shook her head and drummed her fingers on the worktop thoughtfully. SJ wondered if she'd matched her nail varnish on purpose. That was pretty extreme. She was about to cite this as an example of extremism when Didi said, "I do have quite long sessions at the gym, though. I'll usually stay there between four and five hours."

SJ gasped. "Blimey! That sounds exhausting."

"Well, yes, it is. But I do like to do things properly – and as I'm there it makes sense. I usually start with two hours on the weights, then I do an hour dance class and some spinning. Then eighty lengths in the pool and then the sauna and jacuzzi."

SJ felt her mouth drop open. "No wonder you're so slim."

"I need to keep slim for my job. And anyway, alcohol is very fattening. I've found it more difficult to balance the two as I've got older. I'm thirty-five." She frowned. "I put on weight really easily, these days."

"So what would you drink on a normal day?" SJ asked, preparing to double it. People who drank too much never told the truth.

"A litre of vodka – maybe a touch more – it depends very much on what I'm doing."

"Bloody hell, Didi, I don't even want to add up the units for that lot. Honey, you're killing yourself. Have you any idea of the harm you're doing to your body?"

"I don't drink every day." Didi waved a careless hand. "Sometimes I can go three weeks without drinking." She turned and looked SJ straight in the eyes. "So I can't be an alcoholic, can I? I regularly stop drinking." There was something in her eyes – almost a pleading. And this, SJ realised, was the reason she'd been brought round here. This was what Didi had wanted all along. Reassurance that she wasn't an alcoholic.

SJ took a deep breath, aware that Didi's life might depend on how she answered this question.

"I'm afraid I can't tell you if you're an alcoholic or not." She heard Kit's words echoing down the years at her. "Only you can decide that. But what I can tell you is that it's perfectly possibly to be an alcoholic who's a binge drinker."

Didi looked disbelieving and SJ went on softly, "It's quite a common misconception." She knew she sounded pompous, but she couldn't think of another way of saying this. "But all alcoholics stop drinking if you think about it. We sleep, we pass out, we run out of money. Life makes us stop. Binge drinkers just stop for longer periods."

"But that doesn't make sense," Didi said. "I thought the whole point of being an alcoholic was that you were a daily drinker – a man with a fat belly who props up the bar and gets uppity if he can't have his fix. Are you saying that it's something else? That there's another definition?"

"Yes. I'm afraid I am." SJ paused. "There are lots of definitions. But the best one I've ever come across is that it's someone who can't control their drinking once they start. If they have one drink, they need to have another. They don't just want it. They need it. If someone came along and offered them a choice? A million pounds or a drink? They'd take the drink." She looked at Didi. "Is that you?"

Didi didn't reply. The red and black kitchen filled up with silence. A smartphone which was on the worktop in front of them beeped. Didi glanced at it. "I'm so sorry, I need to go and get ready for my client."

"Sure," SJ said. "I've got to go too. I have a class tonight."

"Ah yes – you're a teacher, aren't you? What's the subject?"

"Poetry and a Pint." SJ smiled. "It's as it sounds – a fun class for adults. I hire a back room at The Crown in Hackney and people bring along a poem to discuss."

"Can we talk again?" Didi asked, as they walked back into her hallway. "I really appreciate you coming here. Should I pay you for your time?"

"No," SJ said, slightly shocked that Didi thought that might be why she'd come. "I'm here because I want to help. Because people helped me when I needed it – you know." She hesitated. "You've got my mobile number. Phone any time. I usually

88

have it with me. If I'm working it's on silent, but I'll call you back."

"Thank you." Didi looked as though she meant it too. She smiled and the fine lines around her lovely black eyes creased a little. SJ felt warmed.

"What is it you exactly do in the theatre?" she asked, curious to find out in case they never met again.

"I'm not really in the theatre," Didi said. "Although sometimes it can get pretty theatrical." That brittle little laugh again. "I'm a professional dominatrix, SJ."

Chapter Eleven

SJ had wanted to ask Didi so many questions after her casual little throwaway exit line, but there hadn't been time. Perhaps that's why Didi hadn't told her until the last minute. Perhaps Didi too had decided they wouldn't meet again.

The first thing she'd wanted to ask had been the same as when Didi had mentioned her white phobia, which was, "Are you serious?" But she had known, as she'd looked into Didi's sloe black eyes that she wasn't joking.

Somehow, Didi being a dominatrix made perfect sense.

Not that SJ was an expert on the subject, she thought, as she hurried towards the station. Like most of her friends her knowledge of bondage and sadomasochism had quadrupled overnight when she had read *Fifty Shades of Grey*. A dominatrix, SJ imagined, tied people up and then did heinous things to them with whips and possibly melting candles. She could feel herself blushing at the thought. Bloody hell. Why was it so easy to imagine Didi in that role? Was it the presence she had? Her slightly imperious manner? The effect she had on men?

The Overground was crowded with rush hour commuters. As SJ clung to a hand rest she thought about the way Number Ten Tim and Half Pint Hughie had reacted to Didi. Both of them had looked at her with a kind of reverential awe.

Shit – what if they were clients? For a sudden awful moment she had an image of Half Pint

Hughie handcuffed naked to a giant bed while Didi strutted around in a black leather basque or whatever she wore flicking at his scrawny limbs with her whip.

The image was so distracting that SJ's hand slipped off the hand rest as the train pulled into a station and she cannoned into a man in a pinstriped suit in front of her.

"Sorry," she said to his stiffening shoulders.

Several people, including him, disembarked onto the platform. SJ grabbed a free seat by the doors. The woman beside her was drinking something in a takeaway plastic carton via a straw. It smelled strongly of peaches. It was making SJ feel slightly sick. Or maybe that was the image of a naked Hughie spread-eagled on Didi's four-poster. Not that it probably would be a four-poster as the posts would get in the way of the whip. But then again maybe that would add to the excitement. *She whips me, she whips me not. She whips me, she whips me not!*

The cracking of a whip sounded and SJ jumped out of her skin before she realised it was only the sound of her fellow commuter crushing the plastic cup. She must have finished the vile peach drink.

Her neighbour shot her an apologetic smile. SJ forced herself to smile back. No, of course Hughie wasn't a client. He never looked as if he had two pennies to rub together. No way would he be able to afford Didi's prices. Judging by the house she lived in she must charge a fortune.

'You're doing an awful lot of judging, SJ'. She could hear Dorothy's sensible sponsor voice in her head.

It irritated her how much that happened. Even when Dorothy was away on a flaming cruise she couldn't avoid her. Still, she supposed Dorothy's voice was an improvement on the demonic Alco's.

'You've no idea how Didi pays for her house,' Dorothy continued pleasantly. *'She might have an independent income. She might have been left it by a relative.'*

SJ wondered if telling Dorothy about a member of AA being a dominatrix was breaking their anonymity. Probably – which meant she'd have to keep it to herself. She couldn't tell Tanya either. That was a shame. Tanya might know something about bondage.

Actually, that was unlikely. Cross-dressing and bondage weren't the same thing probably. Even though they were both fetishes – were they both fetishes? She suspected that any odd sexual behaviour that got people going was a fetish. Still, there was no reason to think cross-dressing and bondage were in any way connected. Her head spun. Luckily, by the time they reached Hackney Central she'd calmed down. Her heart had stopped pounding, her hands no longer felt clammy. The whole thing was beginning to seem a little surreal.

As she hurried home – there was just time for a quick change before her class – two thoughts still circled her mind. The first was that she was never now likely to meet Ant and Dec. What a pity. That would have been so cool.

The second thought was more persistent. How on earth did Didi manage with all those white naked bodies? Surely that must be really difficult with a white phobia. Maybe she got around it by insisting all her clients had tans. If they ever met again, SJ decided she would ask her.

It was hard work having two jobs, SJ mused, as she arranged the tables and chairs in The Crown's back room and got out her paperwork: one folder of plastic loose leaf display sleeves, which contained her latest poems; a thick A4 notepad; her iPad because The Crown had free Wi-Fi, and a translucent pink pencil case, which was home to several pens and an oven timer. What on earth had possessed her to buy pink? She wasn't really a pink sort of girl. Possibly because the pink one had been a bargain 50p and the cooler blue and grey ones had been £1.99.

It was hard work being so broke too. When she'd been a practising alky she'd lived in a smart London house, with a gorgeous garden and an endless amount of tasty food and drink, none of which she'd had to pay for. Now she was sober she lived in a much smaller rented flat in a not very salubrious part of Hackney, which cost an arm and a leg, and she quite often had beans on toast for tea. Not that she didn't like beans on toast – especially if they had HP sauce mixed in with them. She was actually quite good at existing on next to nothing – when she and Tanya had been at uni together they'd lived on avocado on toast, which they'd bought from the market. How had they managed that? Avocados always seemed so bloody expensive, these days.

On the plus side she'd been happier these last four and a half years than she'd ever been. And actually she preferred the room at The Crown to the one she'd hired previously at The Red Lion. The Crown's room was more authentic somehow. It smelled of dust and old furniture and mysteries. There was also a rumour that Byron had regularly drunk there. Or so Jaheem, the landlord, had claimed when he'd said she could hire the room.

"He and the other guy – Sheila – they always coming in here."

"Sheila?" SJ had repeated, puzzled. "Um... a female poet...?"

Jaheem shook his dreadlocks with a frown. "No. You know who ah mean – the guy with the drug problem – they always on the pipe – smoking the big O – Opium."

"Ah, you mean Shelley," SJ said in sudden understanding.

"Shelley – that's him." Jaheem gave her a wide grin, showing his very white, rather pointed teeth. SJ had already decided he'd been a vampire in another life. "Those guys – they top poets, yeah?"

"Yeah." SJ had hired the room for his cheek. And also because he let her have it for a pittance and only threw her out if he needed it for a wake, which was rare.

Out of curiosity she had once Googled The Crown and could find no reference to Byron and Shelly ever having been in it. But who was to say they hadn't? There was a lot more chance they'd been in The Crown than The Red Lion simply because it was older.

And it had been quite good fun discussing the possibilities with her students when they'd first moved over.

Dorothy, who wrote blockbusters for a living and was the longest standing attendee of Poetry and a Pint, as well as being her sponsor, had laughed her head off.

"That Jaheem could sell sand to a sheik," she had said, wiping tears from her eyes. "I heard him telling someone at the bar the other day that Jack the Ripper regularly came by for a tomato juice."

"Christina Rossetti probably came in here, though," said Bruce, another of her poets. "She was only up the road."

"She probably wrote *In The Bleak Midwinter* in this very room," Sybil, his wife added. "Do you reckon we can get Jaheem to turn the heating up, SJ? It's freezing in here."

"Wear layers," one of the performance poets advised her.

"Cold is good for the soul," someone else agreed. "Poets do their best work in a freezing garret."

"I thought that was artists and writers," SJ said. "I'll ask Jaheem about the heating." Though she didn't hold out much hope, seeing as she hardly paid him anything. In the end he had lent her a knackered old paraffin stove, which he said she could have as long as she supplied the paraffin. It was probably illegal – according to Sybil they'd all been banned in the seventies – but it kicked out loads of heat.

While she waited for her students to arrive – because, despite her meeting with Didi she had got here too early – SJ decided to write an experimental poem on her iPad, based on a list.

Things to do before Friday (it could do with a better title – ho hum, it was a work in progress.)

Text Didi and see if she's okay
Phone Tanya and arrange another day
To go out.
Give Alison a shout
About
Dad's seventieth.

Hmmm. She'd had to leave out the numbers and cheat quite a lot with the ends of lines, which was a bad sign. And while she encouraged her Poetry and Pinters to cheat if it made the poem amusing, she couldn't say she'd even done that.

Maybe she would stick with pen and paper. Nothing in the world ended with seventieth. Or birthday. Not properly, she'd checked before. And talking of Dad's seventieth she should chase up his present, which she'd ordered from eBay and which hadn't yet showed up. EBay was usually very reliable and the seller had a 99.7% reliability rating.

She could probably get eBay into her poem – lots of things rhymed with bay – day, hay, lay, may, pay, say, way. SJ smiled. She could get a fine bit of doggerel out of eBay, she was sure. She could possibly even complain about the late delivery of Dad's present in verse.

Hey, eBay,
It's Dad's Birth-Day
But his present's
Not headed my way.
I did pay!
Hey, eBay,
What d'ya say?
Will it be here
By Satur-day?

Mmm. Maybe she'd forget the eBay poem. If she sent the seller a rhyme like that he might report her and get her sectioned.

Fortunately, the parcel arrived the next day so she didn't have to resort to the poem. There was plenty of time to wrap it up before Saturday when the whole family were going out for a meal at The Vineyard in Romford, close to where her parents and Alison lived. The whole family being Mum, Dad, Alison and her husband Clive. Sophie and Kevin, Alison's kids, apparently had other plans. SJ was sorry about this. Particularly about Kevin. At least she could have had a bit of fun with him. They were on pretty much the same wavelength – both of them being black sheep and not very conventional.

Much as she loved her parents, the prospect of spending a whole evening watching them get tipsy – because that's what usually happened at family celebrations – filled her with dread.

It was relatively easy not to drink as long as she wasn't too stressed. She always felt stressed when she was around her mother. And Alison had the ability to push her stress button to unlimited heights – if she was in wind-up mode, which SJ couldn't predict in advance. She would just have to keep her fingers crossed. And pray!

Chapter Twelve

On Saturday morning, the day of the meal, Alison rang.

"I just thought I'd phone and tell you you're welcome to stay over at ours later if you like. Save you having to traipse back to town afterwards. Not that drinking and driving's an issue for you, is it, Sis?" She gave a tinkling little laugh that made SJ want to thump her. Alison just couldn't resist the chance to have a little jibe.

"No it isn't an issue. Seeing as I haven't got a car." Ha – put that in your pipe and smoke it, annoying little sister.

"Oh no. I forgot. You had to give it up."

"I didn't *have* to give it up."

This was not entirely true, but she had no intention of admitting it. "There just didn't seem much point in keeping it. You don't need a car in the centre of London." Calm down, SJ. Change the subject. Don't rise. You know she enjoys it. She took a deep breath. "Anyway, what have you bought Dad?"

"A set of darts. Top of the range," Alison said smugly.

Crap. That's what SJ had bought him too. But hers were bound to be inferior quality because Alison and Clive were a lot better off than she was.

"How about you?" Alison went on.

"Oh, this and that," SJ said, wondering if there would be time for her to get something else before they all met up. Not if she wanted to fit in a lunchtime meeting as well. Which she did if she was going to be surrounded by alcohol all night.

"See you later then." Alison hung up. SJ felt sad. She wished she and her sister got on better. Still, at least they could go out for a family meal, these days, which pleased her mother.

By the time she set off for Romford that evening she was feeling a bit less despondent. She had decided not to change the darts – they were already wrapped up – and besides, hadn't her father once said it was impossible to have too many sets of darts? But she had got him an extra present – she'd spotted it as she'd walked past a gift shop on her way home from the meeting – a novelty mug, inscribed *The evolution of a darts player*. It would make Dad smile anyway. She'd also got him a large blue helium balloon with *Happy Birthday Spring Chicken* on one side. And *70 Today* on the other, which she hoped would survive the train journey across London.

The Old Vineyard was, despite its name, a brand new restaurant adjacent to a car park. Maybe the car park had once been a vineyard, SJ mused, although that seemed pretty unlikely in the middle of Romford.

Everyone was already sitting at the table in the packed restaurant when she arrived. Alison looked gorgeous as usual in a pale blue low cut top and huge hooped gold earrings. Although she also looked as though she'd put on weight. So did Clive. The perks of going out on too many posh dinners. Maybe there were some advantages of being broke, after all. SJ tried not to feel smug.

100

"Hi, everyone. Happy Birthday, Dad. Are you feeling old?"

"Hello, SJ, love. And yes. I'm feeling one day older than yesterday. And one day younger than I'll feel tomorrow. Ta." He took the blue and white striped gift bag she gave him and looked a bit alarmed at the size of the balloon, which SJ tied to his chair, thank goodness it was still in one piece. "What's all this then? I hope you haven't been spending all your money on me."

"Of course I have," she said, aware of Alison's gaze and of the fact that Dad already had a gift wrapped package by his plate that was exactly the same size as hers.

"It smells good in here," she said, breathing in the scents of garlic and spices. "Have you already ordered?"

"No. We were waiting for you." Her mother looked impatient. "But if you'd like to look at the menu, Sarah-Jane?"

"I'm not late, am I?" Why did she always feel as though she was slightly out of step with her family? As though they were a close knit unit and she was on the outside looking in. Maybe it was because she didn't have any children. No partner now either. She was the first person in their family who'd ever had one divorce, let alone two, before she was even forty – she wasn't exactly conventional. No wonder she didn't fit in.

"Move that bottle," her mother ordered, as SJ sat down in the space beside Clive. "Sarah-Jane doesn't want that under her nose."

101

Oh and she was a recovering alcoholic too. Thanks for the reminder, Mum. Still, at least her mother actually acknowledged the fact now. It had taken her ages to properly accept her daughter had a drink problem. Although they still didn't talk about it. Unless you counted indirect little remarks like that.

She had a contrary urge to move the bottle back so that it was under her nose again. But she resisted. Clive was smiling at her. "Good to see you, SJ."

"You too." Shit, how she wished she was at an AA meeting where no one bothered with niceties. They just got straight down to whatever was important. They spoke about how things really were for them. They spoke about their truths. Even if their truths showed them up to be pretty flawed people with lots of little gripes and jealousies.

If she had been at an AA meeting and her family had been AA members this is what everyone would have been saying:

Clive: Thank God SJ's finally here. I'm starving.

Alison: I can't wait to give Dad the presents. I bet he's going to like mine best. But then that's only right – I am his favourite daughter. I am his princess, after all.

Dad: I wonder if I can get away with a steak? Should I try for the twelve-ounce rib eye as it's my birthday? Or maybe even the mixed grill?

SJ smiled to herself. Ho ho ho. She was definitely right about Dad. He had a dreamy look on his face. She might be being a bit harsh about Alison, but she didn't think so – her sister was looking incredibly pleased with herself. The only person she couldn't read tonight was Mum – she looked a bit agitated.

It was traditional in their family to open the presents after the meal so it wasn't until they were drinking coffee that Dad finally got to see his birthday gifts. He opened Alison's present first, his face breaking into a broad smile as he clicked open the small rectangular box, which contained the darts, having pretended up until that point to have no idea what his present could be.

"Lovely quality," he said, weighing them in his fingers while Alison preened.

"Do you like them, Dad? Are you sure you like them?"

"They're grand, love. Absolutely grand."

"There's something else," Alison said, just as he was about to go on to his next present. She was rummaging around in her handbag, which was on her lap, and then she produced a small red envelope with a flourish.

"As it's a special one, Clive and I bought you this too. I hope you like it."

Along with everyone else, SJ leaned forward expectantly as her father fumbled with the envelope and drew out a piece of white card. SJ could see the gold lettering on it but not what it said.

"Bloodeh hell," her father said, his mouth opening and then shutting again. "Bloodeh hell, love." He always lapsed into his Yorkshire accent when he was flustered. "You shouldn't have." He ran out of words. His face had turned a brick red colour. Alison clapped her hands together in glee. "It's tickets for the Hinckley Darts Tournament in Essex," she said for the benefit of SJ and their mother. "For two, Mum, so you can go if you like. Or he can take one of his darts cronies. But we thought you might like to go with him, so we bought a package that includes a stopover at the hotel. It's really posh."

Excitement buzzed around the table. Dad was still opening and shutting his mouth. Clive was smiling magnanimously, Alison was giggling and their mother was fanning her face with a paper serviette. "Well I never," she was saying. "That's ever so kind of you two. I had no idea, Jim. No idea at all. Why didn't you tell me, love?"

"We wanted it to be a surprise," Alison said. "We didn't want to give the game away, did we, Clive?"

Clive shook his head.

Alison preened her hair. If she'd had a crown she'd have been twirling it, SJ thought, and then berated herself for being such a cow. Alison had every right to be pleased with herself. It was a brilliant present. The ultimate present. Thoughtful, insightful and way, way out of SJ's price range. She couldn't have afforded it even if the idea had occurred to her.

Not that she begrudged her dad such a brilliant present for one second. Of course she didn't. She was smiling and clapping like everyone else, so why did she feel so utterly bereft?

Maybe it was because her paltry set of darts and her silly novelty mug and her tacky blue balloon paled into insignificance beside this. They seemed shabby and a bit mean. She wished Alison had said something – maybe even given her the chance to have contributed. That would have been good, but Alison hadn't said a word. She clearly had wanted to keep it a complete surprise.

SJ chewed the inside of her mouth and wished she didn't feel so choked up. When she glanced up she realised Alison was looking at her for the first time since Dad had opened the surprise present. Her sister's clear blue eyes were triumphant. They said, *beat that.*

After that, SJ would have quite liked to spirit her presents away before Dad had a chance to open them. She couldn't, of course. And Dad being Dad admired her darts and her mug every bit as enthusiastically as he'd admired Alison's gifts. When her sister got up to go to the loo and there was a gap, Dad even reached across and squeezed her knee under the table.

I love you, that squeeze seemed to say.

SJ smiled at him. "Are you having a good time?" she mouthed.

"I'm having a grand time."

SJ was about to say something else when there was a flurry of activity at the kitchen end of the restaurant. She glanced up to see Alison coming back with a waiter, who was carrying a birthday cake festooned with candles and sparklers. That at least she had known about. Although Alison had refused to let her contribute to that, too.

"Happy birthday to you," began Alison and the waiter and soon the whole restaurant was joining in with great gusto.

"Happy birthday, dear Ji-im." Only, apart from their table, there was that awkward gap where his name should be because no one else knew who they were singing for. "Happy birthday to you."

There was a smattering of clapping and, straight after that, the strains of "For he's a jolly good fellow."

SJ was beginning to feel very weary. The noise levels had gone up considerably since they'd arrived and they'd been bad then. Now she was suddenly, painfully aware of the alcohol in the restaurant. The whole restaurant was a tableau of drinks:

- Her mother's half full glass of rosé.
- Her father's pale ale.
- Clive's cider.
- Alison's empty wine glass.
- Even a bottle of champagne in an ice bucket on the next table. (They'd only drunk half of it – amateurs clearly.)

In front of her was her own glass, (she'd been drinking tonic water) which held a soggy bit of lemon atop melting ice. She'd have given anything for a drink. Well, almost anything. Not her four and half years of sobriety. Not that.

It was time to go. She reached for her bag beneath the table and checked her phone, which she hadn't looked at all night. There were three

106

missed calls from Didi. That was odd. She hadn't heard from her since she'd been to her house that time.

The last call had been less than an hour ago. Then it had been followed by a text which said, in block capitals. *I NEED YOUR HELP.*

To SJ's surprise, she felt quite uplifted. At least someone needed her. She would phone Didi on the train on the way home. She glanced at the flushed and animated faces of her family around her. They'd come in taxis – so they'd all let their hair down tonight. Letting their hair down meant one and a half glasses of wine for her mother, and a couple of pints of pale ale for Dad and she wasn't entirely sure what Alison had been drinking.

Suddenly, despite the longing for a drink, she felt all warm and fuzzy towards her family. Even Alison's Game, Set and Match at one-upmanship didn't seem so bad. After all, she'd been playing that game since they were both small. SJ wasn't really surprised she hadn't grown out of it. She, on the other hand, was mature enough to rise above it. Anyway, what did it really prove? That Alison and Clive had more money than she did. That was all.

Dad knew how much she loved him – he wasn't shallow enough to be bought off by a couple of tickets to a darts tournament. Pah!

SJ felt quite proud of herself as she kissed everyone goodbye. She must be growing up. She was a lot more mature and sensible than she'd supposed.

"See you soon," she said as she kissed Alison.

"You must come over for dinner," Alison said. "You're welcome to bring a plus one."

"Thanks. I'll do that." SJ could play the 'let's pretend we're close' game just as well as her sister.

"Have you got a plus one then?" Alison's eyes were guileless.

"Maybe."

"You've kept him quiet. Mum…" she yelled across the table. "Did *you* know Sarah-Jane had a new boyfriend?"

"No, love. Have you really, Sarah-Jane? That's good. I worry about you – living in the city on your own."

Bloody hell. In one sentence they'd elevated her plus one (who didn't exist anyway) to a significant other who was likely to move into her flat and protect her from the evils of London. How had that happened?

She glanced back at Alison's smiling face. The warm fuzzy feelings were dissipating fast.

"I'll let you know about dinner," she said and turned back to her parents. "Thanks for a lovely evening. I'll phone you soon."

"Make sure you do. And bring your man over. Where did you meet him? It wasn't on one of those dodgy dating sites, was it?" Mum's voice was anxious.

Dad was smiling, as though he knew it was all one big wheeze. Or maybe it was because he'd had his steak and his piece of birthday cake and he was surrounded by his family, which was what he liked best in the world.

SJ blew him a kiss. "I'll call you soon." It was a relief to leave the overheated restaurant and escape into the cold night air. She was glad she hadn't accepted Alison's offer of a bed for the night, even though it would take her an hour to get home.

Whatever Didi wanted, it was bound to be a breeze compared to talking to her family.

Chapter Thirteen

Didi didn't answer her mobile when SJ tried it during her stroll to the station. SJ felt slightly irked. Clearly she wasn't that much in need of help then. Well, it was a good job she hadn't just left something important to call her back then, wasn't it. Oh get over yourself, SJ. Perhaps the emergency, whatever it was, had passed. SJ hoped it hadn't been a 'shall I drink this bottle of vodka?' kind of emergency. She hoped she wasn't too late to stop Didi doing that.

Not that she could have stopped her drinking a bottle of vodka if Didi had set her heart on it anyway. SJ had been working a twelve-step program for long enough to know that she was as powerless over anyone else's drinking as she was over her own. The only thing she had any power over at all was the choice of whether or not she took the first drink.

It was an odd thing that, SJ thought, as she waited on the platform for the train. For years and years she had thought it was the fifth or sixth or seventh drink that did the damage. It had been Number Ten Tim who'd put her right.

"Look at this way, SJ," he'd said. "If you jump off the platform into the path of an oncoming train, which of the carriages is going to kill you? Will it be the twelfth carriage or will it be the first one?"

It was a good analogy, SJ thought, as the train whooshed into the station, its front end looking mighty damn solid and unstoppable and not the kind of thing you'd want to leap in front of, at all. And it wasn't one she was ever likely to forget, living in London. Sometimes she felt as though she spent her whole life on trains.

She found a seat that wasn't in the quiet zone and called Didi again. This time she answered immediately.

"Yes?" Her voice was very clipped. SJ was slightly taken aback. Still, at least she didn't sound drunk.

"You were trying to get hold of me," she began, "I've been out with…"

"SJ. Thanks so much for calling. Yes, yes I was. SJ what is a sponsor?"

"Er – well." SJ glanced around the carriage. She didn't really like talking about AA stuff in public. Across the aisle, two seats in front of her a guy in a baseball cap was playing some game on a tablet. She could see the reflection of an older couple's heads in the window in the row of seats in front of him.

"It's someone who helps you out, gives you advice about um stuff and takes you through…" she lowered her voice. "…the steps."

"Steps. Hmmm – what are they?"

"You can read about that on the literature I gave you," SJ said, remembering it with relief. "Or we can have another chat if you like. It's tricky at the moment. I'm on a train."

"Was that the ghastly little white book you gave me?" There was a shudder in Didi's voice. "Ugh. I had to throw that away."

111

"Right," said SJ. "Well, maybe I could phone you back when I get home."

"No need. Just give me some more information. How do I go about getting a sponsor? Do I have to pay for sessions? Is that how it works?"

"No," SJ said. "You don't have to pay. You just ask someone you think will do a good job. And then you keep your fingers crossed that they'll say yes. It can't be a man," she added. "In case of romantic involvement. It has to be someone of the same sex."

"I see." There was a pause.

"You don't have to decide now. In fact, you shouldn't really rush it. It's quite important to get the right person."

"Will you be my sponsor?" Didi asked. "I don't know anyone else in AA so it'll have to be you."

SJ hesitated. This wasn't quite how she'd imagined she'd feel when someone asked her that for the first time. People like Penny and Dorothy who'd been sponsoring people for years always said it was a real privilege, an honour, to be asked. It showed that people trusted you and wanted to be like you.

"It should be someone you admire," SJ said. "And someone you trust. And someone you like a lot too," she added for good measure. No point in letting Didi think she was a complete pushover. "Maybe you'd like to think about it for a while."

"I don't need to think about it. I'm asking you. So will you do it or won't you?"

"I'll do it," SJ heard herself saying. So much for not being a pushover.

"Good," Didi said. "So when shall we have our first session? Shall I text you some dates when I'm free?"

"It doesn't really work like that," SJ said before realising she was talking to thin air. The display on her phone was blank. No signal. What crappy timing that had been. The signal was always bad on this part of the track. So she probably wouldn't be able to call Didi back for a while.

Never mind. She had her first sponsee. How exciting was that! They could sort out the finer details later.

It was the following morning before it struck SJ that it might be a good plan to ask Dorothy's advice about sponsoring Didi. After all, sponsoring someone was pretty important stuff. Life and death stuff – more important even than manning the helpline. What if she did something wrong?

She wondered where Dorothy was. She hadn't actually heard from her lately and she didn't want to wake her up in the middle of the night again. Maybe she should send a text. After some thought she typed into her phone, *Hope you are good. Been asked to sponsor someone. Get me! Please can we discuss when you're free? SJ x*

A few minutes later her phone beeped with the arrival of an answering text. Except when she looked it was from Didi, not Dorothy, and it said, *ARE YOU OKAY TO MEET AT CAMDEN THIS PM?*

Well, no actually. She couldn't just drop everything and trek over to Camden at the drop of a hat. Except that actually she was free and it wouldn't involve dropping anything. She quite often saw Tanya and Bethany on Sunday afternoons because Michael played badminton, but this weekend they were all away at Tanya's parents. SJ realised, with a slight sense of irritation because it meant that Didi was calling the shots again, that she might just as well go to Camden.

No sense in letting Didi think she was in total control, though. It was high time she set some boundaries. She decided to leave it ten minutes before texting back.

Her landline rang and she snatched it up. "Look, Didi, I know you're keen to get started, but I'm afraid I can't…"

"Sarah-Jane, it's your mother here. You really should answer the phone with more care. Haven't I taught you any manners?"

"Sorry, Mum – I thought it was someone else. How's things? And thank you for the lovely meal last night." Damn she should probably have phoned Mum first thing to say thanks. Alison had probably sent flowers by now.

"You're welcome, love – look I wanted to talk to you last night, but you dashed off."

"No, I didn't. It was nearly half past ten."

"Alison stayed until midnight."

"Bully for Alison."

"I'm sorry?"

"I said good for Alison. What did you want to talk to me about?"

"I'm worried about your dad."

"Oh?" SJ felt a little chill go through her. "In what respect? He seemed fine to me. I thought he had a great time last night."

"Well, yes he did. We both did. We had a lovely time."

"So why are you worried?"

"He's not been so well lately. It's a bit sensitive but he keeps getting – you know – clogged up."

"Clogged up?"

"With his business – you know?"

"You mean he's constipated?"

"Yes," said her mother in relief. "Thank you, I couldn't remember the word."

"Well, has he been to the doctor?"

"No, he won't go."

"Why not?"

"He's too embarrassed. You know what your father's like."

Yes, SJ knew only too well. He wasn't the kind of man who talked about bodily functions. He found the whole subject excruciating. He was proud of the fact he'd never changed a nappy in his life – not that a lot of his generation had, SJ guessed.

He predated the New Man era. Poo, wee and sick were all off limits and when she and Alison had started their periods he'd leave the room if the subject was mentioned. He didn't even like fart jokes. Once, when Alison had put a fart cushion on his chair at the dining table, he'd not spoken to her for two days.

"Poor Dad," SJ said with a little sigh.

"One of those thingie tests came through the door the other day," her mother went on. "I couldn't get him to do that either."

A thingie test – SJ thought hard and there was a little silence during which she could hear Mum's anxious breathing.

"The ones where you have to send them a sample," her mother said, with obvious embarrassment. "Of your…"

"Yes," SJ said to save her the discomfort of spelling it out. "Right. Well, he really should do that one, Mum, you both should. Isn't that test so you can spot the early warning signs of bowel cancer?"

"I know what it's for, Sarah-Jane. " Her mother had gone into stiff and formal mode as she always did when she felt awkward. "But I can't make him do it if he doesn't want to, can I?"

"No. I guess not."

"Will you talk to him?"

"Me?" SJ gasped. "What makes you think he's going to listen to me?"

"Because – oh I don't know, but he won't listen to me. And I asked Alison and she said no, point blank. She said it was too icky and she didn't even like talking to her children about icky stuff let alone her father. And honestly, Sarah-Jane, I'm at my wits end."

So as usual she was the last to be consulted, SJ thought with a little dip of her heart. For one mad second there she'd thought maybe Mum had decided that as she was the older sensible sister she might have something to offer. But no, she was just the last resort.

"Right," SJ said. "Well…"

"Please, Sarah-Jane. I don't know what else to do. What if he's really ill?"

"Of course I'll talk to him," she said with a little sigh. "If you think it will help." She couldn't bear to think of her father being ill. Her lovely, gentle bear of a father, who'd been a quietly solid presence her entire life. Okay, so he might not have been on hand for what Alison called the icky bits of their childhood illnesses but he'd been there for bedtime stories, 'checking under the bed for monster' duties, and for nightmares. SJ had gone through a phase of having terrible nightmares when she was about eight. *A Nightmare on Elm Street* had been showing at the pictures and Tommy Jones, a boy at her school, had convinced her she would be killed in her sleep by a razor-wielding monster.

The super-sensitive, eight-year-old SJ hadn't been able to sleep for weeks. Mum had lost patience with her in the end, but Dad never had. He'd sat by her bed, night after night, stroking her forehead with his warm, rough hands and reassuring her that there wasn't a monster in the universe that could get past him. She had felt safe when he was in the room and he'd never once sneaked away before she had fallen back to sleep even if it took hours for her to fall.

"Of course I'll talk to him," she said again, aware that another text had just flashed up on her mobile. Hopefully it was Dorothy.

117

"When's a good time to come over?"

"I was thinking maybe Tuesday evening, pet, if you could." She could hear the relief in Mum's voice. She must really be worried. "I'll give you your tea – it's steak and kidney pie, Tuesdays."

SJ smiled. "Sounds nice." It meant she would have to skip off phone service a bit early, which would annoy Penny, but it couldn't be helped. Dad's health was more important. Much more important.

"See you Tuesday then, Mum."

As she disconnected and reached for her mobile, another text came through. The previous one hadn't been from Dorothy but Didi. This one was too.

CAN YOU CONFIRM PLEASE, SJ. I AM VERY BUSY.

She texted back. *Yes, that's cool. Where and when?* So much for setting boundaries, but she was too worried about Dad to be concerned about making a point to Didi now.

Chapter Fourteen

Where to meet had proved to be a lot more tricky than *when* to meet. This was because – thanks to Didi's white phobia – an awful lot of places were out of bounds.

They'd ended up in a tiny coffee bar in one of the labyrinth-like tunnels of Camden Market. The décor was red and black. The waitresses wore red and black too and SJ nearly missed Didi altogether, she blended in so perfectly. It was only when she unfolded herself from a black chair that SJ spotted her.

"Hi," she said, as SJ went across and pulled out the chair opposite. "I've ordered a cafetiere of coffee. Is that okay with you? I may have something to eat too." She consulted the menu.

SJ, who'd opened her mouth to say coffee was fine, shut it again, as her opinion clearly wasn't being sought anyway.

"Great," she said. She was going to have to lay down some ground rules. In fact, now was probably as good a time as any to do it.

"Didi," she began. "We need to talk about how this usually works…"

Didi gave her a sweet smile. "I can't tell you how grateful I am that you've agreed to be my sponsor," she said, and there was such genuine warmth in her voice that SJ was momentarily disarmed.

"Yes. We must talk," Didi continued. "I can't keep getting you over here like this. I know that. I'm sure you've got far better things to do."

"No, it's fine," SJ said. "I mean, yes I have obviously got lots to do, but I didn't mind today. It was actually quite a good time as it happens."

Didi nodded seriously. "Thank you. Thank you so much."

It took SJ a moment or so to realise she was no longer talking to her but to the waitress who had arrived with the coffee and two blue oversized cups and saucers – very similar to the ones Didi had at home.

"We'd like to order if we may," Didi added. "I'll have my usual burger with a fried egg on the side, please, and French fries, well done. SJ, how about you?"

"I've already eaten," SJ said. "But I'd like some milk please for my coffee." She sneaked a glance at Didi and saw that she was smiling.

"It's fine," she said. "They use blue jugs in here. I won't watch while you pour. But thank you for being so sensitive about it."

"How do you get on with the fried egg?" SJ asked as soon as the waitress was out of earshot. "Doesn't that cause you a problem?"

"Not if the yolk's broken. Chef will do that for me. I know him quite well." She raised her eyebrows and SJ felt her eyes widen. Did Didi mean…?

Before she had a chance to ask Didi said, "Yes, he's my Monday man. That's his day off and he likes to spend it ironing."

"Ironing?" SJ shook her head, puzzled. "I thought for a moment you meant he came to you for – um – professional services."

"Indeed he does. Oh, SJ, you really are an innocent, aren't you. It's not all about handcuffs and chains, you know. In fact, it is not about that at all. My saucy chef…" she lowered her voice conspiratorially. "Well, he likes to do my ironing. I whip him while he does it, of course. Well, I do if he doesn't do it perfectly. And, believe me, he never does it perfectly. I have very exacting standards."

"Gosh." SJ couldn't think of a single other thing to say. She looked at Didi in admiration. "Does he pay you a lot? I mean, not that it's any of my business, of course, but…"

Didi waved a hand. "It's okay – we're friends. I'll tell you. He pays me…" she paused for dramatic effect while she poured out her coffee, "…around four hundred pounds a session."

Fortunately, SJ wasn't holding the cafetiere or she was pretty sure she would have dropped it. That was more than she got in a week at Mortimer's. "Four hundred pounds!" she mouthed. "Bloody hell."

Didi picked up her cup and sipped with delicate precision, her little finger stuck up in a way that reminded SJ of Alison when she was trying to act posh. Only on Didi it clearly wasn't an act.

"But now…" she breathed, "we must change the subject. His girlfriend's coming back."

SJ shut up hurriedly. Good grief – surely Didi didn't mean the waitress. But there was no one else in the vicinity. The waitress, a pretty blonde with very long eyelashes and a mole on her cheek, put the milk jug in front of SJ and smiled at Didi

121

before bustling across to another table to take their order. She clearly had no idea that she was serving her boyfriend's mistress. His mistress in every sense of the word, SJ thought.

"So sponsorship," Didi went on. "I was hoping you could fill me in on all the things I need to know. I did do a little bit of research – on the internet, you know. After we spoke before."

"That's a good start," SJ said surprised. "And what did you discover?"

"That, as you said, a sponsor is able to take you through the steps according to the big book. Would that be the Bible?"

"No," SJ said. "It's the name they give to a book written by the two guys who founded AA. Bill Williams and Dr Bob. They were a stockbroker and a doctor."

"How interesting," Didi said. "So were they experts or something?"

"No, they were alcoholics – the same as us." SJ kept her voice low. "That's if you've decided you are an alcoholic, have you? Last time we met I don't think you were sure."

"I did what you suggested," Didi said, pausing to refill her cup. "I went out for a drink with some friends and I decided to limit myself to just the one."

"One glass of vodka?"

"Bottle."

"Bottle of vodka!" SJ gasped. This was worse than she thought.

"No, of wine. I don't drink spirits when I'm out."

Thank heaven for small mercies. SJ recovered her composure. "And did you manage?"

"No. I think I'd drunk two bottles of wine before we even got to the restaurant. We met in the bar first."

"And that convinced you?"

"Yes. I don't remember the end of the evening. That's happened a lot lately. In fact, I don't remember much past nine o' clock. My friends poured me into a taxi at around midnight apparently. I *hate* it, SJ." Suddenly her voice, although still low, was savage and her black eyes glittered. SJ drew back a little from the table. "I *hate* being out of control. I *hate* the feeling of not knowing what I've done. I can't bear it."

For a moment she was locked rigid. Her eyes slightly glazed. As if she was looking at herself properly for the first time and hating what she saw. SJ remembered that feeling very well. Compassion overrode her alarm at the strength of Didi's reaction.

"It's not much fun feeling ill all the time either, is it?" she said, in a bid to lighten the mood.

"I don't get ill that much. Not in the way I used to. Although I do find wine is worse than spirits. I think my tolerance must be quite high."

"It sounds like it." SJ paused. "I overdosed once on a litre of gin. I ended up in hospital having my stomach pumped out."

"A litre – heavens. I can do that in a few hours. Though I try not to." Her voice had gone a little dreamy. "It's a very good pain reliever, alcohol, isn't it? That's why I started drinking, I think." She

123

broke off, as the waitress arrived with her burger and fries and an egg, with the yolk broken so it was more yellow than white. "Thank you, Laura. That looks perfect. Please pass on my compliments to the chef."

"Sure," Laura said. "He'll be pleased. You know he has a soft spot for you."

"And I for him," Didi said. "He is very skilled. Do tell him I said so."

SJ listened to this exchange in silence. Every word Didi said seemed full of ambiguity. Already, she felt out of her depth. She wished Dorothy would text her back or phone so she could ask her advice. But so far there'd been no word from her. She glanced back at Didi, who had unwrapped the serviette (blue) that her knife and fork had been wrapped in and was laying it out on her lap. What would Dorothy say if she was here?

'Treat her as you would any other first-timer,' probably. 'Treat her as a very sick person.'

SJ cleared her throat and wished she didn't feel so intimidated.

"Right then," she began. "Where were we?"

"You were telling me why you started drinking?"

"Was I?" SJ blinked. "Well, that's quite a long story. But getting back to sponsorship. I think that's where we started."

Didi nodded.

"A sponsor guides you through the steps. They're on hand to offer you advice and guidance. We don't have any professional qualifications and we're not counsellors. We just have our own experience."

Didi nodded again. She had her mouth full so SJ decided to take full advantage. "How that works is that we arrange to meet – usually once a week. You would come to mine at a time that's convenient for us both. Before a meeting works best because then once we've chatted we both go to the meeting."

Didi's eyebrows shot up. "I don't want to go to any meetings."

"Well, I'm afraid that's part of the deal," SJ said firmly. "Anyway," she added, slightly puzzled. "You've already been to one."

"One was enough." Didi waved a hand as if the matter was closed. Then, as if she'd suddenly become aware that this might be a deal breaker, she changed tack.

"What if I meet someone I know?"

"What if you do? They'll be there for the same reason as you are – so it doesn't matter. From an anonymity point of view you'd both be on the same level."

"You don't understand." Didi put her knife and fork down and wiped her mouth delicately. "What if I meet a client?"

"The same goes for clients. The anonymity thing really does work quite well."

"It wouldn't work for me. My profession requires me to be in a position of power – authority. I cannot be on the same level as a client. I cannot be in a room where we are equals." She blinked slowly. "You can see that?"

"I can't sponsor you unless you come to meetings. I'm sorry, Didi. It just won't work." She picked up her bag. A sense of relief was stealing through her, mixed with disappointment. It would have been good to help but she had learned enough to know that she couldn't do it alone. Nor should she. As she rose to her feet Didi rose also.

"Don't go," she said, in a voice that was more command than plea. But the panic was back in her eyes. "I really do need your help. There must be a way we can do this. We are both intelligent women. Will you please just discuss it with me?"

Every instinct SJ had was urging her to say no, there was no other way. To walk out of the strange little red and black café, to get away from the darkness that was Didi back to the normality of an everyday Sunday. In her bag, an incoming text sounded. Was that Dorothy finally? She ached to look. But she didn't. Neither did she walk out.

She sat back down again.

Chapter Fifteen

Ways to help Dad without him guessing Mum put me up to it

The sensible approach

1. Tell him he's looking a bit peaky (even though he isn't).

2. Mention he seemed a bit quiet on Saturday night (even though he wasn't).

3. Tell him one of my friends found out they had bowl cancer just in time, thanks to a lifesaving test.

SJ considered her list. Number three was top favourite so far – well it would have been if she'd put *bowel* cancer rather than *bowl* cancer. Considering she'd once been an A-Level English tutor, her spelling was appalling. Unfortunately, the friend story was also complete fabrication. She didn't know anyone who'd ever had bowel cancer, which could be tricky if her father wanted any details. She was hopeless at lying.

The not so sensible approach

1. Book a doctor's appointment and then trick him into going to it by saying it was just a coffee/darts game/present buying expedition etc.

2. Blackmail him into doing the test by saying she was terribly afraid she had a genetic illness and the only way to test it was by collecting a sample of…

3. Knock on the bathroom door at a carefully timed moment and…. (No … No… Definitely not. She couldn't even finish the sentence.)

SJ sighed. She was getting nowhere fast. She had been thinking about the problem ever since Mum had asked her and she was no further forward. And now it was 4.30 p.m. on Tuesday, and very shortly her mother was expecting her to stroll in and eat a steak and kidney pie dinner and resolve everything. Well, she probably wasn't actually. She probably thought SJ would muck it up, which was why she hadn't asked her in the first place. And that was a self-fulfilling prophecy, if ever there was one, because that was exactly what was going to happen.

She snapped the cover of her iPad shut. She could only do her best.

For once the train was relatively quiet. She found a half empty carriage and sat and thought about the conversation she'd had with Dorothy last night.

Dorothy's first reaction had been pleasure. "Well done, pet. I'm surprised no one's asked you to sponsor them before."

"You are?" SJ had said in surprise. "Why?"

Dorothy had laughed gently. "Ah, SJ, why are you still so down on yourself? Do you know I've never heard anyone say a single bad word about you. That's rare."

"You can't have been speaking to the right people."

"Stop it. Now tell me about this wee girl."

SJ had planned to give her own sponsor an edited version but she found herself telling the truth. How she was a little afraid of Didi – how she could never quite seem to get control over their conversations, and how Didi had said she couldn't attend any meetings. "Is it even possible to sponsor someone who won't go to meetings?" SJ had finished.

"Anything's possible," Dorothy had said thoughtfully. "But it would certainly be harder because it's through going to meetings that she'd pick up how the Twelve-Step Program actually works. If she doesn't go then the job of explaining that would be entirely down to you."

"Right," SJ had been surprised to hear Dorothy even considering it. Her sponsor was very pro AA. She'd been involved with the fellowship for years. SJ had fully expected her to be against the idea of sponsoring anyone who refused to go to meetings.

"I'm not going to tell you what to do, pet," Dorothy had finished. "It's really your call. What are your instincts saying?"

"They're saying I probably should run a mile." SJ hesitated "But I also get the feeling that she's had an awful lot of pain in her life and I want to help. My instincts aren't very trustworthy though," she finished sadly.

"Maybe you should think about it for a few days," Dorothy suggested. You don't have to decide straight away. Do you?"

The only part SJ had left out was Didi's profession. Although she was desperate to tell

Dorothy this, it didn't seem that relevant. It would have felt like gossiping. SJ was well aware that the gossip train worked as well in AA as it did in any other faction of society, but that didn't mean she had to get involved in it.

Didi hadn't said her profession was a secret either but SJ didn't think she'd want it bandied about. The one thing she did know for sure was that if she was going to try and help Didi the only basis they could do it on was one of complete trust.

When her mother opened the front door SJ was hit by the scent of home-made steak and kidney pie. She took a deep breath and let it fill up her senses. If a single smell could conjure up home then this was hers. It was Mum's signature dish and it threw up a thousand memories of her childhood.

"Hello, love." Mum had a wooden spoon in her hand and she looked hot and pink and a little flustered. "Dad's in the lounge. I've left the gravy on," she called back over her shoulder as she hurried back into the kitchen.

SJ followed her. "Have you said anything else to him? Why does he think I'm coming over?"

"For your tea. I know you don't visit us that often but it's not unheard of."

Ouch. "We only went out on Saturday," SJ protested.

"That was a special occasion – they don't count." She stirred the gravy forcefully. "Now, do you think you should talk to him before dinner or after?"

"After, definitely," SJ lifted a lid off a saucepan and discovered some steaming spuds. "Shall I mash these?"

"No – go and say hello to your father."

"All right." How was it that mums always made you feel about ten years old? Not that SJ had anything against saying hello to her dad but it would have been nice if she and Mum could have had a cosy chat first. Cosy chat – who was she kidding? Cosy chats were definitely reserved for Alison – they had more in common. SJ felt that little dip in her heart again and she pulled herself up. She wished she wasn't so bloody sensitive. She was here. Her help was required. She should be pleased about that.

"You do have a game plan, don't you, Sarah-Jane?"

"Course," SJ said, crossing her fingers as she went out of the room.

Dinner was nice. They sat up to the table and Mum put the peas and the carrots in little serving dishes like she did at Christmas. SJ decided to enjoy the feeling of being an honoured guest without having Alison around to usurp her.

Her father did seem quieter than usual. He was smiley enough, though. Perhaps Mum was imagining things about him being ill. Surely she was. And then suddenly it was the end of the meal. Mum cleared the plates – they'd had a shop-bought strawberry flan for afters, which was a little disappointing – then she left the room and closed the door pointedly behind her.

131

"So what's all this about then?" her father said, looking at her hard. "I'm not stupid. I know you two have been plotting something. Out with it."

SJ was about to deny this but one look at his face stopped her.

"Mum's worried about you," she said, feeling her face burn. Oh what the hell, in for a penny in for a pound. "She said you'd been having constipation a lot lately and you won't go to the doctors about it."

"Did she?" Dad's face was unreadable. He didn't look at SJ but at the table, long and hard, as if he was trying to remove a stray gravy-covered pea that was stuck to the tablecloth by willpower alone.

There were no sounds from the kitchen. SJ wondered if Mum was listening outside the door. She had an urge to leap up and fling it open, but she was too scared she'd find her on her knees, an empty glass pressed to the other side of the wood. Not that there was the slightest reason for her to be on her knees, but that's what seemed to happen in sitcoms.

She looked around the room instead. On the mantelpiece there was a picture of Alison and Clive on their wedding day. On either side of that were pictures of Kevin and Sophie – the type where a photograph has been superimposed on canvas. They looked relatively new. Probably Christmas presents. There were other pictures of Sophie and Kevin when they were younger dotted about the walls and there was one of Alison standing in her beauty salon holding up a glass of champagne and smiling. It had been taken on the salon's launch day, SJ remembered. She hadn't been to the launch because she and Alison hadn't been speaking at the time.

There was just one picture of SJ. One very old, very small school photo.

"Did she?" her father said again and when SJ looked at him he was nodding thoughtfully.

"I'm worried about you too," she said. "To be honest, Dad. I mean I know you don't like discussing stuff like this but what if there was something wrong? It's got to be better to know."

"There's nothing wrong."

"How do you know?" She decided to forge ahead. At least they were having a conversation. Sort of. "Mum said you won't do the test thingie they send around – the one that can detect if you've got bowel cancer."

"I have not got bloodeh cancer," Dad said, banging his fist on the table so hard that the dishes still on it clinked in response. He looked up from the table, meeting her eyes for the first time since this conversation had begun. "And I wish she'd stop going around telling people I have."

"I'm not people," SJ said with an ache in her throat. "I'm…" she paused. She had a ridiculous urge to cry. This was all going horribly wrong. She'd known it would. She was crap.

She blinked several times. "I'm worried about you too," she said, but the ache stopped her voice from working properly and her father didn't respond.

She shifted her chair along a bit so that she was closer to him. "When I was little," she began, "you always kept me safe. Do you remember when I had nightmares and you would come into my room and you would sit by my bed?"

He still didn't reply but he looked up and she could see herself reflected in his eyes.

"You told me no monster would ever get past you. And I believed you. I trusted you completely." She hesitated. "And do you remember when you did the Father's Day race at Sports Day and you came last, but that was only because Matthew Bradford's dad slipped over in the mud and you stayed back to help him?"

He nodded then, and she stumbled on. "I know Mum said you were mad and that Matthew Bradford's dad shouldn't have entered because he was too fat, but I didn't think you were mad. I was really, really proud of you that day, Dad."

She didn't even know what she was trying to say but the words were coming anyway: a higgledy-piggledy jumble of them that had nothing to do with constipation or cancer and everything to do with love.

"And then on Sunday when Alison gave you that amazing present." This one was harder. SJ could feel the ache in her throat threatening to overspill into tears, but she couldn't stop now. She didn't dare because he was listening.

"Well, you made me feel as though it didn't matter. As though it wasn't about the money and that you loved my present just as much."

"I did, lovie," he said quietly. "I did."

"I couldn't bear it if you were ill," she finished. "I just couldn't."

There was another little silence. There were still no sounds from the kitchen. What on earth was her mother doing out there? SJ wiped at a stray tear that seemed to have appeared on her face.

Their chairs were so close now that they were almost touching. How had that happened? She leant against the solid Aran-jumper warmth of him and after a moment or two he put his arm around her and squeezed her shoulder.

"All right," he said. "If it makes you happy. I'll go and see the bloodeh doctor."

Chapter Sixteen

The following Friday at Barney Hall, SJ told a roomful of people about the conversation she'd had with her dad. Not word for word. They didn't need to know the intimate details and besides she couldn't remember all that she'd said. But she gave them the gist because it was still so much in her mind: a rattling of feelings that had been whizzing around in her head and stirring her up ever since.

"I wouldn't have been able to do that once," she finished. "I'd have shied away from being so honest. I'd have still worried about Dad, but I'd have drowned how I felt under a few gallons of Chardonnay."

There were lots of nods. The young girl sitting next to her squeezed her hand.

After the meeting Number Ten Tim came and gave her a hug.

"You may have just saved your dad's life," he said. "My dad died of bowel cancer. No one knew he had it until it was too late. He was only sixty-three."

"I'm so sorry."

"Shit happens." He smiled. "Sorry. I should probably rephrase that. How the subconscious works."

SJ smiled back. "It's okay – you're right. It does."

"When is he going for his appointment?"

"He went this morning. They checked him over. The upshot of that is that his GPs referred him to a specialist at the hospital so he can have some tests. There's a waiting list, of course. But she said it shouldn't be more than a fortnight or so."

Tim frowned. "When I'm in Number Ten I'm going to make all appointments that have anything to do with cancer top priority. No one will have to wait longer than a week."

"I guess it's down to funding. Or lack of it!"

He nodded. "My ex was a lab technician. She said there's always a queue, but some people get bumped straight to the top because of who they are or what they've paid. There should be a fairer system than that."

SJ bit her lip.

"Hey," he said catching her expression. "He's probably absolutely fine. And if he isn't – then you'll have caught it. Stop worrying."

'Stop worrying' had to be the most ignored advice in the English language, SJ thought half an hour later, as she hunted through her bag for her front door key. The most ignored advice in any language probably. With the possible exception of 'don't lose your front door key', which she did on a regular basis.

Where the hell was it? She'd had a system for a while where her key ring had been attached to a little looped clip on the inside of her bag, but the loop had broken recently so now they were loose again and free to disappear into any dark cranny. Dark being the operative word. There were no street lights near her flat and the outside light was broken again. There must be a fault – she'd only recently replaced the bulb. Or it could be vandals – or would-be thieves carrying out Step One of Mission Mugging – plunge victim into darkness. Step Two – sneak up on them in the dark. Shut up, Overactive Imagination.

It would have helped if she'd had a smaller bag but this one, which she loved and which was very old, was also what Tanya had once described as 'approaching cavernous'. It had four different compartments for stuff to get lost in. She sat on the step outside the main entrance of her flat. She would have to take everything out, piece by piece, and conduct a methodical search. It was the only sure fire way.

Purse – check.
Pack of mints – check.
Diary – check.
Mobile phone – check.
Pack of tissues – check.
Emery board – check.
Miss Dior – check.
No key.

She had definitely had it when she'd come out. She remembered locking the door. She went into compartment two.

Cheque book – check.
Mini notepad – check.
Very small folded up rain hat – that could have come in useful if she'd realised she'd had it.
Comb – check.
Pack of staples – check. (What!)
Nail clippers – check.
Mini stapler – (Ah!).

Scrunched up tissue – chuck.

No key.

The back compartment was empty apart from some change, her Oyster Card and a boiled sweet, half unwrapped and very sticky. Nice!

She dug deeper. There was an inner pocket with a zip, which she didn't use any more because the zip was broken. Maybe it had somehow got in there.

Business card with a phone number on the back – check.

Hair band – check.

Hair slide – check.

Round metal thing – her heart gave a little thump as she realised it was the identity disc from Ash's collar.

Miniature pen – crap, for a moment she'd thought that was her key.

USB drive – check.

Pack of love hearts – shit, she'd forgotten all about keeping those.

Her own heart faltered. Kit had given them to her on one of their early dates. They'd gone to see some crappy film – she couldn't even remember the name of it – but she had a powerful image of him coming back across the foyer towards her from the in-cinema sweet shop.

"For you," he'd said handing her the love hearts. They were the type with silly messages written on them. His eyes had been curiously shy as if he'd thought she might laugh or tease him, which she would never have done in a million years, even if she hadn't been totally touched.

She had given him a hug in the crowded foyer and cinema viewers, anxious to buy tickets, had flowed around them like the Red Sea around Moses and his staff.

She hadn't seen Kit for more than three years yet suddenly he felt close. And she felt bereft. She closed her eyes. His face swam in front of hers in sharpest clarity: the slight stubble on his chin; the lived-in tiredness in his eyes; his compassion; his concern. Then, somehow, Kit's face was morphing into an older, ruddier face, a face with tiny broken veins on the nose, another face with compassion and roughness in it – her dad's.

For a moment they were tangled up together and SJ realised that Kit and her father were the only two people in her life who had ever made her feel truly cared for, truly safe. And now Kit was heaven knows where – she hadn't even seen Ebby lately. Maybe she should call him. A part of her was always a bit scared to call Ebby in case she got news she didn't want. Did that make her a coward? Probably.

She prayed every day that Kit had conquered his demons. And Dad, her lovely, lovely dad, well now he had to conquer his demons too.

She knew just how much it had cost him to go to the doctors this morning. More than embarrassment – he had a deep-rooted terror about the invasion of privacy. He had, according to her mother, insisted on going to the surgery alone. Then when he'd come home he'd refused to speak about what had happened at all and decamped to the garden shed to clean the tools.

All he would say was that the GP was getting him an appointment with some specialist at the hospital.

"Shall I come round?" SJ had asked.

"No, Sarah-Jane. I don't think that would help at all."

And she still hadn't found her flaming key.

There were footsteps on the pavement behind her – a scraping of boots on tarmac – and SJ jumped. She felt suddenly very cold, very exposed and very vulnerable. Fear skittered around her heart. Most of her valuables were on the step. That had been a really smart idea.

Well, hello, mugger, just help yourself. She grabbed her purse and her phone and scrambled to her feet, wondering if she could be seen from the pavement, or whether she would be lost in the shadows of the house. The figure was heading her way with slow deliberate strides. Maybe it was the tenant of the downstairs flat. She was a nurse. No, it didn't look like her – too tall. The figure reached the flats, paused and turned towards her.

"SJ?" The voice was husky and for one wild beat of her heart she thought she'd conjured up Kit – but it wasn't Kit, she saw, as the figure came into proper seeing distance. It was a woman. It was Tanya.

"SJ – what are you doing?"

"Looking for my key." The relief that it was Tanya and not some faceless stranger was so dizzying she wanted to laugh. "What on earth are you doing here?"

141

"I thought you might fancy a coffee." Tanya's voice didn't sound quite straight and SJ stepped over the small pile of her possessions and went towards her, concerned. "At 10.00 p.m. Are you okay?"

"Not really."

And now she could see the gleam of tears in Tanya's eyes in the dimness and hear the cracking pain in her voice.

"I've left Michael, SJ. I texted you earlier. Did you not get it?"

"Oh, honey. No. No, I didn't. Sorry. I think my phone's still on silent – I was at a meeting." They hugged and then SJ drew back. "What happened?"

"I'll tell you. But not out here." She tugged her coat around her and shivered. "Can we not get in?"

"I can't find my key. I think I must have dropped it or something." She bent down and began to pile things back into her bag.

"Have you turned out your pockets?"

"Yes, but I never put it in my pocket. It's always in my bag."

"Shall I check?"

SJ shrugged off her jacket and gave it to Tanya while she zipped up compartments. She was still shivering. It was awfully cold. "Did you drive over?"

"Yes. I suppose we could go and sit in my car."

"My landlord has a spare front door key. I could phone him. That'll be a fun conversation."

"SJ – there's a hole in the lining of your pocket. Quite a small one. Did you know?"

"What – no – are you sure?" SJ looked up. Tanya's face was intent as she felt around the bottom edge of the faux leather jacket. "It can't be in there. I always keep it in my bag on a loop."

Tanya smiled as she produced something with a flourish. "Clearly not always. Would this be it?"

SJ blew out her breath. "Thank you. Thank you. I'm an utter plonker. Don't I keep telling you I'm a plonker."

"You're not a plonker," Tanya said softly, as she handed over the key and waited for SJ to open the door. "Just a bit scatty. It's a good job I came round."

It was a relief to be inside. In the light and the warmth and the cosiness, even if it did mean that SJ could now see Tanya's face and she did not look very well. There were smudges of black beneath her eyes – where had they sprung from? They hadn't been there last time they'd met. They stood side by side in the kitchen while SJ made tea.

"I'd offer you something stronger but I haven't got anything."

"It's fine. Drinking won't help." Tanya's hand shook as she spooned in sugar. She wasn't wearing nail varnish at all now – was that a good sign? SJ shook herself slightly. She had a feeling they'd gone past the barometer of nail varnish.

143

"Let's sit in the other room," she said, taking the mug from Tanya's unsteady grip. "And we can talk properly."

Ensconced on SJ's squashy, comfy settee SJ waited. For once in her life she didn't want to say the wrong thing. Tanya didn't say anything either, but it wasn't silent. Rooms were never silent in Hackney. There was endless traffic and endless people noise. SJ's flat was the top half of a house – not a block like the one where Kit lived – and her neighbour worked long shifts, and wasn't in much, but it was never that quiet.

The sounds of the street seeped in through the old sash windows: a muttered voice; the odd bark of a dog; the sounds of black cabs and red buses and the distant whistle of a train.

"So," Tanya began. "Where do I start?"

Chapter Seventeen

It was extremely hard to resist the temptation to say, 'at the beginning,' but SJ managed it. She had already decided there would be no flippancy, no putting her foot in it, no assumptions. She would just let Tanya talk.

"We went to Mum and Dad's last weekend," Tanya said at last. "Did I tell you that?"

"Yes, honey. You said you were going. Did something happen there?"

Tanya paused and bit the edge of her thumb in a curious little gesture of pain that SJ had never seen before.

She frowned. "Are your parents okay?"

"What? Yes, they're fine. We had a good time – they love Bethany. And she loves them. It was all fine – well apart from the fact that Michael seemed a bit quiet. Then on Saturday afternoon, just after we'd had lunch, he disappeared."

"Where to?"

"He said he was going to the pharmacy. He wanted to get some indigestion tablets – I mean Mum said she had some but Michael wanted to get a certain type. To be honest, SJ, I didn't really believe him. It was such an odd thing to do."

"I see. So what happened?"

"I followed him."

"Where did he go?"

"To the pharmacy."

SJ nodded. She was obviously missing something, but Tanya looked so distressed and she didn't want to ask stupid questions. She waited.

"I suppose he had to go there. It was his cover, wasn't it?" There was such a long pause that eventually SJ felt compelled to say something.

"So did he meet someone at the pharmacy?"

"No. But he phoned someone. I was watching him from outside. He was on the phone for at least five minutes."

This didn't sound too terrible either. SJ frowned and wondered if there was a way she could say this very gently.

"I'm sure he was talking to Andy," Tanya said. "I wish he'd just tell me the truth, SJ. All these lies. It's breaking my heart."

She began to sob. Empty little sobs full of pain. It was unbearable to watch. SJ shifted along the settee and put her arms around her best friend and Tanya didn't resist. She lay against SJ's chest, her shoulders heaving.

"It'll be okay," SJ told her, over and over again. "It's going to be okay." She didn't know if this was true. But there were no other words to say.

When Tanya stopped sobbing and half sat up to wipe away tears, SJ reached for her bag and just for once the universe was on her side. The pack of tissues was right at the top. She passed it to Tanya.

"Danks." Tanya blew her nose and coughed a couple of times and shook her head. "I'm sorry, SJ. I didn't mean to go to pieces like that on you."

"It's okay. It's absolutely fine. You can go to pieces on me any time you like."

"It keeps happening," Tanya said with another little sniff. "I keep bursting into tears and I can't stop."

"I know," SJ said. "I mean, I know what it's like when someone you love does – well…." She paused. "But how did you come to walk out? Did you have a big bust up with Michael?"

Tanya nodded. "Not straight away. He was still denying it. Then yesterday when he'd gone to work. I phoned up Andy." She blew her nose again and wiped away more tears. "I told him that I knew he was having an affair with Michael and that I wanted it to stop. I was quite calm about it. I wasn't rude or anything. I didn't rant and rave. I just told him that we've got a daughter who we love very much and that he must leave us alone." She paused. "You'd have been proud of me, SJ."

"What did he say?"

"He said they weren't having an affair. He said the exact words that Michael said, which just proved to me that it wasn't true. They obviously have the same story. They've obviously rehearsed it."

"What did he say?"

"'There's nothing going on. I swear to you.' That's exactly what Michael said. But I know there is, SJ, I know. They wouldn't be having all these cosy chats if there wasn't. Michael wouldn't have lied about going to the pharmacy. I checked his phone. He was definitely talking to Andy in there." She took a sobbing gulp of air. "I miss Bethany."

SJ, who had moved her arm, because it was aching a bit, put it back in position. "Sweetie, you're obviously tired out, and you're in shock. We will get this sorted out. You could have brought Bethany, you know. Do you want to go and get her? I can drive your car."

Tanya looked brighter at this suggestion. Then she shook her head. "No, it's not fair. She's asleep. She doesn't even know I've gone anywhere."

"If you go back early in the morning she never will."

"That's if Michael lets me in."

"Do you think he might not?" This didn't sound like the Michael SJ knew, although she supposed you never could tell. The Michael she knew wouldn't have had an affair either – not in a million years. He'd never had eyes for anyone but Tanya.

"He was furious that I phoned Andy. He started banging things around in the dishwasher. Said he couldn't cope with how I was behaving any longer. He said I should see a doctor. That's why I left, SJ. I think that's his plan. I think he wants to try and prove that I'm imagining all this so that he and Andy can…" Her voice broke again.

SJ frowned. This whole conversation was getting slightly surreal yet Tanya was so deeply distressed and she wasn't the type to imagine things. SJ had never known her to be anything other than rational and down-to-earth. She wasn't the type to get melodramatic. She didn't do paranoia. She was one of the sanest people that SJ knew. She squeezed Tanya's shoulder gently.

148

"Sweetie, it's getting really late. I think we should sleep on it. I'll pull out the sofa bed. Then in the morning we can talk some more. If you like I can go and talk to Michael. How does that sound?"

It was the very last thing she felt like doing, especially as she was due for a shift at Mortimer's at 8.00 – someone else's shift not hers – but Tanya was nodding. She looked vaguely peaceful for the first time since she'd arrived.

She would have to cancel the shift. Friends were more important than work.

To SJ's relief when she got up and went into the kitchen at 6.40 the next morning Tanya was already there drinking coffee and she looked a lot brighter.

"Sorry – did I wake you?" she asked. "I couldn't sleep."

"No, you didn't. It's fine."

"SJ, did you mean what you said about talking to Michael? Would you really talk to him? He might listen to you."

SJ couldn't think of a single reason why he would listen to her but she nodded. "Of course I meant it," she told Tanya confidently. "Toast?"

If she'd have felt even a quarter of the confidence she was pretending she'd have been a lot happier, SJ thought, as she walked up to Tanya and Michael's front door in Bermondsey just after nine.

They'd agreed that Tanya would drop her off and then sit in the car outside, but slightly up the road, while she spoke to Michael. Tanya didn't want Michael to come rushing out to have a row in the street.

SJ couldn't imagine Michael rushing out and causing a row in the street but as she'd already had one row this morning with the girl whose shift she'd promised to cover and now couldn't, she didn't want to take any chances.

Michael didn't keep her waiting. When he opened the door she saw surprise, swiftly followed by relief and then concern, flash over his face.

"SJ is Tanya with you? She walked out last night. She was in one hell of a state. I've been worried sick." He leaned out of the front door to scan the street.

SJ shook her head. "It's okay. She's fine, I promise. She's just up the road. She asked me to come and talk to you. She… Well I know it's a bit weird and I don't want to interfere, but…" Oh crap, she should have thought this through – she was aware she wasn't making much sense. But at least she had his attention.

"Can I come in?"

"Yeah, of course."

He gestured her through to their kitchen, which was the room SJ had always thought of as the centre of their home. It was much bigger than hers and full of gadgets and warmth and pictures Bethany had crayoned, some of which were stuck to the fridge. Bethany was at the table. She'd clearly just finished her breakfast – she had a milk moustache – and she didn't look as though her hair had been brushed, but she smiled when she saw SJ. Everything looked totally normal. Except that Tanya, who should have been here, making coffee and bustling around, was sitting subdued and tearful in her car up the road.

"What's going on?" Michael asked, and SJ looked at him in surprise.

"I was hoping you could tell me."

"To be honest, SJ, I haven't a clue." His voice was quiet. He glanced at his daughter and SJ wondered if he was worried about talking in front of her. Then he frowned and rubbed at his slightly receding hairline – when had that happened? – and for the first time she noticed how tired he looked. He took a deep breath. SJ waited.

"I expect she's told you she thinks I'm..." he hesitated, "...doing things behind her back."

"Having an affair." SJ's face burned. She couldn't bring herself to say 'with Andy'. It felt surreal sitting here talking to her best friend's husband about such things. It also felt so totally unlikely. She'd known Michael for as long as she'd known Tanya. She just couldn't imagine it. Mind you, she supposed you never truly knew people. She'd been pretty shocked when Tanya had told her he liked to dress up in woman's clothes. She'd been pretty shocked the first time she'd seen him actually dressed as Lizzie. But it had been okay. He'd still been Michael. He had been so relaxed about it that he'd made her feel relaxed too. Was it such a quantum leap to think that having dressed as a woman he now wanted to be with a man?

"I'm not having an affair," Michael said. "I know what you're thinking. It's written all over your face. But it's not happening. It never has, it never will. And I am not gay. I really need you to believe that, SJ."

She looked into his eyes. There was only truth there, and tiredness and a sort of quiet pleading. Unease started somewhere in her gut. All her instincts were telling her to believe him. But she already knew that instincts could be so wrong. She chewed the inside of her mouth and blinked a few times. Oh crap, crap, crap. She had thought – hoped – that talking to Michael would make things better but it was making them worse.

He made no more attempt to convince her. He got up and took Bethany's empty cereal bowl from the table to the sink, emptied away the milk and slotted the bowl into the dishwasher.

"Wake Mummy?" Bethany asked, and he smiled at her, his eyes warm, a doting dad smile.

"Not yet. Mummy's very tired. She's having a lie in. I told you."

So that was why Bethany wasn't fretting about Tanya. She didn't know she wasn't here.

"Can I do Lego?"

"As long as you promise to do it quietly, sweetheart."

"Okay." Bethany slipped down from her chair. She was wearing the same denim shorts and pale blue tee shirt she'd worn at Kew, and SJ felt a pang of memory. Tanya had been so wonderfully supportive that day, even though she'd been so troubled about her marriage, and now she was

152

relying on SJ to help her. And SJ had no idea how. What would Dorothy do? Now she actually wanted Dorothy's advice, her sponsor's voice seemed to have vanished from her head.

She turned back to Michael who was still standing at the sink. "It's not like Tanya to imagine things that aren't happening," she said carefully.

"I know." He sighed and came back to the table. "I'm very worried. I've been doing some research."

"What kind of research?"

"Hold on. I'll show you." He disappeared from the kitchen and came back a few moments later with a netbook, which he put on the table in front of them. He typed swiftly into a search engine and SJ felt the unease kick off again. Was he about to try and persuade her Tanya was losing it? Was all this concern just part of some brilliant plot? Bugger, she was buying into the conspiracy theory herself now and it didn't sound very likely. Did conspiracy theories ever sound very likely, though?

Michael turned the netbook around so she could see it properly. It was headed up *Post Partum Depression – Signs and Symptoms.*

"I think it's possible Tanya may be suffering from this," he said. "I did actually have a word with a pharmacist about it last week. He advised me to get Tanya to talk to her doctor. But so far that hasn't gone very well."

"Is that the same as post natal depression?" SJ asked. "I thought that was something that came straight after you had your baby. Wouldn't you have noticed something before?"

"It most often happens then but nothing's black and white, is it? I don't know whether it can happen later." He looked at her. "When Bethany was born we were over the moon. You know that, though, SJ. You know how long we'd waited for her." His voice grew a little husky and he was obviously struggling.

SJ put her hand over his. She felt horribly guilty – the last thing Tanya had said to her was 'don't fall for any of his lies,' but he was so clearly distressed.

"Having Bethany… Having Bethany was brilliant but it also stirred everything up. It…meant… Well, it meant we went through a lot of emotions. You know – about Maddie. It sounds weird but I think Tanya went through the pain of losing her all over again." A tear ran down his cheek. SJ had to swallow very hard several times to stop herself joining in.

Michael rubbed his face. He didn't seem aware of the tear. "It hit Tanya harder than it hit me. It sounds crazy but we both felt guilty. Why had Bethany survived when Maddie hadn't?"

"Have you talked to Tanya about this? What you've just said to me, I mean. Surely she would get it. It makes a lot of sense."

"She won't listen to me. She's so convinced I'm lying. She's obsessed with this idea I'm seeing Andy. But I'm not, SJ. I swear I'm not. I love the bones of her. I would never cheat on her." He clasped his fingers together and rested his chin on them. He looked like he always looked – lovely, straightforward, gentle Michael.

He was telling the truth. She was absolutely sure of it. But where did she go from here?

"Will you tell Tanya I'm not lying? Will you tell her I love her and I want her home? Please, SJ. She might listen to you."

She found herself nodding. "I'll do my best," she said.

Chapter Eighteen

SJ was at her third AA meeting of the week. Going to more meetings often helped when she was troubled about something. Listening to other people's stories helped to put things into perspective.

And if she'd ever needed to get things into perspective it was now. Yet again, she ran over what had happened last Saturday.

When she'd finished talking to Michael, which hadn't taken more than about fifteen minutes, she'd gone back out to where Tanya was sitting patiently in the car.

"Hey," she said, seeing Tanya was sobbing quietly. "No need to cry. This is going to be sorted. I'm sure it is."

"What did he say?" Tanya pulled another tissue from her bag, which was open on her lap. "Did he admit it?"

SJ shook her head as she slid into her seat. "No. He said the same to me as he said to you. But I think he's telling the truth, Tanya. I really do."

Tanya blew her nose loudly. "He's not."

"He loves you, honey."

"I used to think that too." Tanya twiddled with the ends of the tissue she was holding. "But if that were true, he wouldn't be doing this – he wouldn't be seeing Andy. I'm not making it up, SJ. I'm not mad."

"Of course you're not." SJ took a deep breath. "But...do you...well...maybe think...?" Bugger, how the hell did you tell your best friend that they might not be seeing things as clearly as they thought they were? Especially when your best friend was the sanest, most rational, most down-to-earth person you knew. Indeed, that you'd ever known.

For one crazy moment she considered telling Tanya that she was right. That it was plain as day that Michael and Andy were shagging each other senseless – the bastards! And that Tanya should get the hell out of there and file for divorce – in fact, why didn't she and Bethany come and stay with her. It would be cramped but they'd manage. And she did get pretty lonely at times. It would be good to have Tanya around 24/7. Just like the old days when they'd shared a house at uni.

But as she looked back into Tanya's pain-racked eyes she knew that she couldn't do this. Sometimes that was what being a best friend was all about, wasn't it? Telling the truth – even when you knew they didn't want to hear it.

"Tanya," she said quietly. "Michael's really worried about you. And I am too. Maybe it would be a good plan to go and see your doctor. Not because you're mad or anything – but just to have a proper chat."

She saw the light fade out of Tanya's lovely green eyes. Saw her expression go from hope to disappointment to resignation and finally to anger.

"I see," she said and the words, *Et tu, Brute* hung in the air between them.

Before SJ could move or do or say anything else, Tanya was tugging at the door handle. She was in such a hurry to get out of the car that she dropped her bag and a lipstick fell out and rolled into the gutter.

She didn't pick it up. She was too anxious to escape. Half running, half stumbling she raced along the pavement. Not in the direction of her house but the opposite way. SJ retrieved the lipstick – russet gold, Tanya's signature lipstick – and then she started the car and went after her friend.

She felt like a kerb crawler. She wound down the window and pleaded with Tanya to get back in the car.

But Tanya wouldn't even look in her direction. After they'd gone a few hundred yards and were nearly on the main road, SJ gave up. It was probably best to give Tanya some space. When she'd calmed down she would try again, and again, and again: and however many agains it took to get Tanya to speak to her. They'd been friends for far too many years to let something like this break them apart.

They were no nearer to speaking now than they'd been a week ago, but at least SJ knew Tanya had gone home. At least she was safe. SJ knew this because later that same day, worried sick and still feeling like a Brutus, she had texted Michael to check.

She's okay, he'd texted back. *Thank you for trying. I'm sure she'll be in touch soon.*

SJ still wasn't sure that she'd done the right thing. Telling the truth was a lot harder than she'd ever thought it would be. Telling the absolute truth, that was, because you knew it was the right thing to do. Even though you also knew it might have shitty consequences. Even though you knew you were going to look like the bad guy.

She sighed heavily and the woman sitting in the chair in front of her, turned round and smiled. "Bad day, huh!"

SJ came back to the present – and the meeting – with a start and gave her a wry smile back. "Bad week."

Luckily, she didn't have to elaborate because the main share of the evening was just about to start. Number Ten Tim was in the chair, she saw, and was pleased.

Despite his nickname, which he actively encouraged, and the fact that he could go on a bit, he was very wise. He had a dry, dark sense of humour, which SJ was in the mood for tonight.

"On the day my doctor told me I had six months to live, I was furious," Tim began. He shook his head and smiled before he continued. "I couldn't wait that bloody long. I wanted to die there and then, preferably in the next 24 hours – end of the week, absolute tops."

There was a ripple of laughter. Only in an AA meeting would people laugh at such a statement, SJ thought. They all laughed at the most horrific things. Last week in this meeting they'd listened to a girl who'd warned them that stabbing yourself was not a good suicide choice – not unless you had disproportionally long arms.

"You simply can't get enough force behind the thrust," she had complained, stretching out her

159

arms and making stabbing motions at her chest to demonstrate. "Stabbing myself was yet another thing I failed to get right."

SJ knew now that they held up their darkest moments for laughter because they had survived. They had all survived things that the average person would go pale simply to hear about. SJ had heard someone describe it once as going not just to the gates of hell, but a great deal further: and not just once, but many, many times.

Her own rock bottom, her own overdose on gin, agonising as it had been, paled into insignificance compared to what lots of her fellow members had suffered. Sharing traumatic experiences with others who'd been through similar things bonded you.

The same thing happened to the survivors of plane crashes and ship wrecks; the survivors of natural disasters and cancer. Shared survival bonded you in a way nothing else could.

Today was no exception. Listening to Tim talk about how he'd got through the shock death of his father without picking up a drink was inspiring. By the time he'd finished she felt more optimistic about her friendship with Tanya. Okay, so Tanya might hate her now, but it wouldn't always be so. She would just have to keep trying until things were right again.

After the meeting she was talking to Penny when Tim came across.

"Good share," she said, turning to smile at him. "Very entertaining. I'm glad you didn't die."

"Me too," he said and winked. "How's your dad?"

"He's okay. He's got his appointment date through. It's in a couple of weeks."

"That's good news." He looked at her, considering. "You look like you could use a day out. What you doing on Sunday?"

"I usually see a friend," SJ said guardedly. Not that she would be seeing Tanya this Sunday – not as things stood between them at the moment anyway. "Why do you ask?"

"A group of us are going to the seaside – we've hired a minibus. There's supposed to be a heatwave this weekend. Fancy it?"

"I'm not sure. Maybe."

"Penny's coming," Tim said. "Aren't you, sweetheart?"

"I am indeed." Penny's eyes sparkled. "I'm looking forward to it. Tim's right, SJ, you should join us. It would do you good. If you don't mind me saying, you are looking a bit peaky."

"I feel a bit peaky," she said, suddenly feeling a bit tearful too and blinking rapidly.

"Be at the Hackney Empire at 8.30," Tim instructed. "I'll save you a seat. All you need is a bikini – preferably a skimpy one." He dodged out of the way as she gave him a mock punch on the arm.

"In your dreams, Tim."

He sighed. "You're right there – in my dreams. But seriously, SJ, come."

It was only as she was walking round to the Empire on Sunday, in the sultry beginnings of what promised to be the hot day that had been forecast, that it struck SJ that she hadn't asked what beach they were going to. She assumed the closest, which meant Southend, so it was quite a shock when Tim told her cheerily that they were going to Bournemouth.

"Well to be precise we're going to Boscombe," he said, "which is just up the road. Because it's a little bit quieter and in my opinion a little bit nicer. And as I organised the bus, I had the final say."

"I know it well," she said. "I was brought up in Bournemouth. But then my parents moved up here. Wow – I haven't been back there for years."

She couldn't remember the last time she'd been on a minibus either. It was a twelve-seater and as well as Penny there were a couple of other girls she knew, who waved at her cheerfully as she and Tim climbed aboard.

"Our seats are at the back," he told her. "Because there's slightly more leg room."

Because it's the only place he can fit, SJ observed wryly, as he went ahead of her, dipping his head to avoid scraping the roof of the bus. Until Tim got into a confined space you tended to forget how tall he was.

This had been a good idea, she decided, as they drove out of London. Already she could feel her spirits lifting at the prospect of getting completely away. It was a long time since she'd been to Boscombe beach and years since she'd actually swum in the sea. Not that she was definitely going to do any swimming. It would probably be freezing. But she wore a bikini beneath her cut-off

162

jeans and tee shirt and in her bag was a bottle of sun tan lotion and Dorothy's latest blockbuster, which she'd been meaning to read for a while.

"I used to go to Bournemouth quite a bit," Tim said conversationally, as they hit the M25. "My gran lived there. Me and my brother went for school holidays."

"Whereabouts?"

"Studland."

"The posh bit," she said, not really surprised. Tim was down-to-earth, but there was also a polish about him that was roots deep, not overlaid. "I'm surprised we're not going to Studland then – that's one of the most beautiful beaches in the country."

"Yeah, there was some talk about that. But it adds a fair bit of time on to the journey. The ferry across gets jam packed in a heatwave. So we decided against it." He turned to look at her. "So how's things, SJ? How are you?"

For a moment, as she met his kind black eyes, she wondered if she could get away with saying, 'Fine – everything's fine.' Probably not. They had the back four seats to themselves. The minibus was full of chatter and ribbing and laughter. No one was listening. And Tim was not a fool.

"You've not been your usual cheery self lately," he prompted. "Feel free to tell me it's none of my business. But I've a hunch it's not just your dad, is it?"

"No," she said. "It's not." And she told him about Tanya. All of it – Tanya's suspicions, her talk with Michael, Tanya's reaction.

"She was so terribly upset. I felt as though I was letting her down. Actually I felt like I was betraying her. We've been friends for so many years and there I was believing everything Michael said – even though Tanya had warned me what he'd say."

"But you have to make a judgment call in these situations. And the only place you can make that is here." He tapped the left side of his chest. Black fingers spread wide against the whiteness of his tee shirt. "That's what you did, SJ?"

"I know." She swallowed. "But what about our friendship? She won't speak to me. She thinks I'm siding with Michael, and I can't bear the thought that this might be the end of it. We've been through such a lot together. Especially the last few years. Tanya was there for me all through my drinking. I let her down then too – I betrayed her trust."

She paused. She'd had no idea she was going to pour her heart out to Tim like this but in the confined space of the bus – which seemed, right now, like a little cocoon of safety – it was easy.

She didn't question the fact that she could trust him. She knew she could. Number Ten Tim might talk a lot of old nonsense about all the things he planned to do when he became Prime Minister, but he didn't gossip. He'd been sober for about nineteen years and she'd never heard him say a bad word about anybody – or they about him.

"I blurted out one of Tanya's darkest secrets to a roomful of people when I was in a blackout," she went on softly.

For a moment she paused and looked out of the window. They'd finally got off the motorway and were going through the New Forest. She could see ponies and walkers dotting the landscape. The wide green and brown spaces brought back her childhood. Everything had seemed so simple then.

"Michael had just started cross-dressing," she went on softly. "They were both struggling to come to terms with what that meant for their marriage. And I told everyone. Including my husband at the time, who was a good friend of Michael's – well he was until he knew that."

"Not a good friend at all then," Tim said, blinking slowly.

"I guess not."

The noise levels were rising. Then someone at the front of the bus started to sing. *"Oh, I do want to be beside the seaside."*

It was hard to remain sombre. SJ smiled. "I'll shut up. You didn't invite me along to moan."

"Better out than in."

The rest of the bus had joined in with the song now. It was way too noisy to carry on chatting. SJ raised her eyebrows and Tim smiled and in the next breath, they were singing along too.

Chapter Nineteen

Boscombe Beach may not have been as jam packed as Bournemouth, but it was pretty damn busy today. As she strolled with Penny and a crowd of others along the prom next to the vast blue sparkle of the sea, SJ realised she actually felt happy. The shrieks of children, the squawks of seagulls, the overriding shush of the sea, the buzz of dozens of people chattering – all of it so different from the hectic thrum of London – felt like a layer of insulation between her and the sadness.

Dad's problems and the fall out with Tanya both seemed a long way away. She took a deep breath of the ozone-scented, burger-flavoured air and decided that for today at least, maybe she could forget about sadness for a while.

"Nice to see you smiling again," Penny said, flicking her fair hair off her face. "This is lovely, isn't it? Apparently they've got an artificial surf reef here. You can't tell, can you?"

"I've never seen such a flat sea," Tim said, catching up with them. "I wouldn't mind trying that thing they're doing with boards though – what is it?"

"It's called SUPing," said Sha, one of the younger girls. She turned around to talk to them. "Short for Stand Up Paddle-boarding. My boyfriend does it a lot. It's really cool. And massively easier than surfing. You can probably hire the boards somewhere. We should have a go."

166

"I'm up for that," Tim said.

"I'll try anything once," SJ added recklessly.

Massively easy weren't the first words that sprang to mind, SJ thought, as she wobbled around on the cumbersome, rocking board. It was like trying to balance on an unstable curved plank of wood. Her tee shirt and shorts were already soaked through, thanks to the fact that she'd spent far more time in the freezing sea than on the board. Another wave slapped over the lower half of her body – she hadn't managed to get off her knees yet. "Jeez!" Where had all these flaming waves come from anyway? It had been totally flat when they'd been watching from the shore. No one else seemed to be having a problem standing up, either.

Tim, who was on a board close by, gave her a cheery wave as he glided past. "You're supposed to use the paddle," he shouted. "It helps with the balance."

Oh yes, the paddle. She kept forgetting about that. "Thanks," she said in the most sarcastic voice she could manage. Which must have been pretty damn sarcastic because in the next moment he was beside her.

"Would you like me to give you a few tips?"

"Nope. I'm perfectly fine." She stood up in order to prove exactly how perfectly fine she was. The board tilted, wobbled dangerously, and in the next breath she was in the sea again. Breath being the operative word – because she tried to take one at just the wrong moment and got a throatful of bitter salt water. Coughing and spluttering, she scrambled to her knees – fortunately, the water wasn't much more than thigh deep – and opened her stinging eyes to see Tim, still on his board, bent double with laughter.

"So you thought that was funny, did you?" She had the advantage because he was laughing way too much to defend himself and she was way too cross, not to mention way too wet, to have anything left to lose. With a swift sideways movement, she flipped Tim's board, and consequently Tim, into the sea.

He was still laughing when he emerged, which enraged SJ even more. She made a lunge for him and he ducked and in the next moment there was a major water fight going on – they weren't the only ones who'd got soaked, there had been quite a bit of collateral damage during the shenanigans.

Sha and a couple of guys SJ didn't know very well were using their paddles to fire swathes of water at each other. Penny, slightly more dignified, was kicking water, mostly at Jason, a teenager who SJ had seen around but didn't know. Two other girls were using the boards to slap water into the air – they seemed to be aiming at Tim but SJ was getting caught in the crossfire.

"Stop it. Stop it right now. STOP!" It took until the third stop before SJ realised that someone was seriously upset. It was the guy who'd hired them the boards, she realised. Oops. He was striding through the shallow water towards them, waving his arms furiously, his face a fiery red that clashed violently with his pink Mohican, and he was yelling at the top of his voice.

"All of you. Out. Right now! I won't have my boards abused. Session aborted! OUT!"

Blimey, SJ thought, feeling marginally guilty, partly because she had started it but mostly because no one was taking the slightest bit of notice of Mohican Man. They were all having far too much fun. Water was flying everywhere. You couldn't see through the spray.

"Um guys – guys…I think we'd better – um – Guys…"

Tim, noticing suddenly what was going on, came to her aid. He was perhaps the only person who could have come to her aid. He was at least a foot taller than Mohican Man and much more imposing.

"Enough's, enough. Fun's over, people." He stood up in the centre of the group and put his hands in the air, which made him even taller and seemed to make his voice more authoritarian than usual.

"Session aborted," SJ yelled for good measure. She hadn't meant to take the mickey but she couldn't stop giggling. And it had been a strange thing to say.

"If any of those boards are damaged I'll be keeping your deposits." Mohican Man was spluttering with rage now.

"Sorry, mate." Tim gave his shoulder a friendly slap, but he wasn't in the mood to be placated.

"I bloody mean it. They're good boards. They're not bloody toys. If there's any damage…"

"We really are sorry," Penny said, flicking a strand of wet blond hair from her face and doing her best 'fluttering eyelashes' look. It seemed to work. Slowly, slowly, he let himself be placated by her motherly niceness, although he did still insist the session was over.

"At least we got our deposits back," Sha said, as they headed back up the beach to where the rest of the group sunbathed.

"I'd have paid a tenner for that," Jason said. "I'd have paid double. It was worth every penny."

A man with a grey pony tail slapped him on the back. "Enjoying yourself without a drink, hey buddy? Who'd have thunk it!"

"Typical alkies," said one of the girls on the beach, shielding her eyes and looking up at them. "Can't go anywhere without causing trouble."

Tim peeled off his tee shirt and wrung it out over the sand. "I've been kicked out of a few bars in my time," he muttered. "But I've never been thrown out of the sea."

SJ laughed. "I'm sorry. But you did start it."

"Moi?" He put his hand across his heart – the exact same gesture he'd made earlier – only this time it was skin against skin. He had a nice chest, she noticed idly. Muscled and not too hairy – he may have worked in an office but he certainly took care of himself. She felt warmed and it wasn't just the sun, which was still beating down on them.

She had known Tim for years but he'd only ever been on the periphery of her world. Strange how that happened sometimes with people. She had never realised how nice he was. She glanced at his face and suddenly they were locked in a gaze that was more than casual – as if they had just noticed each other for the very first time.

"At least we shouldn't take long to dry off," she said, feeling suddenly shy of his gaze and looking up at the cloudless sky.

"Yeah." He took her cue and looked up too and the moment – if ever there had been a moment – was gone.

Lying on the beach, wriggling her toes in the hot, gritty sand, feeling the glare of sun against her closed eyelids and listening to the sound of the waves shushing against the shore, reminded SJ of her childhood. Sometimes in the holidays, if she and Alison had nagged enough, Mum would pack up a picnic of scotch eggs and sandwiches and take them to the beach.

It had always been sunny then. There had always been ice cream. And they usually built a sandcastle after lunch. The best days were when Dad had come with them. He was ace at building sandcastles. While Mum read her paperback on a deck chair, Dad would help SJ and Alison find a suitable patch of sand near the sea, but not too near.

"The trick is to judge whether the tide's going in or out," he'd say.

"How do you know that?"

"You watch. And you wait." He'd hunker down beside them in his stripy trunks and shield his eyes and stare out at the horizon.

"What are you watching?"

"I'm watching to see if the seahorses under the waves have their heads pointing towards me or their tails."

"What sea horses?" Alison would say. "I can't see any sea horses."

SJ couldn't either, but she didn't want to disappoint Dad so she'd shield her eyes too and wait.

"You can see the flash of their eyes if the tide's coming in," Dad said. "They have silver eyes." He'd point. "There – do you see? Just at the point below where the waves break."

And every so often SJ fancied that she could see a flash of silver as a wave broke and her heart would beat very fast. "I saw one, Dad, I saw one." And he'd reach over and ruffle her hair with his big hand.

"I saw one too," Alison would yell. "A big one – and it's got pointy pink ears."

"Has it, love?" Dad would say and he'd ruffle Alison's hair too and then the three of them would walk back to a point on the sand. Alison usually got to choose the exact spot because she was the youngest and they'd start to dig.

Dad would kneel beside them. Totally tireless he would dig like a terrier with both hands going madly, spraying out the sand behind him, so that if anyone walked past they'd be in danger of being buried. But no one ever did walk past. SJ realised, years later, that Dad made sure they were always in a spot away from the rest of the families before he started digging.

And because she was the eldest he also told her one day that the real way you could tell if the tide was coming in was to remember that seahorses only liked to gallop on soft sand.

"They're sensitive critters – they don't like hurting their hooves. So what you have to do is walk just in front of the sea. If the sand's hard, then it means the tide will be on its way out. Seahorses don't like galloping on hard sand. And if the sand's soft, the tide'll be on its way in."

Crap, SJ wished she hadn't started thinking about Dad. Life had seemed so very simple then. Summers had seemed endless, she'd believed in seahorses who galloped along beaches and she'd thought her parents were immortal.

They went in different directions for lunch. Some of the group had brought sandwiches, but SJ, Penny, Tim and Sha queued up to go in the Urban Reef, which was on the prom and was three levels high and had outside seating, even on the first floor. Huge parasols shielded the tables but SJ could feel the sun on her bare shoulders. The scents of pizza and burgers mingled with the scent of the sea. It was bliss.

"Boscombe's gone upmarket," Sha remarked as they drank home-made lemonade and shared two plates of nachos. "When I was a kid they only had burger bars here."

"There used to be trampolines and a fun fair," Tim said, his face a little reflective. "With those swing boat things that took two people. Me and my kid brother used to see how high we could get them."

Sha smiled. "I bet you two could get them right to the top."

"Yeah we could," Tim said. "Happy days."

"Are you still close to him?" SJ asked as she levered a cheese-covered nacho from the pile and popped it into her mouth.

He shook his head. "He died when he was fourteen. Meningitis."

There was a sudden hush around the table. Penny, who was sitting next to Tim, stroked his arm. Sha blinked. SJ wished she could take back the question. Suddenly they were all close – held within a bubble of bittersweet empathy – which Tim broke.

"Hey, guys. It's cool. It was a long time ago." He smiled around the table. "Yeah, I miss him. He'd have loved the board thing we were doing. He loved the sea."

He paused to attract the attention of a passing waitress. "Could I get another one of those lemonades please – how's everyone else fixed for drinks?"

SJ wondered if it was his brother's death that had started him on his journey to alcoholism. There was often a tipping point. But no more was said. The atmosphere notched back up into carefree.

It was hard not to be carefree on such a fabulous day.

The minibus was picking them up from the car park at five, and around half past four Tim started to pack stuff into the rucksack he'd brought. "Think I'll take a stroll," he said.

"Want some company?" SJ asked. "Or would you rather…" she'd been going to say, 'be alone,' but that sounded a bit OTT. He hadn't mentioned his brother again but she'd wondered if he'd come here in order to lay some ghosts.

"Company's cool," Tim said. "More the merrier."

In the end a few of them strolled back towards the pier, past blue and yellow beach huts, past Mohican Man who didn't glance up from his paper as they passed. All his boards were out but clearly he'd hired them to responsible adults this time.

Just before the pier were a circle of giant sand coloured boulders. "They're for kiddies to play on," Sha said. "Quite a cool idea, don't you think?"

"Don't get any ideas about climbing them," the man with the grey pony tail told Jason with a wink. "We don't want to get barred from the beach as well as the sea."

Tim turned to SJ and said, "Do you play any musical instruments?"

"Um, no." She glanced at him puzzled because the question was so out of context. "Why? Do you?"

"Is the pope Catholic?" His eyes were suddenly alight with amusement and he put on a pseudo black voice. "Sister, you ever know a black man who ain't got the rhythm in his soul?" He began to click his fingers and moonwalk along the sandy promenade.

He had the rhythm all right. Even though he was taking the mickey. She bet he was a great dancer. She laughed. Penny shook her head in mock amazement.

Sha and Jason immediately joined Tim. Soon there was a whole crowd of them moonwalking towards the pier but it was Tim who led them through the archway on to the wooden slatted boardwalk. A queue of moonwalking alcoholics. SJ wondered how long it would take for them to get barred from the pier.

She was so diverted that she didn't see the silver drum on its triangular stand beside the central aisle of the pier until they were almost on top of it and then the only reason she noticed it was because Tim paused in front of it and rapped out a tune.

Rapped was an understatement. Even though the drum had a musicality of its own, even though a child could have played it, Tim made it sing.

"It's a babel drum," Jason said, reading from the board above it. "Magic."

"Look, there are instruments the whole way along," Penny called in delight, heading towards the next one – a set of tubular chimes. "What a fabulous idea. Tim, did you know these were here?"

He smiled and didn't answer.

"I've heard about this," said the man with the grey pony tail. "It's a percussion trail. There are all kinds of different chimes and other oddities. Pretty cool, aren't they? A musical pier."

"I think they're for children," SJ said. "Not great dollops like us."

"I am a child," Tim called above the chimes of a perfectly played arpeggio. "Who's with me? This needs two players."

By the time they got to the last set of chimes, which was close to the entrance but on the opposite side to which they'd come in, they were all breathless. SJ couldn't remember the last time she'd had so much fun.

"This one is the pièce de résistance," Tim said. "And it needs four players. Who's up for it?"

SJ found herself being nudged forward.

"But I'm not musical," she protested.

"You are, SJ, trust me." Tim steered her to the far left of the instrument and gestured to a sign on the board in front of them.

Suddenly understanding, she smiled at him.

"All you have to do is hit the chimes, one at a time, left to right." His voice was in her ear. She picked up the soft covered red baton that was there for the purpose and waited until the other three players were in place.

"Ready?" called Tim. "Okay then, SJ – over to you. Do you remember the tune?"

She would have done – even if they hadn't sung it several times over on the mini bus.

Anyway, a child could have done it. The chimes had been designed for a child – all you had to do was hit them in order and they played a perfect rendition of, *'I do like to be beside the seaside.'*

It was silvery and uplifting and SJ laughed aloud as she played the beginning of the old familiar tune. Beside her, Penny took up the next part and Jason and Tim played the final two parts.

A small audience of families with kids had gathered to watch and they were urged to play an encore. When they finally finished they were all breathless and laughing.

SJ looked out at the glittering sea. A seagull, its chest a dazzling white, soared across the sky. A gentle breeze caught her hair, and a warmth that had nothing to do with the sun lifted her soul. There was a part of her that fully expected to see seahorses galloping in on the tide.

Chapter Twenty

SJ was at Mortimer's when she got the phone call from her mother. Or to be precise the three missed calls, none of which she saw until she checked her bag in her break.

Crap, crap, crap, why hadn't she looked before? It must be something to do with Dad. What if he'd taken a turn for the worse? Or been rushed to hospital? Or he'd had his appointment and it was bad news. No, his appointment wasn't until the following Monday. She had the date circled in her diary. Even *she* couldn't have got that wrong.

So why else would Mum be phoning her mobile, which she only did in emergencies because of the cost? With sweaty fingers and her heart pounding she called back. There was no answer. SJ left a message telling them she'd be at work for another couple of hours and then she'd be home and could come round if needed.

She couldn't carry the phone around while she was waiting on tables because there was no pocket in her skirt, but she kept racing back to the cloakroom to check it.

"For heaven's sake, sweetie," Miguel, who was her boss and very camp, berated her. "You're like a cat on hot bricks. Whatever is wrong?"

"My dad's not very well and I'm a bit worried," she said guardedly. Miguel was unpredictable. He could go from being incredibly kind to viper sharp in the space of five minutes. And you could never be quite sure what mood he was in.

His black eyes narrowed and he glanced at his watch. "You can bugger off if you like," he offered. "We're not too busy."

"Are you sure? Thanks. I'll make up the time," she called over her shoulder, as she headed for the back to get her stuff. It was probably best to go before it got busy and he changed his mind. It was only 1.30."

Outside in the muggy air – it was still unseasonably hot for May – SJ tried her parents again. No answer. Maybe she should go straight there. But that was pretty pointless if they were out. Maybe she should go to the hospital. But what hospital? No, that was definitely overreacting, even for her.

For heaven's sake, calm down, she told herself. You don't even know if there's anything wrong.

She wished she didn't feel so on edge. She wished she could roll back time to Sunday – to when they'd been still on the beach. The water fight, the music on the pier – it all seemed a long time ago.

The sense of peace she'd felt after her day at the seaside had been smashed about an hour after she'd got back and found a message from Tanya on her landline.

It had been short and not at all sweet.

'SJ. Don't keep calling me. I thought you were my friend. But we both know that's not true. Let's just leave it at that.'

The curt little message had broken SJ's heart. She had instantly reached for the phone and then stopped again. The one thing she wanted to do the most – dial Tanya's number and sort this out – was the one thing Tanya was asking her not to do. And she had, after all, already phoned about sixteen times. Well, maybe not quite sixteen, but definitely a lot of times. Never once had Tanya picked up.

Dorothy, when she'd been consulted, had advised her to leave it too.

"Give her time," Dorothy had said. "She's hurting. And if her husband's right and she does have post natal depression then the good thing is that it will get better. It is only temporary. The best thing you can do, right now, hen, is wait. Let it lie."

Why was it so bloody difficult to let things lie? Why did she not have any patience? Why did the world seem to be conspiring against her at the moment? The people she loved the most were hurting and she couldn't do anything to help them.

She was at home, making a cup of chamomile tea in an attempt to calm down, when her phone rang again. She snatched it up. She didn't recognise the number, which was even more worrying. Maybe Mum was calling from hospital or someone else's mobile.

"Hello?"

"SJ, it's Ebby."

It took her a few seconds to register who Ebby was. He hadn't phoned in ages and she'd been so sure it would be her mother.

"Ebby, hi. Sorry. I didn't recognise your voice."

"Hope I haven't caught you at a bad time?" He sounded unusually subdued.

"No, you haven't. It's fine. Are you okay?"

"Yeah, I'm good. I'm cool." His voice was guarded and she knew in the next breath what he was going to say. "It's my boy, Kit, he's not so good. You said you wanted to know an all…"

"Yes, yes I did. I do." She sank onto the edge of her sofa. There was a strange sense of stillness in the room. As if someone had just pressed the pause button on time. The television screen looked dusty. In contrast, the framed picture of Ash on the wall behind it looked stark. Her own tongue felt too big for her mouth.

"What's happened? Is he okay?"

"No. He's in hospital. I'm here. SJ, you might want to come."

"I'll come. I can come right now." She grabbed the notepad from the telephone table and wrote down the details Ebby gave her. Afterwards, when she looked at her own writing she was amazed how coldly neat it was. As if she'd been practising for a handwriting test. As she sat on the tube on the way to the hospital she wondered if her writing had been so neat because in that moment it had been the only thing in her life she could control.

Ebby met her at the entrance of the ward. He had green paint on his jeans and some on his arms, the type that's used on garden fences – he must have rushed straight from a job. His face was very grave.

"My boy – he don't look so good, SJ." He gave her a brief hug and she felt his dreadlocks brushing her face.

"What happened? Was it the…?" She couldn't bring herself to say cocaine.

"He was attacked," Ebby said, as they walked side by side along a corridor. "Got himself into a bit of bother."

"Bother? But how?" SJ was horrified. "Do you mean a mugger? Did someone attack him in the street?"

"No, honey. This weren't no random beating. Way I heard it was that he owed a lot of money. And I mean, a lot of money. To the wrong sort of people. You don't want to go owing the wrong sort of people money, SJ. Not in Kit's line of business."

"So, they beat him up? Oh my God." She glanced at him. His face was very grave. "He's going to be all right, though, isn't he? I mean, he's going to get better?"

Maybe this was the wake-up-call Kit needed. Maybe this was his rock bottom. It could even be a blessing in disguise. Hope skittered about in her heart. She imagined sitting next to him, as he had once done for her. She imagined him giving her that wry smile, making some dark edged comment about her not seeing him at his best. But before she could get too carried away on this fantasy, Ebby added. "They did a lot of damage. He weren't in no fit state for it either. The neighbour who found him on Sunday, he thought he was dead."

183

SJ felt sick. At the door of ICU, Ebby put a hand on her arm. "He don't look too pretty… He's not – you know – conscious or nothing. I'm kind of having second thoughts about calling you. I'm kind of thinking maybe you might want to remember him – as he was."

"It's all right." She met his gaze steadily. "I want to see him. You did the right thing calling me."

He nodded. "Okay."

They went into ICU and she followed Ebby into a private room where a figure lay motionless beneath a blue blanket. For a second SJ thought they'd come into the wrong room. She wouldn't have recognised Kit if she hadn't known it was him. His face was a mass of purple and black. His eyes were closed and his thin bruised arms were festooned with drips.

He was breathing through a tube. His chest rose and fell in the faintest of movements: his only concession to life.

She would not cry. Not out loud. She would not cry, because somewhere inside his battered, ravaged body was the man she had once trusted with her soul and she was terrified he might hear her grief. But she couldn't stop the tears from rolling down her face and soaking into the collar of her blouse.

"You can hold his hand," Ebby said. And they both stepped closer, she to the left of Kit's head and he to the right. They held a hand each and Ebby said, "We can talk to him. The nurses said he maybe can still hear. Hey, big guy," he looked at

Kit, and his eyes were hugely tender. "I brought a special lady in to see you. I brought you the SJ – don't say I never do nothing for you, man."

Kit's fingers felt cool in her hand. As though they were already in some other place – a place that was nearer to death than it was to life. SJ squeezed them anyway – very gently, so as not to hurt, which seemed absurd, yet also right.

"Hello, my love," she said. "I thought it was time we caught up – you know, long time no see." Her voice had gone artificially high with the strain of not letting it break and she knew the words were banal. But there were no words for this. None had ever been invented.

Kit's eyes remained closed. SJ doubted he could have opened them even if he'd been conscious. His face was still. His hand unresponsive. His breathing was the only sound in the white room.

"He's not in pain," Ebby said.

"That's good. That's very good." She stroked the back of Kit's hand. He had told her once that if ever she got the chance she should try a hand massage.

"You wouldn't think it – but they're the best." His eyes had warmed as he'd spoken. "Very soothing. My sister always has them at the hairdressers."

SJ didn't know whether it gave him any comfort, the hand massage, but it gave her some, doing this for him. A rhythmic stroking, not too light, she didn't want to annoy, and not too hard – she didn't want to cause him any more distress.

185

Once long ago when she'd been in a hospital room, not dissimilar to this, he had brought her boiled sweets. He had understood that her throat would be sore from where they'd had to push the tube down to pump out her stomach.

He had understood so much about addiction. He had understood so much about her. She remembered there had been a time when she'd wanted him to have understood because he'd been there – experienced the crazy, raging control of the demons himself. Yet right now she would have given anything for him to have *not* understood. For him to have only empathised because of what he'd read in a text book: for him to have only empathised because he was a kind and sensitive man.

Because it seemed inconceivable that this man who had been so strong, who had guided her – and so many others – step by painful step away from the insatiable demon of addiction, was now dying at its hand.

SJ didn't know how long they stayed with Kit. Only that the sky outside the windows slowly darkened to rose and then to deep purple and then to black. She was aware that her mobile beeped a few times with texts, but she didn't check them. She knew they might be from her mother. She was aware that her parents must have got her message by now but nothing else seemed as important any more as being here in this room.

Eventually it was Ebby who made her leave.

"We can't stay here all night, girl." His eyes were gentle. "We can come again…"

186

"Yes," she said. And she wondered if they said such things because they were trying to remain hopeful – or because they actually believed they would happen.

Ebby had driven to the hospital and he insisted on giving her a lift home and seeing her indoors and making them both a chamomile tea.

"I'll let you know – if there's any news," he said.

"Thank you."

They hugged again at the door. "Take it easy, sister," were his last words.

SJ agreed she would. Then she shut the door and when she was finally alone she sobbed for the man who had saved her life, the man she had loved so much, the man she had once thought was her soulmate.

Chapter Twenty-One

SJ phoned in sick the next day. It was not something she often did. Especially when she wasn't actually physically ill. In fact, she couldn't remember ever phoning in sick since she'd stopped drinking. Luckily, she had the constitution of an ox and was rarely ill. Not that she looked terribly well, she decided, as she studied her reflection in the bathroom mirror.

There were blotchy patches on her face from all the crying. No amount of make-up was covering those up, and her eyes were so puffy she could hardly see. Miguel probably wouldn't want her going in looking like this anyway. She'd put off all his customers.

She had phoned the hospital first thing. Kit was the same – still unconscious, which meant surely that there was some hope. Her heart told her that, even though her head – and Ebby when she spoke to him – told her that there wasn't much.

She had also seen last night, when it was too late to do anything about it, that she had two texts from Alison. They both said. *SJ, where are you? Mum can't get hold of you. PHONE ME.*

The texts had been sent an hour or so apart so either Alison thought she hadn't sent the original or she was just repeating her orders.

There was also a text from Didi. *HELLO SPONSOR LADY, WHEN'S OUR NEXT MEETING. CAN YOU DO WEDNESDAY PM?*

Why was everyone shouting at her? SJ took a few deep breaths, made herself a very strong coffee and called Alison back first.

"I've tried to phone Mum," she began but Alison cut across her.

"SJ. Finally" Where the hell have you been? We thought you'd died or something."

She flinched. "I'm sorry. Is it Dad? Is he okay?"

"Sorry isn't really good enough, is it, SJ. We needed you yesterday and where were you? Working, no doubt. Look, I know you need the money, but family's important...and…"

"Is Dad all right, Alison?" Her voice must have been sharp enough to stop Alison in her tracks – that took some doing – because she did at least get to the point.

"He had to go in for his appointment yesterday with the specialist."

"But Mum said it was next Monday."

"Yes, I know – but it got changed because they had a cancellation. SJ can you just listen to what I'm telling you."

"Sorry," she said automatically. "So, how did it go?"

"They've done some tests. So we have to wait for the results of those. But the specialist is a bit worried."

"Oh." SJ thought she might cry again but there didn't seem to be any tears left in her body. Maybe she would have to fill up with them again like a human cistern.

"SJ, did you hear what I said?"

"Of course." She shook herself and tried to find the right response. "Did the specialist give you any clue as to what it could be?" But what she really wanted to say was, why isn't Mum or Dad phoning me? Why is it you with your self-important, holier than thou, voice?

But that was probably just her being over sensitive, wasn't it? Alison was only keeping her in the loop.

"Well, the specialist did say that there's a few possibilities – apart from the big C of course. Mum and I are keeping optimistic, though."

"What possibilities? What did he think it might be?"

"Diabetes, IBS, something to do with coeliac disease – there's a lot of stuff it could be, I checked on the internet. Poor Dad – this isn't doing him any good. He's in a right old tiswaz. Where are you anyway? Are you at work?"

"No. I'm off sick. I can come over if you like – are you at Mum and Dad's now?"

"Yes, but I don't think you should come over if you're sick. Dad's got enough problems as it is."

"I'm not actually sick – I just…"

"Look, I've got to go. I just wanted to keep you up to speed."

"Can I have a word with Mum?"

But Alison had disconnected. SJ stayed where she was on the settee for a long time, staring into space, thinking about how much of a mess her life seemed to be in at the moment and wondering what she could do about it. There seemed to be a block at every turn. Her best friend wouldn't speak to her. Mum and Dad didn't want her over there and Kit – Kit was probably dying. Oh, Kit, why didn't you let me help you? Why hadn't she kept in closer touch? She hated to think of what he must have gone through to get to this point. He must have been in so much pain, not just physically, but mentally. On Sunday when he'd been beaten so badly he'd been left for dead, she'd been down the beach sunning herself. Laughing.

How utterly selfish she was.

She was only roused into action when her phone rang again.

It was Didi. "Are you ignoring me?"

"No, of course not. Sorry. I'm having a bit of a bad day."

"Oh dear." Didi hesitated. "Did you get my text about meeting up later? Would it be best to leave it till another time?"

Probably, SJ thought. But then again she had no wish to sit and mope about in her flat all day either.

"No, it's fine. You can come over here this afternoon if you like?"

"I don't suppose we could meet in Camden Market again, could we? That would suit me better."

SJ felt like saying that it wouldn't suit her in the slightest, but she didn't have the energy. Besides, maybe it would do her good to get out.

At least Didi needed her, she thought, as she walked through Camden Market. It was busy and crowded. The noise of the shouting stall holders

191

hurt her ears and the vibrancy of the shops and people hurt her eyes, even though she'd put on sunglasses. The sunglasses also hid her puffy face. It had been quite dark in the red and black café. She might have to take them off in there or she wouldn't see a thing. She hoped Didi wouldn't comment.

On the other hand, SJ was beginning to realise that Didi was so self-absorbed she might not even notice the mess of her face. Rather bizarrely this thought cheered her up. At least she wasn't like that any more. At least she cared about other people today. Sometimes she thought she cared too much.

She hadn't spoken to Dorothy about Kit, although she'd badly wanted to ring her again. She was too aware that she'd phoned Dorothy up more times lately than she did when she was at home and Dorothy was supposed to be on holiday. She was supposed to be having a rest from all the hassles of home. Besides, she was back in three and a half weeks. They could catch up properly then. The thought warmed SJ as she went past a shop that looked as though it sold the kind of outfits Didi bought.

A mannequin dressed in a black leather basque and thigh length boots pouted out at the world. It was only when she crooked her finger at SJ and lifted an eyebrow that SJ realised she was real. Blushing, she hurried on, past a shop with a giant Nike Air trainer stuck to the wall and another where a woman had her feet in a tank of piranhas

– or whatever the fish were that bit the hard skin off your feet. Yuk. Poor fish.

By the time she reached the entrance to the labyrinth which was Camden Market, SJ was beginning to feel quite cheered. It had been a good idea to come out. Especially to somewhere as distracting as Camden. It was so full of life and shoppers.

She brushed past a stand of bags and one of them fell off its hook and landed at her feet. Pausing, she bent to pick it up. Gosh, it was gorgeous and she needed a new bag. Could she stretch to £22? Maybe not this month. Shame. She put it back on its hook.

With a wry smile, she turned round and walked slap bang into Miguel. Oh crap, crap, crap. He looked almost as shocked to see her as she was to see him. Which wasn't surprising as when she'd phoned in sick this morning she'd insinuated she was at death's door. This hadn't been that hard. Her voice had been croaky from tears and although she hadn't intended to say she had flu – she'd intended to give him a potted version of the truth – the flu thing had kind of slipped out.

This was not going to be good.

"SJ – what a surprise!" He was in viper mode, his black eyes flashing. "And there was I thinking you were tucked up tightly in your bed. There was I feeling all sympathetic – feeling sorry for you with your ill father and your terrible flu. Ha!" He peered at her sunglasses. "You think you won't be recognised if you put on those ridiculous glasses and go shopping!"

"No," SJ gulped. "I'm sorry, Miguel. It's not how it looks…" Her voice didn't sound in the least bit croaky now. Typical!

"You are *not* going shopping?" He plucked the bag she'd been looking at from the rail it was on. "You were *not* just going to purchase this lovely bag? You did not lie to me this morning and leave me in the lurch?"

"I did lie, yes. I'm really sorry. But not to come shopping."

"So where *are* you going then?" His eyes narrowed as he glanced at her black skinny jeans and dark jacket with flecks of red that she only put on when she needed an injection of confidence. "A job interview perhaps? Is that why you're here?"

"No!" she said, horrified. "Of course not. I'm meeting a friend." Oh crap, that was possibly worse – even than a job interview. It sounded like she'd skived off and let him down on a whim.

"I see." He stood with his hands on his non-existent hips, one foot slightly at an angle, which he was tapping on the cobbles. Tap tap tap. Glare. Tap tap tap. Glare.

A woman with a small dog was looking over at them and tutting self-righteously.

"Please – don't let me hold you up from meeting your friend." Tap tap tap. Glare. "Heaven forbid that a little thing like your job should stand in your way of coffee outings." Tap tap tap. Glare.

"Miguel, if I could just explain?" She reached out a hand to touch his arm.

He stepped backwards before she made contact. "No explanation necessary. Run along." He made a brushing away motion with his hands. "Oh and, SJ – please don't trouble yourself to return to work. Your services are no longer required."

SJ didn't move. She was too shocked. And Miguel was already, spinning around. She had expected him to be angry. Expected him even to throw a hissy fit – he was renowned for it. But she had not expected him to sack her.

She was one of his best waitresses. They both knew that. And this was the first mistake she had ever made. Ever. Not once had she ever phoned in sick. Not once had she not showed up when she was supposed to – oh, apart from that one time recently when she was supposed to be covering someone's shift and she'd had to change it because she'd gone to see Michael for Tanya. That had caused a few ructions and even though it wasn't her shift – so technically she wasn't responsible – it had been a Saturday, which was Mortimer's busiest day. And word had got round that she'd backtracked on the shift cover at the last moment. Miguel was probably aware of that. Not much got past him.

Even so, surely he had to at least give her a warning? Evidently not. Her hands felt sweaty. She felt like bursting into tears. Her body had clearly had time to manufacture some more.

What the hell was she going to do without that job? She had a couple of months' emergency money in the bank, and that was that. She glanced at her watch. It was five minutes past the time she'd agreed to meet Didi. And although it was the last thing on earth she felt like doing now, she really needed to get going.

A short while later she stood in the red and black café. There were a few people in today and a blond waitress was serving. Was that the one called Laura who'd been here before? SJ couldn't make up her mind. One thing was apparent though. Didi was not here. SJ rummaged in her bag. There were no texts from her either.

Could she have been and gone? She was only ten minutes late – okay maybe twelve, so it didn't seem that likely. She waited until the blond waitress was free and then casually intercepted her. Yes, it was Laura. The same mole on her cheek, the same pretty smile. Thank goodness.

"Um," SJ began haltingly. "I'm supposed to be meeting a friend in here – I think you might know her." She'd been about to say, 'her name's Didi' when she was struck by a horrible thought.

Didi's real name was Carol – they had laughed about it once – *how many dominatrices do you know by the name of Carol?* Didi had said.

Well, none, but then I don't think I know any dominatrices anyway.

It's my professional name. Although a lot of people do know me as Didi, these days.

Madam Didi. It made total sense. The thing is which name would Laura know? The last thing SJ wanted to do was to cock up something else. To disclose private information to Laura – especially in view of the fact that Didi and Laura's boyfriend did ironing and whipping and things together. Oh crap. Her face was burning.

Laura was smiling patiently.

"I – um – can't remember her name," SJ said. "Senior moment, you know. But she always wears black. She has a phobia about the colour white. She can't even put milk in her coffee and the chef has to break the yolk on her egg so it's not white. He did a very good job last time we were in. Very clever." She was babbling but she couldn't stop and her face was so hot that her sunglasses were now slipping down her nose.

But at least Laura was nodding. "You mean Didi?" she said. "No, I haven't seen her today. She was in yesterday, I think. About this time. Are you sure your meeting wasn't yesterday?"

SJ was about to point out that she wasn't stupid. She knew what day their meeting was when she remembered she'd just told Laura she couldn't remember her friend's name. So actually it wasn't such a quantum leap for her to think she might have the wrong day. Clearly someone who suffered with name amnesia might very well suffer with date amnesia too.

She pushed her glasses back up her sweaty nose and they fell off altogether and hit the stone floor with a smack.

Double crap. She and Laura both bent to pick them up. Laura got there first. "Oh gosh," she exclaimed, straightening. "I think they've cracked. It's the floor. It's harder than it looks. Can you see okay without them? Are they prescription ones?"

SJ shook her head. To her humiliation she could feel tears welling up again and now they were rolling down her uncovered no doubt blotchy and swollen face. Could this day actually get any worse? No, actually, it probably couldn't.

Despite the fact she was worried sick about Kit, she had made a massive effort to come over here. She had upset her parents. She probably should have gone over there instead of Camden. She'd managed to get fired from her job in the process somehow and Didi – bloody Didi – had not even bothered to show up.

Chapter Twenty-Two

She decided to go straight from Camden to the hospital where Kit was. She hadn't heard from Ebby today, which meant there was still hope. If there was any justice in the world – if there was the tiniest scrap, if there was such a thing as a Higher Power, which she was certain there was or she wouldn't be sober, then she would find that Kit had turned a corner.

He would be sitting up in bed, saying, "Sorry about that, SJ. That was a close one. Phew. Down but not out – so how have you been? Hey, don't cry. I'm good. I'm still here."

Okay, maybe that was a bit of a stretch. Even for her. Her mind ran another more feasible scene past her. He would still be quite out of it. He would still be lying down all wired up. But as she walked in and took his hand, his eyes would flicker and the nurse would pop her head around the door and say, "I think he's going to make it. He has a very strong heart, that one."

This little scene cheered her until she got to the tube station and found that the line she wanted was closed.

Cursing she phoned Didi while she made her way to the next platform. There was no answer.

SJ tapped out a furious text and then another. And Didi finally responded with a curt reply. *SORRY. GOT HELD UP.*

Not that SJ was letting her get away with that.

WE NEED TO TALK, she'd texted back, typing in the same block capitals Didi used in case that made a difference. She'd read somewhere that communicating with people in the same fashion they communicated with you built up empathy.

No answer.

Time to get tough. *PHONE ME, DIDI. NOW. OR WE'RE FINISHED.*

Rather to her surprise, Didi did phone her about five minutes later and it was immediately clear why she hadn't made their meeting. She was drunk. She was also tearful and hugely apologetic.

"Please don't say you don't want to be my sponsor any more," she'd begged. "Please give me another chance, SJ. I promise faithfully that I will never let you down again. You have my word."

"Huh!" SJ said, high on the power of finally getting Didi's attention. "And how much is that worth?"

"It is worth something. At least it is normally. Please, SJ. I can't carry on like this." Didi sounded like the frightened girl who had first phoned the helpline and not at all like her usual imperious self.

Against her better judgement SJ agreed to carry on sponsoring her. But not before she'd told Didi what the trip to Camden had cost her.

"Oh gosh," Didi said. "But don't worry – he can't just sack you like that. It's illegal."

"I bet it isn't. I lied. I said I was sick when I wasn't. And then I got caught."

"So it's not exactly my fault then," Didi said.

SJ was about to protest that it was entirely her fault when she realised that actually she was right. She should have just told Miguel the truth in the first place. If she had then she wouldn't be in the mess she was in now! She disconnected with a little sigh.

She was nearly at the hospital anyway. One more stop. And no news was good news. Ebby still hadn't phoned. And he would have done if anything had changed.

By the time she crossed the road to the main car park, which fronted the hospital, she was feeling hopeful again.

The first thing she saw was Ebby's car, in a space close to where they'd parked the previous day. Ebby was beside it. He was puffing on a cigarette, standing straight and tall like some dark sentinel. As she got closer to him, he got his phone out of his pocket and began to tap something in to it. Then he glanced up and saw her. And she looked at his face. And she knew. She knew straightaway from his eyes that she was too late.

He held out his arms and she collapsed into them. For a very long moment she laid her head against his chest, breathing in the unfamiliar musk of him, feeling his dreadlocks brush her face, while he held her up because her own legs were suddenly too shaky to be up to the job.

"When?" she said, when she could finally speak.

"Half an hour ago." He stroked her hair. "My boy's at peace now."

"Were you with him?"

He nodded. "He never woke up."

"That's good, Ebby, that's good isn't it. He wasn't scared." She could feel herself starting to sob. But it was as though it was happening to someone else. Another girl who stood in a Rastafarian's arms in a bleak little tarmac car park.

"No more fear now, sister. No more pain."

She didn't answer. She couldn't speak now. Although she was shivering it was still quite warm. A little distance away she was aware of a couple getting out of a car with a helium balloon which said *Congratulations, it's a girl*. The woman laughed as the man bent to say something to her.

Life and death – SJ thought – side by side in the same car park. How did that work? How could that be possible? What a very odd place the world was.

"Let's make a move," Ebby said eventually. "I'll take you home? No sense in hanging out here."

She didn't remember the journey back. It was as though her mind had switched off – or at least on to auto pilot. So that she lived in a little bubble of numbness where nothing that happened really touched her or felt real.

She didn't remember much about the days that followed either.

A whole fortnight somehow got lost. She did function. She got up, she made toast. She did her Poetry and a Pint class without remembering a word of what anyone said. She phoned her mother. She felt as though she was an actor in a play performing someone else's lines. It was like being an understudy in her own life.

The only thing that really registered was Ebby phoning up the first weekend and telling her the funeral wouldn't be arranged until after the inquest, which there had to be because of the circumstances of Kit's death.

"He had family," she told him. "He had a sister and a niece and he had parents too. Where were they?"

Her voice shook with anger. "Why weren't they there in the hospital? Why weren't they with him, Ebby? It's not fair."

Ebby had sighed. "The relatives – they're often all gone by the end, SJ. You can't blame them. They all would have had a gutful of it – they don't want no more pain, you know?"

There was a part of her that could understand that. When the anger had gone she understood it better. No one wanted to see their loved ones die the slow and painful death of addiction. No one wanted to see their loved ones die by their own hand. Because she knew that Ebby was right. Kit's life may have been ended by a beating, but he'd been dying anyway. In the final reckoning it had been the consequences of his addiction that had killed him.

She had heard someone say in the rooms once that losing someone to an addiction was like watching them commit suicide before your eyes – over and over again – until they finally got it right.

It was people like Ebby and Number Ten Tim and Dorothy who visited dying alcoholics and held their hands and attended their funerals. They did it because they cared and because they knew that next week it could be them. No one was safe. There was no such thing as recovered. Only recovery, which was ongoing and day by day and sometimes in even smaller time capsules than that. Sometimes in the midst of blackness it was minute by minute.

SJ was amazed she hadn't picked up a drink herself. She hadn't wanted to drink. Although she had wanted to stop living. Maybe she had stopped living in a way. She was in the darkest place she'd ever been. Darker even than when she'd been in hospital, after her own overdose. Darker than the moment she had seen Kit snorting coke – because back then there had been hope. There had been a future that wasn't blocked out in grey.

She hadn't been alone, back then, either. She wasn't completely alone now, she reminded herself. She still had Dorothy – and there was Didi – although she hadn't heard from Didi since she'd spoken to her after her no show at Camden. And there was Dad.

Her dear, sick dad. And it was thoughts of Dad that finally roused her back into life – or at least roused her enough to get back into making lists. Banal and stupid lists that didn't mean very much. But that she made because the numbers on them were her stepping stones back into the world.

Chapter Twenty-Three

Ways I might get my job back at Mortimer's

1. Go round there and grovel big time (probably not enough).

2. Offer to do a shift with no pay (probably not enough either).

3. Offer to do a week with no pay (good in principle but it wouldn't help with the rent). And do I really need to go crawling back on my belly?

SJ abandoned this list and started another one.

Ways to convince Mum I'm not a bad daughter

1. Phone up and apologise profusely for not being available when Mum had called. (again).

2. Offer to accompany Dad to his next appointment. (again).

3. Send a good luck card.

4. Turn up on the doorstep and offer to take them out for a 'cheer up' lunch.

She'd already tried the top two without success. Mum was being really sniffy with her at the moment. Goodness knows what Alison had said. Sending a good luck card seemed trite and banal. And turning up on the doorstep to take them out for lunch wasn't going to work because she was flat broke. She could barely raise the train fare to get over there, let alone the money for lunch.

Maybe they could come here? She could cook them something. Yes, fine plan, SJ – they're going to love beans on toast. She hadn't yet told Mum about losing her job. Partly because she didn't want to land her with anything else to worry about. And partly because she felt ashamed. Especially as she'd have to admit that the reason she'd lost it was because her boss had caught her shopping when she was supposed to be in bed with flu. Not that she'd actually even been shopping – but she may as well have been.

Mum would have the same opinion as Miguel on the actual truth. Going for a coffee – even if you were trying to save someone's life – was not going to hack it.

Her mother would be very disappointed. She'd say it too. "I'm very disappointed, Sarah-Jane. Why can't you be more responsible like your sister?"

SJ didn't think she could bear being held up and compared to perfect Alison. Not right now when her entire life seemed to be getting more imperfect by the day.

She abandoned the second list too and started a third.

Ways to tell Didi she didn't want to sponsor her any more

1. I'm sorry, Didi, but this isn't really working out, is it?

She couldn't think of a single other thing she could say. And yet somehow she couldn't bring herself to say it.

Had all of the disasters that had happened lately been her fault? She started another list.

Things that ARE my fault

1. Losing my job.

Then another…

Things that are NOT my fault

1. Dad getting ill.

2. Didi being a nightmare sponsee.

She also wrote down two more things on her iPad – but she had no idea which list they should go on. The first one was:

Tanya not speaking to me.

Was it her fault that Tanya thought she was the queen bitch from hell? Had she been totally insensitive? However many times she went over it she couldn't think of a way it could have turned out any differently.

Not unless she'd lied to Tanya, humoured her in the interests of their friendship. And what sort of friend would she have been then?

SJ concluded that Tanya not speaking to her was probably not her fault.

The other thing she'd written on her iPad was a much greyer area.

Kit dying.

Had that been her fault?

She'd only been going to AA for a couple of years when she'd attended her first funeral. It was the funeral of a guy who'd been a binge drinker.

"I'm not sure I'm really an alcoholic," he'd said to SJ and a group of others after a meeting one night. "The last time I had a drink was four months ago. And the time before that was six months. And the time before that was..." He spread his hands wide and shrugged. "Can't even remember, to tell you the truth."

"So why are you here?" One of the younger guys in the group had challenged.

"Dunno really." Steve grinned. He had a cute little dimple, SJ had noticed, and his smile was infectious. He was what Penny called the classic cheeky chappie.

"I don't even drink that much." He'd looked around at them all. "It's not like I'm down the pub every night."

"What happened the last time you did drink?" Number Ten Tim had asked idly. "Did you have fun?"

"Yeah sure I did." Steve had frowned a little then. "Great fun. I was with this real cute chick. She looked a bit like you, SJ. Lovely dark hair and legs up to here."

SJ blushed. She never had got the hang of compliments.

"We had a ball."

"And you woke up in your own bed the next day – no regrets?" Tim prompted.

"No. I woke up in a cell." Steve frowned as if he'd only just remembered that bit. "That wasn't so good."

"What happened?" A new girl on the periphery of the group asked. "Did you get drunk and hit someone or something?"

"Hey, babe. I don't do violence." He gave her a wink. Then his face sobered. "I drove my car into a wall. Shit – that wasn't good. Lucky there was only me in it. Huh."

"And what happened the time before that when you had a little drink?" This was from Half Pint Hughie. "Was that more fun?"

"Yeah – sure it was." His face brightened. "I was – at a party – met this really gorgeous little chick. We were having a lotta fun. Then we went back to her place." His eyes glazed. "Man, I can't tell you…"

"And you woke up in her bed the next day – no regrets," Tim prompted.

Steve rubbed at the bristle on his chin self-consciously. "No – I… I – woke up in hospital."

SJ could see a pattern beginning to emerge. Someone asked the obvious question. "What the hell happened?"

"I slipped in her shower – so they said. Bashed my head open." He pushed hair back from the side of his head to reveal a thin pink scar. "Twelve stitches. I don't remember much about it."

"Because you had drunk so much you were in an alcoholically induced blackout," Tim said relentlessly. "There seems to be a common denominator here, Steve."

209

"Women," said one of the guys. "Always causing trouble." Everyone laughed.

"I've been unlucky, though, guys. Hey – accidents happen to everyone."

"I used to have a great many accidents when I was drinking," Half Pint Hughie said. "I accidentally wet my bed most nights. I never planned on doing that, so I didn't."

Steve screwed up his face in disgust. "Shit – that's gross. I've never done that. No way, man."

"Yet," said Number Ten Tim. "That's what you mean, isn't it, Stevie boy. You've never done that, *yet*?" His voice was mild but his face had gone utterly serious. "All we're saying here is play the whole tape. If you're a normal person you drink, you have fun, you wake up the next day, perfectly fine, in your own bed. If you're an alky, you drink, you have fun, you drink some more, you get into trouble. That doesn't mean you do it every day. But it does tend to be how things pan out. Next time you're thinking about drinking Steve – be a bit more honest with yourself. Think about how it usually pans out."

Three weeks later Steve tried drinking again. He would have woken up in his own bed this time, SJ heard on the grapevine. Only he'd choked on his own vomit in the night and died.

He was just thirty-three. It had shocked SJ hugely. Until that moment she had almost believed that Steve had indeed just been unlucky. That alcoholism wasn't so dangerous. Wasn't so sneaky. That – hey – everyone had the odd blackout when they were having a good time.

Alco's voice had whispered in her ear. *'Hey, you weren't that bad, SJ. You were never a proper alcoholic.'*

So your average drinker overdoses on a bottle of gin then, do they? SJ had hissed back. 'Your average drinker sits down one Sunday lines up every tumbler in the house – no swigging it out of the bottle – and then systematically downs the lot.'

'You were depressed,' Alco purred. *'It was a cry for help.'*

Sometimes it was oh so tempting to believe Alco was right. That she wasn't a proper alcoholic. That she could drink again safely. And it would all be all right.

"It's the disease that tells you it's not a disease," Dorothy told her. "Lots of alkies think they can drink safely – even when every single piece of evidence points to the fact that they can't."

SJ had known a few people who had died since then. Some of them, like Steve, had never known they had a problem. Others had known because they'd been sober for many years but then they'd tried it again – for whatever reason, maybe they'd had their own Alco whispering in their ears. And they hadn't survived.

"Couldn't we have done more for them?" she'd asked Dorothy. "Couldn't we have – I don't know – stopped them somehow?"

"No, hen." Dorothy had looked a little sad. "The only person we can ever keep sober is ourself."

So perhaps Kit's death wasn't her fault either. SJ had spent a lot of time torturing herself about this.

When she'd finally gone to his funeral, which had been hugely well attended, she'd also felt humbled. Three people had given a eulogy. One of them had begun his with the words, "I am a recovering heroin addict and Kit Oakley saved my life." His voice cracked a little. "I know I am not the only one. I know there are many others." For a moment, he had raised his eyes to the congregation. Total silence had filled the packed crematorium as he'd looked out at them, his gaze travelling slowly from row to row. During the twenty second or so stillness that enveloped them he had made no attempt to wipe away the tears that were rolling down his face.

Emotion washed through the congregation in waves. You could feel it. It was one of the most powerful and moving moments that SJ had ever experienced. Beside her, Ebby closed his eyes and didn't open them again until the man at the podium cleared his throat and continued quietly.

"We all thank you for that, Kit Oakley," he said. "We thank you from the deepest place in our hearts."

SJ had leaned on Ebby's shoulder, her own heart breaking with pain, and he'd put his arm around her and squeezed her tightly.

When she'd got home she'd rummaged through her bedside table. She'd recently moved the little packet of love hearts from her bag and had put them beside Tanya's Russet Gold lipstick in the top drawer.

With fingers that trembled she carefully peeled back the pink foil to reveal the message on the top love heart.

She'd been hoping it would say something like, *Be Mine* or *First Love.* She'd been hoping for a message from beyond the grave. A message from Kit. Something that would make her feel better.

What the top love heart actually said was, *Don't cry.*

Chapter Twenty-Four

"I'm so very sorry," Dorothy had said when SJ told her about Kit. "What a tragic waste of a life. Are you okay, hen? Why didn't you phone me before?"

"You're on holiday. And I keep phoning you up. You must be sick to death of me."

"That doesn't matter," Dorothy said and SJ wasn't sure whether she meant the fact that she was on holiday or that she actually was sick to death of her phoning.

Before she had time to clarify this Dorothy said, "How are things with your dad? Is there any good news there?"

"Yes, actually. There is." Jolted back from the jaws of self-pity, SJ smiled. "Very good news. All of the tests he's had so far have come back clear. We're still waiting for the results of the MRI scan, but the specialist says she doesn't think there will be a problem. Everything's looking really good."

"That's super news," SJ had heard the pleasure in Dorothy's voice across the hundreds of miles that separated them. "That's absolutely brilliant." There was a pause and SJ wasn't sure whether it was the signal or whether Dorothy had just gone very quiet. "Well, hen, I'll love you and leave you. My battery's not holding its charge very well. I think I need a new phone."

"You needed a new phone in 1971," SJ pointed out.

"Don't be so cheeky. It works, doesn't it?"

"Only just, by the sound of it. What if I want to phone you and it's packed up?"

"Oh ye of little faith. I'll be back in a couple of weeks anyway. "

"I wish you were here now," SJ complained and then felt guilty. Dorothy must be dreading leaving the lap of luxury and coming back to the reality of her sponsee's moans and groans full time. She had about 160. Well, maybe not quite 160 but she certainly had a lot. SJ had enough trouble with just the one!

"Just keep on working the program," Dorothy said before she disconnected.

It had taken SJ ages to work out what people meant when they said 'keep working the program.'

"It's all up there," they would say enigmatically at meetings and point towards the Twelve-Step scroll on the wall.

SJ considered herself quite au fait with the English language. She'd taught it at A-level for several years. She could read the twelve steps as well as the next man or woman. She understood what they said. They were written in English, after all, albeit rather archaic English. How they made up a program and how you actually worked it was a completely different matter.

"It might help if you boil each step down to a single word," an older member had once told her. He produced a crumpled list from his pocket and gave it to SJ. "Here – check this out. I call it my quick reference guide."

1. Honesty
2. Hope
3. Faith
4. Courage
5. Integrity
6. Willingness
7. Humility
8. Brotherly Love
9. Self-Discipline
10. Perseverance
11. Awareness of God
12. Service

SJ looked at it and then back at him. "You try to live in accordance with these principles," he went on with a beatific smile. "Copy it down if you like, so you'll remember them."

"You'd be a saint if you could live in accordance with that lot," SJ said, her fingers itching to slap the smug expression off his face. So much for Brotherly Love – she'd failed already. She'd spotted a couple of others that were going to be deal breakers too. Self-discipline – she was rubbish at that – and Awareness of God. Unless that meant you were aware that God was a tricksy bugger who liked lulling you into a false sense of security before whipping the rug from under your feet with a flourish.

She had a feeling it didn't, though. She had a feeling she was going to get a whole pile of 'God knows what's best for us' and 'Everything in God's world is exactly as it's meant to be' platitudes that she didn't want to hear.

As the time had gone by, though, SJ had to admit it had started to make a bit more sense. The principles in the twelve steps, Dorothy had explained patiently, basically boiled down to one very simple piece of advice. "Accept what you can't change – which was everything in the universe except yourself. And do the next right thing."

Oh, and don't pick up a drink, of course.

She had been trying to follow this advice for the last four and three quarter years. And on the whole it had worked. She had slowly grown to know herself better. She had slowly grown to like herself more. Her self-esteem was sky high compared to what it had been when she had come in. She had been happy. Now was just a rough patch, she consoled herself. Everyone had rough patches.

She glanced at her watch. She was seeing Didi at six o'clock after she finished phone service. Didi was coming to her flat – which was a first – SJ had de-whited it this morning. This had involved walking around and putting out of sight every single white item she could find. This had been easy when it came to things like her white coat on the back of the door, or the white notepad by the phone. But the kitchen was pretty tricky: white fridge, white cooker, white kettle, white blinds, white walls. Or were they magnolia? Was magnolia okay? The floor had grey tiles but they had white flecks in too. She decided they'd have to avoid the kitchen.

The lounge wasn't too bad. The walls in there were a pale lemon. Very warming. The carpet had a whitish background but with splodges of green and brown – she hoped that would be okay. There were a couple of pictures with white frames, including the one of Ash, on the walls. She took those down. They left ghostly squares.

The bathroom could be an issue too. It had a white bathroom suite – not a modern one – an antique nineties style one, which had just come back into fashion again. At least that's what her landlord had told her when SJ complained that it needed updating.

She could drape the bath and the sink with throws – she had a couple of huge burnt orange coloured ones she used for the sofa. But there wasn't much she could do about the loo. Although it did have a pine seat. That might help. The loo roll was white too – because that was cheapest. SJ wondered whether she should warn Didi about that – so that she could bring her own.

No, she couldn't. She didn't even know how to phrase it. 'Please bring own loo roll, as mine is white.' She was not going to text that. Besides, Didi must come across that problem all the time. She probably carried her own supply.

Anyway, she'd gone to enough trouble already to accommodate Didi's ridiculous phobia. She felt a twinge of resentment. It was crazy. And all because she'd been scared of going to hospital as a child. Not that SJ wasn't sympathetic to irrational fears: she'd had plenty of her own – *The Nightmare on Elm Street* killer, for one. She seemed to remember she hadn't liked hospitals much herself either. She'd had her tonsils out when she was seven.

That had been pretty nasty. But she hadn't developed a flaming phobia about flaming white things. Even Alison wouldn't have got away with that one. Mum would have given either of them a slap if they'd so much as mooted the idea.

The clock on the lounge wall, which SJ suddenly realised had a white face and would have to be moved too, showed five to four. She had a last swift recce. All clear. Didi would probably be late anyway. She was flaky at the best of times. Although, SJ conceded, Didi had tried a lot harder since her 'No Show' at Camden Market. She was currently texting SJ a daily update on her No Drinking Progress.

Not that this was a major concession as she didn't drink every day anyway. Or maybe she was being unfair on that score. Didi might be a binge drinker and not a daily drinker, but her binges did take place fairly regularly. She rarely had a gap of more than about eight days.

Currently she was on Day Six. So they were coming up to critical point. Didi had asked her to go into more detail about the steps today. And SJ had got out her AA literature. On impulse she had also printed out the Quick Reference Guide that she'd typed out from her handwritten copy. She glanced at it again.

1. Honesty
2. Hope
3. Faith
4. Courage
5. Integrity
6. Willingness
7. Humility
8. Brotherly Love
9. Self-Discipline
10. Perseverance
11. Awareness of God
12. Service

Maybe she could put this lot into practice on Didi. Then she might have a chance of staying sane in her 'nutty as a fruitcake' sponsee's company. Oops, failed on Brotherly Love (Number 8) already.

The entry phone buzzed bang on four o clock. Well, at least she was here on time. "This is not about me," SJ told herself firmly as she released the door catch so Didi could get in the main front door. "This is about helping Didi (Number 12). Which I am very willing to do (Number 6). Okay, God (Number 11) let's go.

Didi strode in with a hand shielding her forehead and her eyes half closed. "White walls in the foyer," she said. "Gave me quite a start. Are there any more?"

"Not if you come into the lounge," SJ said, steering her in the right direction. "I think it's fairly safe in there."

Didi nodded her approval. "Thank you," she said, her gaze sweeping the room. "You've taken some pictures down. Bless you."

SJ felt warmed. This was going to be better than she thought.

"How on earth do you manage when you go round to other people's houses?" she asked, offering Didi the armchair and perching on the sofa. "People you don't know very well, I mean. Do you phone ahead?"

"I don't go out much. And never to houses I don't know."

"Isn't that awfully restrictive?"

"Yes," Didi said simply. "It is." And just for a second SJ saw a flash of terrible vulnerability in her eyes. It was gone in an instant, but it made her feel quite humble. Didi must really trust her to come here.

"How are you doing with the not drinking?"

Didi cleared her throat. "Okay. I don't really miss it until…" She frowned. "Until something crops up – until there's a reason, such as… I don't know. I guess I drink when I'm not feeling confident."

It was hard to imagine Didi not being confident. "I think that's the same with all of us," SJ said gently. "We use it to fill in the gaps. In my case I used it to fill in the gaps where my personality should have been." Blimey – that was a chunk of humility for her. (Number 7). "I don't think I knew who I was at all until I started doing this program." Damn she was starting to sound like Dorothy. "When I was growing up I was just a

221

frightened little girl who didn't know how to deal with the world."

"When I was growing up I was my father's plaything," Didi said softly. There was a quiet sadness on her face. "I would have done anything to please him. Anything to get him to love me. But it didn't matter what I did. It didn't matter how good I was. How hard I tried." She glanced at the carpet, spotted that her boots were on a patch of white and jerked her feet away and up on to the chair.

"Are you okay?" SJ said in alarm.

"What? Yes. Sorry. You must think I'm completely nuts. But sometimes if I'm feeling particularly sensitive..."

"Right. Of course I don't think you're nuts." bugger – there went honesty. (Number 1). SJ hesitated because she wasn't sure she wanted to know the answer to what she was going to ask – but Didi had tossed it out there. "What do you mean you were your father's plaything?"

"He liked to play hospitals," Didi said. "You know how kids do when they're small. It's an excuse to look at each other's bits. Only I was the kid. And he was the grown up."

"Right," SJ said again. She hadn't been expecting this – yet there was a part of her that wasn't surprised. No wonder Didi was – well, how she was.

"He used to put on a white coat," Didi said. "And he used to make me undress. 'Carol Baker,' he'd say. 'I'm afraid you are gravely ill. But don't worry. I have just the tools to make you better.'

Then he would make me lie on a table, covered with a white sheet, and open my legs." Didi looked at SJ calmly. "That's pretty sick, isn't it?" she said. "If you'll excuse the pun."

SJ nodded. She didn't have any words. Not a single one. She thought of her own dad – cuddling her in the night, chasing away her nightmares, promising that no monsters would ever get past him. Safe. Solid. Secure. And then she thought of Didi's dad, bending over his daughter, but not because he wanted to protect her. Turning the colour white into an endless nightmare.

SJ slipped off the sofa and went and knelt beside Didi. "Oh, my God," she said, putting her hand over Didi's. "Oh, honey. I don't know what to say."

"I've never told anyone that before," Didi said, and her voice was utterly blank. "There didn't seem much point. It's so far in the past."

"What about your mum? Did she know what was going on?"

"She died when I was tiny. It was just me and Dad – it was always just me and Dad." She paused. "That's the real reason I kicked off in the hospital that time. I thought they were going to do the same things that Dad did. Only there would be more of them doing them. I couldn't bear it. At least I knew that my dad loved me." Her voice was soft with pain. "I still have a major hospital phobia. I pay through the nose for extortionate medical insurance. If I need to see a doctor they come to me. I control the situation totally. It makes it bearable."

SJ squeezed Didi's cool fingers. Never again would she judge anyone for odd behaviours until she knew what was behind them. Never again would she complain about them meeting in the red and black restaurant.

"Do you still speak to him?" she asked.

"I do." Didi looked at her. "That's probably even sicker, isn't it? I see him regularly. We have lunch at his house. He lives in Primrose Hill. He's a solicitor."

SJ blinked. She had no clue what to say. Or what to do. Whether she should even speak or whether listening was enough.

Didi was so calm, so detached, almost as if what she'd just told SJ had happened to someone else, not her. Maybe that was the only way she could cope. Dorothy had told her once that denial only existed because people couldn't bear the pain that facing the truth would bring.

While SJ was trying to decide what to do next Didi got up suddenly, her movements jerky. "Excuse me a moment." She had her hand over her mouth.

Before SJ could react or even speak, Didi had left the room. SJ got slowly off the floor, which took a while as her left foot had gone to sleep. Had Didi run away? Should she follow her?

She'd barely reached the lounge door when she heard the sound of retching coming from the bathroom. She stood outside the door, her head hurt with trying to decide what to do next. She felt awash with helplessness. She was out of her depth. Not just out of her depth but bobbing in waves that were tsunami high.

After a moment or so she went back into the kitchen and put the kettle on again.

When Didi finally emerged her face was pale. She leaned on the worktop, clearly still visibly shaken.

"Sorry," she said. "I think I may have eaten…" She broke off as if she couldn't bring herself to finish the lie.

"Thank you," SJ said. "For trusting me." She hesitated. "You know you could talk to someone…"

"Don't ask me to go to the authorities," Didi said, turning towards her with a slight smile. "I know there have been cases crawling out of the woodwork left right and centre these last few years. The whole world seems to have been sexually abused – mostly by celebrities." She gave a brittle little laugh. "But that's not the way I want to go."

"I didn't mean the authorities," SJ said. "I meant maybe someone you could talk things through with."

"I'm talking to you."

"Yes, but I'm not qualified. I can't help."

"I don't want your help." Didi spread her hands. "Not with this. I'm telling you because I have to be honest with you, don't I? That's what Step One is – isn't it? And you're my sponsor."

"Well, yes," SJ said, hugely touched. "Yes it is. And thank you for being honest." Would you like a coffee?"

225

"I'd prefer a vodka." Didi said. "But I suppose that's out of the question."

"I'd quite like one myself," SJ said in the same flippant tone that Didi had used. Because if Didi could be so searingly honest, she would make damn sure she was too. "But I'm pretty sure that would only make things worse."

The kettle clicked off and they exchanged a bittersweet smile.

For the first time since she'd known Didi, SJ realised, they had taken a step forward. Honesty (Step One). Okay so that wasn't what Step One said in the official literature – it was to do with alcohol and admitting you were powerless over it. But what lay behind the words was honesty.

For the first time she realised how immensely powerful the principles that underlaid the Twelve Steps were.

It was a revelation.

Chapter Twenty-Five

So far SJ had applied for four waitressing jobs, two washing up jobs and one receptionist job at the Hackney Empire. She'd have liked to get that job. Okay, so she'd never been a receptionist but she was good with people. How hard could it be?

Harder than it looked, she guessed, because she hadn't even been offered an interview. She hadn't got any of the other jobs either. This wasn't helping her self-esteem, which was dropping by the day. She was trying to keep positive. When she was at meetings or talking to anyone on the phone she said she was fine. But she wasn't really. She was still grieving for Kit.

This morning when she'd put on a wash she'd had to empty her pockets of crumpled tissues. The bed had been full of them too, from all the times she had cried herself to sleep. Grief slipped into you like a knife when you were at your most vulnerable, and SJ was at her most vulnerable when she was in bed at night, alone.

Didi was scared of the colour white, which made total sense now after what she'd told SJ. But SJ was scared of the dark. When Kit had been alive – when she'd known he was out there somewhere – she hadn't felt quite as alone. She hadn't done it consciously, but she realised now that there was a part of her that had always believed he would be okay. And that one day when he'd tossed off the shackles off his addiction he would phone her. Come back to her. And they would spend more nights together. All of their nights.

It had been a crazy fantasy. She knew that now. His death had smashed it utterly. He would never come back. He was gone. And she had to move on. But it was hard. Particularly without a job to occupy her. If she didn't get a job in the next month or so she was going to have to dig into her savings, and when they were gone she would have to sign on. She wasn't even sure how to go about this. She had never claimed benefits in her life. The thought was totally depressing.

Thank heavens Dad was all right. Today he had a round up appointment with the consultant at the hospital. According to Mum, last time he'd seen the consultant she'd been very pleased.

"I know we're still waiting for the results of the MRI," she had said. "But I'm not expecting any nasty surprises. Everything else has come back fine."

"So what could have caused the blockages," Mum had asked. And apparently the consultant had just shrugged and said, "Diet's the most likely culprit. Maybe a bit of stress."

"The only thing I've been stressed about is all the doctor appointments," Dad had complained. "And I've never been on a diet."

"I don't think she means you've been on an actual diet," Mum had said, shaking her head in exasperated affection. "She means what you eat, dear." She'd patted his bulging tummy. "Although maybe you should be on a diet!"

Despite his protests, SJ and Mum and Alison were all going along with him to get the results and then they were going for a celebratory lunch at the Harvester up the road from the hospital. Dad didn't know about this last bit. It was a surprise.

SJ used a bit more of her precious Oyster Card credit to get over to her parents.

"Bloodeh waste of time all this," Dad said, as they piled into Alison's car. "No wonder the NHS is so broke. Doing all these unnecessary tests on people."

"It wouldn't have been a waste of time if there'd been something wrong," Alison said, "Now have you got the seat belt done up properly?"

"I'm not a flaming child," Dad grumbled as he finally clicked it into place. "And you're not coming in to my appointment. None of you. It's not a spectator sport."

"I think it might be best if I come in with you, Jim," Mum said. "It's always better if you've got someone with you to write down what they say. It's difficult to take it all in when they're speaking jargon."

"There won't be any jargon because there isn't any problem," Dad said in a voice laced with sarcasm.

"That's not entirely true, though, Dad is it." Alison interrupted. "If they weren't worried then they wouldn't have done all the tests in the first place. And you did have the – you know…"

"The constipation," SJ supplied helpfully. "Has that gone now?"

Dad, who was sitting in the front seat, didn't answer. Mum fidgeted. Alison concentrated steadfastly on negotiating a roundabout. The car filled up with embarrassment.

SJ chewed the inside of her mouth. What was it with her family? Why would none of them just say it like it was? Or was it her? Did she overstep boundaries? Cross lines? Make people feel awkward. Sometimes she felt as though she was out of step with the entire world.

Except for the people in AA. And that was mainly because they mostly told it how it was. They told the truth. However unpalatable. Well, mainly they did. SJ wasn't naïve enough to think people doing a program were any more inherently honest than people not doing a program. But at least they were trying their best to be honest. They had to try their best. Their lives depended on it.

She and her mother exchanged glances on the back seat. At least they were okay again now. At least she was here, part of what was hopefully the final hospital trip. Then her family could get back to normal.

"So, they didn't mind you having time off today then?" Mum said, as they pulled into the hospital car park.

"Not at all," SJ said, relieved that this at least was the truth. "I'll get us a ticket," she said, hopping out of the car before Mum could ask her a more awkward question.

Bloody hell, three quid for two hours – you needed to be rich if you were ill round here. She pushed the coins into the slot and pressed the

230

button for the ticket. *'Stop complaining, SJ.'* That was Dorothy's voice again. *'Be grateful we have an NHS. Be grateful that your father's all right.'*

That was true. And she was: so very, very grateful. She glanced up at the sky as she headed back towards the car – blue and hot – there wasn't a cloud in it. This was the best summer they'd had in years. Thank you, God, she whispered in her mind. Thank you for making my dad okay.

"Chop chop," Alison said, holding out her hand for the ticket. "We haven't got all day. We've got to walk right to the other end of the hospital."

"Take a chill pill," SJ said with a sweet smile. That was one of Kevin's expressions – he was for ever throwing it at his mother – and SJ knew it infuriated Alison no end. Alison glared at her but she didn't care. Sometimes the smallest victories were the most satisfying.

So much for rushing to keep their appointment. They'd been waiting about twenty-five minutes so far, which SJ didn't think was too bad in the big scheme of things. Alison had spent the time flicking through an out of date *Good Housekeeping* magazine and tutting. Mum was sitting very tightly with her bag on her lap and her elbows tucked in to her sides. And Dad, arms folded, legs spread, was staring stoically ahead.

SJ felt a poem starting.

NHS – how I do love thee, let me count the delays.
I love thy plastic chairs and long strip lights.
Receptionists all itching for a fight.

How curious the way that we behave…
All scared out of our wits but acting brave.

Elizabeth Barrett Browning would be turning in her grave by now at this desecration of her beautiful sonnet. SJ was just contemplating her next line when a door opened in front of them and a dark haired nurse peered out.

"Jim Carter, please."

Both Alison and Mum leapt to their feet. Dad was slower.

"You're not coming in."

"I am," Mum said. "I want to hear the good news from the horse's mouth."

"No."

"Yes."

"No."

"Is anyone coming?" the nurse said with a problem-diffusing smile.

Dad rolled his eyes, gave a deep sigh and finally capitulated. "Your mother can come," he said, in a voice so granite firm that even Alison didn't argue. "You girls stay here."

They were gone a long time, during which it got hotter. Perhaps the AC had broken down. SJ couldn't see any but there must be some because the air was over dry. Alison had abandoned the magazine and was texting rapidly into her phone. SJ had checked hers a couple of times but no one wanted her today. Not even Didi who was quite sporadic with her texts but who did always send one at some point to let SJ know she'd had another sober day.

Maybe she should nip outside and phone her. SJ decided against it. Mum and Dad were bound to appear the minute she stepped outside and they wouldn't want to hang around at the hospital.

She had abandoned her poem and was people-watching instead. There were a lot of people here today; mostly they seemed to be in couples or family groups. There weren't a lot of singles. Curious. Several doors led off the waiting room. Each was marked with the name of a different consultant. At intervals one or another of them would open and people would emerge.

Sometimes they would be smiling. Sometimes they would be grim faced and sometimes they would be crying and have a relative's arm around their shoulders. It took SJ a little while to realise that all of these people must be getting the results of tests. There were more smiling faces than anything else. That was a relief. But even so it was a worry to realise they were sitting in a Waiting Room for The Results of Nasty Tests.

She was just relaying this observation to Alison when the door through which her parents had disappeared opened. SJ breathed a sigh of relief. Finally.

But it wasn't Mum and Dad who emerged. It was the dark haired nurse. She beckoned towards them. "Would you mind coming in for a moment, please?"

Alison snapped her phone shut and they both got up. SJ's legs felt slightly rubbery as if her intuition had leapt ahead of her and into the little room where her parents sat. As if it knew what was coming. Knew that something bad awaited them.

On one side of a large desk sat a smartly dressed Asian woman and on the other were five chairs, two of which were occupied by her parents. Dad was sitting, stone- faced, and Mum was saying over and over, "But I thought you said it was going to be all right?"

Alison was across the room in an instant, kneeling beside Mum's chair, putting out her hand to touch her shoulder.

"What's going on?"

The consultant was frowning. The nurse was the only one who seemed to be in control. She gestured towards the chairs, comfy chairs, not plastic like they were in the waiting room. "Please will you sit down," she said, and for the first time SJ noticed she had a faintly Welsh accent.

"I'm Mrs Khan," the consultant said, half standing so she could shake their hands in turn. "I'm afraid there has been a slight development."

"A tumour," Dad said. "That's what she's talking about – a bloodeh tumour."

"What – but I thought everything was fine. You said everything was fine." Alison's voice had the same accusatory tone as Mum's. "There can't be a tumour."

"There is a mass, which didn't show up on the ultrasound," Mrs Khan said slowly, as if this was not the first time she'd said it. "But it did show up on the MRI, which gives us a much more accurate picture."

"What sort of mass is it?" SJ asked and the doctor turned towards her.

"I'm afraid we can't tell you that for sure until we've taken a biopsy, which does involve surgery."

"No way are you cutting me up."

"As I've said, Mr Carter, it's really quite a minor procedure. Not too invasive. We'd only need you to come in for the day. Although I'm afraid you would need a general anaesthetic."

"Nope."

"But Dad it's important." Alison had her bossy voice on. "How soon can he come in?"

"It should be within a fortnight. I'm recommending an emergency biopsy." She turned her attention back to their father. "As a precautionary measure. At this stage we don't know enough to make a full diagnosis. It really is for the best, Mr Carter. The sooner we find out what we're dealing with, the sooner we can start you on a course of treatment."

For a few moments no one spoke. SJ wondered if it was possible for rooms to tremble. It took a little while longer for her to realise that it wasn't the room. It was her. She was sitting on her Dad's right hand side. She reached out for his hand and squeezed tightly. He didn't look at her, not at first; his gaze was fixed on Mum.

SJ wondered what he was thinking. Her amazing dad. Was he worrying about Mum and how this was going to affect her? He didn't deserve this. They should be getting good news. They were supposed to be going for a celebratory lunch. Nothing special – just a nod to the man in the sky, a toast to life, a quick clink of glasses to acknowledge that all was well.

How could they have been so naïve?

Dad still wasn't looking at her, but he gave the tiniest squeeze back in response to hers.

"It'll be okay," she said, only half aware of the hubbub of Alison and her mother and Mrs Khan talking. "It'll be okay, Dad. It will. It will, it will."

Chapter Twenty-Six

No one mentioned cancer. It wasn't mentioned in the overheated car as they drove back. Everyone complained about the temperature instead and how they should have got a car that had AC, only who'd have thought you needed one in this climate?

It wasn't mentioned when they were sitting in her parents' kitchen, SJ drinking tea and Alison and Mum drinking a medicinal glass of port – good for shock, Mum had said, pouring it into thimble sized glasses and flicking SJ an embarrassed smile. "I suppose you're going to tell me you can't drink this?"

"Um, no, Mum, I can't."

It wasn't even mentioned when Dad disappeared out to the garden shed. "Gotta go. Problem with my tomatoes."

"Let him go," Mum said when Alison tried to go after him. "He's best left alone for a bit, love."

Dad had left the back door open. Jasmine sweetened the air, its scent carried on the faintest breeze that drifted in to touch their faces: summer soft. It was a hot blue day out there with not a single cloud. But all of the gratitude SJ had felt towards God when they'd gone to their appointment, all of the hope, all of the positivity, was gone.

The shock was beginning to wear off – despite the fact she hadn't had the helping hand of any port. And into its place surged anger.

"You must let me know what you want me to do," Alison was saying to Mum. "About the hospital visit I mean. Will he need anything to go in with? Pyjamas and things – does he have any? You need pyjamas in hospital."

"I think so, love," Mum was saying. "But they're not very new. I should probably get new." She kept wiping her forehead with a hanky. "I think I'm still a bit shocked. They had said, you know, that nothing was wrong."

"We still don't know if it is," SJ said sharply. "It still might be nothing."

"A tumour isn't nothing." Alison shot her a look. "Everyone knows what a tumour is. He'll have to have chemotherapy and that other thing they do – radiation treatment."

"Radiotherapy," SJ said. "Only if it's…" she hesitated. Was anyone going to say the word? "Only if its cancer," she said. "But we don't know that it is yet. Don't you think we might be jumping the gun?"

Her mother and her sister looked at her. And she thought how alike they were in their worry. Both of them had the same fine hair, the same slightly upturned noses and downturned mouths. No wonder they were so close. Sometimes she thought she must be a changeling with her olive skin and thick dark hair, swapped into the family when she was hours old – and that the real SJ had been spirited away by fairies to a darker realm.

"What else could a tumour *be*?" Alison said. She blinked away the first tears.

"I don't know," SJ said. "But I don't think we should be talking like this. I'm not writing Dad off just yet."

"Neither are we," their mother said, and it seemed to SJ that she straightened her back a little. "But it is very worrying."

SJ nodded. It was. And the last thing that was going to make it better was to sit here and chew over all the awful possibilities of what might lie ahead while Dad did goodness knows what in the shed. She got up and went across the kitchen and hugged her mother.

"I'd better get back," she said. "But I'll phone you later. And you will let me know if there's any more news."

"Of course I will. Yes, love. You go. We don't want you losing your job as well."

"No," SJ said with a hollow smile. And feeling guilty, and as though she was abandoning a sinking ship, but knowing she couldn't stay, she left.

She didn't want to go home to her empty flat. She couldn't bear to cry any more tears. She didn't think she had enough tissues. Or enough strength.

In normal circumstances she would have phoned Tanya, but she couldn't do that either. Or she'd have phoned Dorothy. But Dorothy's antique phone had finally given up the ghost yesterday. She had sent SJ a very short email from a computer on board.

Sorry, hen. No phone for rest of trip. Will be back very soon. Take care.

Very soon meant in just over nine days. An eternity away.

Who else could she phone? As she sat on the Overground she scrolled through her contact list. Ebby's name came up and she hesitated. Maybe she could call Ebby but she didn't know him that well and what would she say? My dad's just got some bad news – only it might not be bad, but it's a shock all the same…

Ebby would say, 'Don't worry. You don't know the score yet.' What else could he say? And she knew he was right. But actually she was more angry than worried. She felt like screaming at someone – well not just a random someone – God to be precise. She felt like opening the train window and shouting out of it into that perfect blue day.

DON'T YOU THINK THAT TAKING KIT WAS ENOUGH?

AND TANYA – THAT WAS A CHEAP TRICK TOO!

AND MY JOB – okay – so I did actually have a hand in cocking that up – fair dos.

BUT DAD? MY LOVELY SWEET DAD WHO NEVER HURT ANYONE IN HIS LIFE. What the hell is that about?

Only she wouldn't have said hell. She'd have said fuck. She'd have said it loudly and in block capitals. FUCK, FUCK, FUCK YOU.

She'd have screamed it into the sky. Until all the pain inside of her was out there instead of flowing around her veins like poison.

Maybe she should call Penny? No. Penny would tell her to calm down in that patronising way she had sometimes. Usually when SJ was in a bad mood. Penny never had bad moods – she was one of those irritating people who was always on an even keel. Who always saw the best in everyone. She was probably the type of person who sung in the bathroom in the mornings too.

Scroll, scroll, scroll through her phone.

Maybe she could call Tim. He'd been very sweet at the beach. But he hadn't been in touch since. SJ had been a little surprised that he hadn't so much as texted her. They'd swapped numbers on the minibus. He was the first man she had really trusted for ages – there had been a moment, just a moment, when she'd even thought they could be more than friends. Who the hell was she trying to kid? Number Ten Tim, despite his idiosyncrasies – or maybe even because of them – was gorgeous. Not to mention rich. He probably had any number of beautiful city girls vying for his affections. He didn't need to befriend a past-her-sell-by date, jobless, saddo alky like her!

'Have a drink,' Alco said.

"What?"

Had she just said what out loud? Was she really talking to herself in an empty train carriage? Actually, a not quite empty train carriage. There was a man across the aisle texting someone. He had his phone on silent but they were obviously texting back because he kept stopping to read their replies, then smiling, then typing another message. He was clearly talking to the love of his life. His face was all lit up. She was probably his wife. They had probably only been married a few months and they were still in that lovely period when you texted each other fifty times a day. Lucky bastards.

Bugger, he'd just looked up and was frowning at her. Had she just said that out loud too? She dipped her head to avoid his eyes, her face flaming.

'Have a drink,' Alco said again, slightly louder this time. *'You know you want one.'*

A drink – yes, that would be nice. It was a long time since she'd thought about having a drink. But summer was the time when she missed drinking the most. Every time she walked past a pub garden and saw all those people sitting outside, chatting and laughing, with bucket sized glasses of wine in front of them.

She usually told herself that it was the chatter and the laughter she missed. Not the actual wine. The feeling of being a part of something – the feeling of belonging. Not the heady, buzzing uprush euphoria of that first sip. She could live without that.

'Wouldn't it be lovely, though? Just the one glass. What have you got to lose?'

'Everything,' SJ replied to Alco properly this time. 'Everything,' she said again in her mind. 'If I pick up a drink I'll lose everything.'

'How ridiculous,' Alco said. *'That's just AA talk. They brainwash you in those meetings. They terrify you into thinking you can't drink when actually it's not true at all. If it was that difficult to stop then you*

242

wouldn't have been sober all this time – what is it now – five years?'

'Mmm, nearly five years.'

'I rest my case. If you were a real alcoholic you wouldn't have been able to do that. Everyone knows that real alcoholics can't stop. They live on park benches. They drink meths, they have no family or friends, they have no homes, they have no jobs.'

'I have no job,' SJ said dreamily. The idea of having a drink – just one drink – was growing within her like some exotic flower. She thought about the jasmine outside her parents' back door, climbing the trellis, insinuating its way around each wooden slat, reaching upwards, reaching for the warmth of the sun. Reaching for the comfort of the rain. Was rain to plants like alcohol to alcoholics? Did they need it to survive?

'A drink would make you feel so much better, SJ.'

'Yes it would.'

It would mean she didn't have to think for a while. She could escape the world and all of its problems, all of its pain.

Did she have enough money? With a sense of rising panic she checked her purse. There was a five pound note and a few pound coins and she planned to buy bread, butter and some of the cheese Mr Singh's had on special offer at the moment. The cheese was really nice – so strong it took the roof of your mouth off. She loved strong cheese. It would go really well with a nice Shiraz. She probably couldn't afford Shiraz. She definitely couldn't afford Shiraz and cheese – no matter how well they went together.

243

Unless the Shiraz was on special offer too. They'd been doing that lately – the shop. A cheese and wine promo – having both on 'Special' and putting up little signs to suggest which wines went with which cheese. How cool was that? Mr Singh had a very good marketing eye. Pity she didn't drink any more.

I don't drink any more.

The words came straight at her like an arrow. 'I don't drink any more.' An arrow, with a poison tip of disappointment aimed straight at her heart.

Getting drunk would be good.

Getting drunk would be brilliant.

What did she have to lose?

'Alcohol is the great remover.' The words filtered through from some ancient share. 'My drinking cost me my job, my driving licence, my friends and family and my self-esteem.'

She didn't have a job.

She had a driving licence – what use was that without a car?

She didn't have any close friends. Well, there was Tanya, but she wasn't speaking to her. And there was Dorothy, but sponsors didn't count. Especially when they were out of the country. *'And out of contact,'* Alco added helpfully.

She had a family. It hurt to think of Dad going under the knife. She blocked out the image swiftly.

She did have self-esteem. *'No you don't,'* Alco said gleefully. *'You're a fuck-up, SJ. Give it up. Have a drink.'*

Alco was right. She was. She was total crap. She'd been doing her absolute best to be a good person for goodness knows how long. She'd been trying to be the best person she could be and God – who was supposed to be on her side, who was supposed to be pleased she was staying sober – just tossed it all back in her face.

And then he stood there and laughed at her – a rip roaring, bent-double sort of laugh. She was reminded fleetingly of Tim on the surf board. Even Tim thought she was a bit of a joke. The git.

So she might as well drink. She got off the train, feeling light-headed and slightly surreal. She caught a glimpse of herself in the train window as she passed. She looked like the wild woman of Borneo. She should have washed her hair this morning but she hadn't wanted to be late for Dad's appointment. Dad's appointment that had begun so well and ended so badly.

Fresh pain swept through her. What was the point of staying sober if life just got crapper and crapper? What was the bloody point? What good did it do?

'No good at all,' chipped in Alco gleefully. 'Shiraz and cheese, SJ. Check it out.'

A few moments later she reached the little shop and with a huge sense of relief she pushed open the door. Only it didn't open. Perplexed, she shoved harder. The door didn't budge. It seemed to be locked. It hadn't been locked this time yesterday when she'd bought some milk. She peered through the glass. There were no lights on either. What on earth was going on? And then she saw the note – stuck just below the sign that told you the shop's opening hours.

Closed for family funeral. Sorry for the inconvenience.

Dismayed, SJ stepped back a pace. They couldn't be closed. She needed her Shiraz. Now she'd made up her mind she was hell bent on getting it. She paused in the coolness of the shop doorway and thought hard. Where else could she go?

There wasn't exactly a shortage of shops that sold booze in Hackney and yet… Irrationally, SJ didn't feel that comfortable going in a shop she'd never been into before. She wanted the comfort of this shop, Mr Singh's smiling face and bad jokes. Mrs Singh's colourful sari and kindness.

She leaned her forehead against the coolness of the door and closed her eyes. Just up the road there was a pub she had never been inside. It was called The Bentley Arms after some famous guy who had once lived in Hackney. SJ had no idea what he was famous for – some invention or another. It didn't really matter. The only thing that actually mattered was that the pub was open all day.

Four minutes later she was standing at the bar. It was the type of pub which had a big screen and no atmosphere and a very long bar, draped with little towels that said things like *Big Ben London Bitter* and *Black Bush Irish Whiskey*. At the far end a handful of guys exchanged banter with the barmaid, who reluctantly detached herself when she saw SJ and strolled up to serve her.

"What can I get you, love?"

"A large glass of Chardonnay please?" The idea of ordering Shiraz seemed mad now. She much preferred Chardonnay. She just hoped she had enough money to pay for it.

"£5.50 please."

SJ handed it over. She couldn't afford cheese now, but hey the shop was shut, so who cared. She had a feeling the wine would go straight to her head. Especially if she drank it at top speed. Then she could go home and she could sleep. Proper sleep with no nightmares. No dreams about Tanya or Kit or her father. Proper oblivion type sleep.

She picked up the glass, which had condensation on the outside. Gosh it smelled good. And she carried it to an empty table, which was slightly in shadow, in the furthest corner of the bar.

Chapter Twenty-Seven

There were no beer mats. SJ felt a fleeting irritation. What kind of pub didn't have beermats on every table? Maybe it was a sign of the times. She hadn't been in many pubs lately. Perhaps they didn't supply them any more. Perhaps they couldn't afford them. Although with wine at £5.50 a glass they should be able to bloody afford them.

The Chardonnay, which was about twelve inches from her nose, glowed softly. She could smell it. She reached for it at exactly the same moment as a shadow fell over her table.

"Hello, SJ."

She didn't need to look up to know who it was. She would have recognised that deep resonant voice anywhere. Even though it was the last place on earth she'd have expected to hear it.

Reluctantly, she glanced up into Half Pint Hughie's face. He smiled pleasantly, giving her a flash of his toothless pink gums.

"Do you mind if I join you?"

Bloody hell. Of all the people it could possibly have been. Of all the flaming people, it had to be one of AA's most die-hard members. Just her luck. Her fingers hadn't made contact with the glass but she itched to pick it up. She hesitated.

Hughie didn't wait for her to answer his question. He sat down opposite. It was clearly too hot for the mac. Although he wasn't dressed for summer either. He was wearing an old fashioned black suit with shiny patches on the elbows and a rather grey-looking shirt from which his long wrinkly neck protruded, emphasising his tortoise like appearance. His solemn gaze met hers steadily.

"You're not going to stop me drinking it," she said.

"No," he agreed gravely. "I'm not."

"What are you doing here anyway?" she said, slightly taken aback. Surely that was why he was here. Unless, of course, he too fancied a sneaky drink. Hey, maybe there were dozens of 'supposedly' recovering alcoholics hanging out in bars all across the country, whilst pretending they were squeaky clean at meetings.

Something in her heart told her this wasn't true.

"I'd get you one too, but I'm all out of cash." Pain found a gap in her armour of flippancy and she heard her voice crack.

"I'm not here for a drink, SJ. I gave it up, so I did." He leaned back slightly in his chair and crossed his right leg over his left – so his right ankle rested on his left knee. It was an attempt at a more casual pose, but it looked ridiculous. He was wearing orange socks and his black shoes, unlike the rest of his rather shabby clothes, were highly polished. SJ wondered if he'd ever been in the army.

"I saw you come in," he added. "I figured you might need a friend."

"Well, I don't," she said. Why did her throat ache so much? Why did she feel so perilously close to tears again? "I just…need…a…drink." She had to say the words very slowly and firmly. She wasn't really sure why. Perhaps because she wanted Hughie to know she meant them. Perhaps because it was getting more difficult to speak.

"I don't think it's a drink you want," he said mildly. "I think it's oblivion you're after. Would that be true, would you say?"

The words were so very close to her thoughts of a few minutes ago that she was jolted. How had he known?

"I AM going to drink it," she said again.

"Be my guest." There was the slightest beat. "If you think it will help."

"It will," she said firmly, even though she was not nearly as sure of this as she'd been a few seconds ago. Hughie was spot on about one thing. She did want oblivion and it had just struck her that this glass might not actually be enough. It certainly wouldn't have been in the olden days. She'd have needed at least a bottle – possibly two to reach the kind of plateau she needed – that fuzzy, warm, don't-care-about-anything feeling.

'It's a great start though,' said Alco.

She picked up the wine.

"What sort of day have you had?" Hughie said idly. As if they were just two friends making casual conversation. As if this wasn't a life and death matter – crap, where had that thought come from. AA, of course. Bloody AA. Drinking didn't kill you. Especially if you didn't have the money to buy any more. Which she didn't. Well, she did actually, but only if she didn't pay her rent, which was already late.

"Pretty rubbish," she said. "You?"

"I've been to a funeral," Hughie said.

Yeah right, SJ thought. Here it came. The scaremongering talk about the dangers of alcohol – the nasty deaths. The memory of Kit's unconscious face burned in her head. She blanked it out swiftly. Hughie was NOT going to sway her with any tragic funeral stories – that's if it was even true. Wow, that wine smelled good. Nectar. Maybe she should tell Hughie to bugger off. She really didn't need a sanctimonious audience.

"I hope it was no one close," she said to be polite.

"It was a friend. Lilian Singh – the daughter of the family who own the corner shop up the road. Nice family – I've known them for donkey's years."

SJ blinked. Shocked, she cradled the wine, which felt gloriously cool between her cupped hands. "I know Lilian too. She used to serve in the shop sometimes. What happened to her?"

"Knocked down by a bus on her way to the shops last week," Hughie said. "That's not how people are supposed to die in real life, is it?"

"No." SJ blinked again, realising suddenly that she was crying. When had that happened? "Her poor parents," she said. "Her poor, poor parents."

"Yes," Hughie agreed. "So what have you been up to, SJ?"

She told him about what had happened at the hospital and he nodded slowly. "I remember you mentioning that before. It was you who got him to go for his appointment, wasn't it?"

She nodded. Bloody tears. They were rolling down her face in earnest now, but she couldn't

251

wipe them away without putting down the wine. And she didn't think she had any tissues in her bag anyway. She hadn't thought she'd need any today. Bloody God.

Hughie fumbled in his pocket and pulled out a spotlessly white handkerchief with a blue monogrammed H in one corner. He held it out to her. She stared at it in amazement. Somehow he was the last person on earth she'd have expected to carry a monogrammed handkerchief.

"I always take one to funerals," he said. "In case anyone should need it. Don't worry, no one did. Your make-up's starting to run," he observed.

SJ put down the wine – close to her in case he got any ideas of whipping it away – and took the handkerchief. "Thanks."

"You're very welcome." Another little beat. "I hope your dad'll be okay. Hopefully if it is something unpleasant, they've caught it early enough, wouldn't you think?"

She nodded.

"And how's that lovely young girl you brought to Barney Hall going along, SJ? Haven't seen her at any meetings lately."

"She hasn't been to any," SJ said quietly. "But she has stopped drinking, Hughie. She's thirteen days sober."

"Ah, that's grand, so it is." Now he was nodding and smiling, his pink gums gleaming. "I expect you've helped her quite a bit, have you not?"

SJ nodded. The thought of Didi was like a shock of cold water in her face. For the briefest moment she saw Didi in her front room, jerking her boots off the carpet onto the armchair: Didi, with her terror of white, clinging on to her thirteen days of sobriety, text by text. She thought about the honesty they'd shared: the thread of trust that was strung between them – such a fragile, gossamer thread.

If she drank that glass of Chardonnay she would have to tell Didi she couldn't be her sponsor any more. How could she help someone else to give up drinking if she couldn't do it herself?

She would be letting Didi down.

Totally.

Utterly.

For a glass of Chardonnay.

What the hell was she doing?

"Oh, Hughie, shit, get me out of here. Please, get me out of here." Suddenly, she was shaking so much she could barely stand up. But Hughie was on his feet too. He was beside her. He had an arm around her shoulders and she leaned against his wiry body, which suddenly felt enormously strong.

Twenty seconds later they were outside in the glare of the sun and she was sobbing and sobbing and sobbing. Hughie's handkerchief was nowhere near up to the job. And Hughie himself clearly didn't have the words for such a situation. Not in the diesel fumed air of the noisy, crowded street. But he did pat her shoulder a few times. And when she finally stopped sobbing, he said, "You live close by, don't you, SJ?"

She nodded.

"I'll walk you back. See you safely inside."

She didn't protest, even though it seemed an odd thing to say when it was still bright sunlight. Keep her safe from whom? Even the Hackney muggers weren't very active at this time of day.

Maybe he meant keep her safe from the glass of wine which still sat on the pub table. Keep her from nipping back in to drink it. Even though she knew now she was as far away from drinking that wine as she was from the moon.

They walked back in the sun, SJ clinging tight to Hughie's arm. And she thought with some distant part of her mind that they must make an odd couple – the girl with the blotchy, mascara-streaked face and the shaky walk, and the man with no teeth who looked like a tortoise in a past-its-best funeral suit.

Chapter Twenty-Eight

Even when they were back in her flat, she couldn't stop trembling. Emotions crawled out of every corner. Despair, grief, anger, self-pity and shame – on and on they came in a swirling vortex she couldn't control, or stop.

Hughie had installed himself on her sofa. He'd been there for the last hour and a half. He looked out of place in her flat, but also strangely at home. Occasionally he got up to make her another chamomile tea, or fetch her more tissues.

"I don't know why I'm so upset," she said, when she had finally cried herself out and was left feeling a shaky kind of grey.

"They're just feelings," Hughie said. "They need to come out. If you're anything like the rest of us, you'll have been trying to pretend they don't exist. Putting a brave face on it – pushing them down. But that's not very good for the alcoholic."

"I think I have been doing that," she said softly. "Things have been getting worse and worse lately. But I kept trying to look on the bright side. I thought I was being positive!"

"It's not compulsory to be positive all the time." He rubbed his chin. "We need to acknowledge that bad stuff happens too."

"I've been crying a lot too," SJ said, thinking of the screwed up tissues in her bed and in the pockets of every bit of clothing she owned.

"Yeah, well crying's good."

"Do you cry, Hughie?" she asked.

He blinked. He had brown eyes. Kind eyes. She had never noticed his eyes before. Apart from to think they were a bit beady. He was one of those people who was always there in the background. Even though he never said much he was part of the fabric of the rooms.

"I cried today, so I did. For that poor wee girl who'll never live out her life as she was meant to. Although if I'm honest I was mostly crying for her parents – it's tough to lose a bairn."

The Irish was getting stronger in his voice. It was because he was emotional, SJ realised suddenly. And then there was a moment in his eyes when she knew.

"It happened to you, didn't it?" she said, before she even had time to question the diplomacy of this. "You lost a child – oh, Hughie. I'm so sorry."

He was nodding. His mouth had gone a little wrinkled up. "Kathleen was about the age you are now. She died in childbirth. That's not supposed to happen in real life either, is it? Not in modern times, anyhow."

"I'm so sorry," she said again. "I'm sure you don't want to speak about it – I've got a habit of opening my mouth before my brain's in gear. I'm crap."

"You're not crap." To her surprise he was smiling. "It's refreshing, SJ. People know where they are with you. There's no artifice. That's a good thing. Besides it was a long time ago. Twenty years ago we lost our Kathleen – and the bairn. I still miss her – of course I do, but it's true what they say. Time's a great healer, so it is."

She felt humbled. And slightly guilty for all the times she'd avoided his puckered up kiss in meetings. Not that she was under any illusions that it was meant to be a paternal kind of kiss. But he must be lonely. Bless him. And he was clearly a kind man.

"I hate the way I've been feeling today, Hughie." She spread her hands. "Pure rage. When I was coming back from my parents on the train I wanted to kill someone. God preferably. I wanted to rage and stamp my feet like – I don't know, like a toddler in a temper tantrum."

"That's when you need to speak to someone, SJ. Anger is bad for us – the biggest killer there is. It takes us straight back to the drink." He paused. "So what are you angriest about today, would you say?"

"It's not just today. I've been angry for a while, I think." She told him about Kit and he nodded.

"That's a tough one, so it is. Losing someone you love."

"And it was such a pointless, pointless death," she said softly. "I know that things are meant to happen for a reason, but, Hughie, I just can't see it."

"I agree that the man had a pointless death, but he certainly didn't have a pointless life," Hughie said slowly. "And I'm thinking that would be a lot, lot worse."

She stared at him. She had never thought about it like that. But his words hit her straight in the heart.

It was true. Kit had done so much good; he'd helped so many people. You had only needed to be at his funeral to see that. It didn't take away the pain of what had happened to him but maybe it made it more bearable.

She blinked several times. "And I'm scared for Dad," she added, almost in a whisper.

"Of course you are." His eyes were grave. "You wouldn't be human if you weren't."

"I felt so utterly helpless today. I felt as though there was nothing I could actually do."

"But there is something you can do. You can be there for your mum and your dad. You couldn't do that if you were pissed now, could you?"

"I suppose not."

"So what else?"

She told him about being sacked from her job and he laughed.

"Well, thanks," she said, slightly hurt. "What's so funny? I needed that job. I'm flat broke."

"If the man was pig headed enough to throw you out after one silly misdemeanour then he doesn't deserve you, SJ. You're better off without him. There must be dozens of jobs out there for a girl like you."

"Well there aren't," she said sniffily. "I keep getting told I'm over qualified – I used to be a lecturer – or that I've not enough experience for whatever it is I'm applying for. How much experience do you need to flaming wash up?"

"Perhaps you should go back to being a lecturer."

"Well, that's a lot easier said than done," she said, although she hadn't actually tried. Because it hadn't actually occurred to her.

"So what else are you angry about?" He was relentless. After another slight pause she told him about Tanya.

"You can do something about that one, too, so you can."

"Like what? She told me not to contact her. I tried about a hundred times."

"Then, maybe you need another approach."

She was jolted. The simplicity of this struck a chord.

"Try a prayer," he advised. "Maybe the man upstairs has the answer."

If he'd suggested God earlier, she'd have thumped him, but now the idea didn't seem as irritating. She was definitely feeling better. The bleak, bleak despair she'd been lost in earlier was lifting.

"Coincidence is God's way of remaining anonymous. Have you heard that saying, SJ?" He raised his eyebrows. "It was attributed to Albert Einstein. It's bandied about a fair bit in recovery circles. Not that it really matters who said it. It's the meaning of the thing that's important."

She nodded. "It's about the fact there's no such thing as coincidences, isn't it? That nothing happens by accident." She paused. "Like me bumping into you today – just at the very moment I was going to pick up a drink and spoil four years and nine months of sobriety. Not that I'm counting," she added under her breath.

259

"I think that might come under it, yes." He put his hands in his lap. "I was brought up in a very religious home, SJ, as you might expect, living in Ireland. To be truthful with you I hated it. And I hated God. I got out as soon as I could. I joined the Foreign Legion to escape."

"I could tell by your shoes," she said.

"What?"

"Highly polished."

He looked perplexed. But after a moment or two he carried on speaking. "It was only when I came into the fellowship that I realised I could have a different approach to God. I started to look upon God, not as a being, but as a driving force behind life. I started to see it as a force that operated through other people."

She frowned. "I would have drunk that wine if you hadn't showed up and stopped me."

"I didn't stop you," he said.

"You did."

He was shaking his head, doing that pursed lip thing again and the room became quietly silent.

On the wall behind his head, SJ noticed that the picture of Ash was crooked. She clearly hadn't hung it straight when she'd put it back after Didi's visit.

She got up to straighten it out and Hughie said quietly, "I saw the change in your face. I saw the moment you made the decision not to drink that Chardonnay, but it was nothing to do with me."

"I stopped because of Didi," SJ said, feeling light-headed. She must have got up too quickly. Her hands on the picture frame felt slippery and suddenly it was if the room, not the picture was slightly askew. "I stopped because I knew if I drank it I couldn't help her any more. I didn't care if I killed myself. I felt so worthless and crappy and shit. But I did care about her. I did care about Didi."

"I think they call that unconditional love, do they not."

She didn't turn round but she could hear the smile in his voice. "That's some people's definition of God, so it is. Did you know that, SJ?"

The light-headed feeling was going off. The room had righted itself again. And SJ felt in some very odd way that her head had righted itself too. That even though she couldn't put her finger on exactly what it was, she had learned something today: something important that she hadn't known before.

"Thank you," she said, turning round to face Hughie again. "Thank you for today."

He was getting up as if he too knew that he wasn't needed any more. He reached for his funeral jacket, which had started to crease – it had been on the back of the armchair for so long.

"Don't mention it. We'll see you very soon, I hope. I don't think I've seen you at Barney Hall for a couple of weeks, have I now?"

At the door of her flat she gave him a hug.

"I'll be there on Friday, Half Pint Hughie, so I will."

"Not a bad accent, Sarah-Jane."

He zoomed in for a kiss.

She turned her face away so his lips landed on her cheek.

He winked. Things were back to normal.

Chapter Twenty-Nine

When she got up the next day, apart from a faint headache – no doubt from all the crying she'd done – SJ felt no echoes of the previous day's blackness.

What she did feel was a strong resolve to sort out at least one of the shitty bits of her life. She had a shower, made up her face, put on her confidence-inspiring pseudo leather jacket and set off. She still had a bit of money on her Oyster Card luckily – certainly enough for what she wanted to do today.

On the train she got Didi's daily text to say she was still sober and she smiled and texted back, *YOU ARE A TOTAL STAR. LET'S MEET V SOON.*

She wished she'd taken Hughie's number so she could phone him and thank him again. Not that he needed her to thank him. It was what people did in AA. They helped each other to stay sober, not just once a week in meetings, but whenever, wherever they were needed.

She'd thought a lot about what he'd said about God. She had always had quite an ambivalent relationship with God. As a child she had vague memories of going to Sunday School a couple of times with Alison, but she had a feeling this had been mostly because it was somewhere for them to go on a Sunday morning out of Mum and Dad's way. She didn't remember there ever being a Bible in the house and her parents certainly hadn't been church-goers themselves, not like some of her friends' parents who made everyone say Grace before eating and do prayers by their beds at night.

Her two abiding memories of Sunday School were the singing – she liked singing – and a picture of God that Tommy Jones had painted.

The picture was of an elderly gent with long white hair and a long white beard sitting on a golden throne on a cloud and wielding a club. Well, the teacher had said it was a sceptre, but it had looked more like a club to SJ. And later on Tommy Jones had confirmed with an evil grin that it was indeed a club.

"For hitting naughty kids with," he'd said. "Like you, Sarah-Jane."

"What have I done?" she said alarmed.

"She stole my chocolate biscuit at break," Alison had supplied helpfully.

"That was my biscuit."

"No, it wasn't. Yours was the plain one. Mum said so. I'm telling on you when we get back."

"God's gonna thwack you with his club," Tommy Jones added gleefully. "God doesn't need to find out – he already knows everything everyone does," and he waved his arms about and made roaring noises until the teacher spotted what was going on and told them to pack it in.

She hadn't given God a lot more thought until she'd joined AA. Unless you counted the kind of praying that everyone did, which came out of being in a desperate situation and usually involved a trade.

'Please God, get me out of this one and I promise I'll never do anything so stupid again. Amen.'

In SJ's experience these kinds of prayers were never answered anyway. So the image of a punishing God who brought down plagues of locusts on bad people had stuck in her head.

When she'd joined AA and seen God mentioned in the Twelve Steps she'd been bitterly disappointed. She didn't think she'd have a hope in hell of getting sober if God was involved, bearing in mind they'd never seen eye to eye before.

But when Dorothy had explained that she should forget any preconceived image she had, and come up with her own personal concept of God, she had seen the whole thing in a different light.

Hughie's suggestion that the word God might actually be substituted with the words Unconditional Love was a new one to SJ.

As was the idea that God might actually work through other people.

"Maybe it was a coincidence that I was put in your path yesterday," he'd said idly, as he'd sat on her sofa yesterday. "Or maybe it wasn't."

"You mean it was God?" she'd said flatly.

"Possibly it was God."

"Or possibly it was the fact that you happened to be passing because you'd just come back from a funeral." She'd raised her eyebrows. "Sorry, Hughie, I mean, don't get me wrong. I'm very glad you were there. I'm incredibly grateful. But it doesn't make any sense."

"Why not?"

"Because… if you take that one to its logical conclusion then it means Lilian Singh had to die a totally pointless, meaningless death, just so you could happen to be passing."

He'd nodded. "And my lovely Kathleen. She died a totally pointless death too. Maybe God thought the deaths of two lovely young women were enough, so he did. Maybe he didn't like the idea of another pointless death on his conscience! And not just you, but Didi – what would have become of her?"

SJ hadn't answered this. It was too 'out there', too whacky. And of course there was nothing to say that she would have died if she'd drunk that wine – she probably wouldn't have died yesterday. But she would have been back on the treadmill of alcoholism, wouldn't she? A treadmill that had very nearly killed her the last time she'd stepped onto it.

And if you followed this train of thought to its logical conclusion it meant that if there was some universal force somewhere moving the pieces, making sense of the chains of events, the connections that threaded people together, then she owed her life to two other young women's early demise.

Or maybe that was all utter tosh and not what Hughie had been trying to say at all. Maybe he'd just meant that something good could come out of the most awful tragedies, if you let it. Yesterday she'd thought she had grasped it, but now her head hurt again. She decided to stop thinking about it. Maybe she was just completely nuts.

Half an hour later, as she walked up the path to Tanya and Michael's front door, she had decided she definitely was. Why on earth should today's visit be any different from any of the other times she'd tried to speak to Tanya? The most likely consequence of her turning up unannounced was that she'd get the door slammed in her face. And she'd have wasted the last of her travel money.

Then again, maybe they weren't even in. If they were in, they weren't answering the door. She hadn't even considered that. But then… had a curtain just twitched in the bedroom? She rang the bell again. Even though all of the resolve she'd woken up with was starting to leach away into the summer morning. It was less sultry today, which was a relief.

She was about to turn away when she saw a shadow beyond the glass and then she heard the click of the door being opened and then Tanya was standing in front of her.

"Hello, SJ."

Her friend looked a little thinner than she had the last time they'd met and maybe a little paler, but this only added to her fragile beauty.

"Hi Tan. Um…" She paused. Her intuition had got her this far, but she hadn't really thought this through. "Can I come in?" she said at last. "I really need the loo."

Oh well done. Classy. Could there be a more inane thing to say? Probably not. But it was, at least, effective.

Tanya opened the door properly and stepped back a pace. "You know where it is."

There was no sign of Bethany, SJ registered, as she went upstairs. How odd.

When she got back down Tanya called her into the kitchen. "Would you like coffee? I've got chamomile tea if you'd prefer?"

"Coffee's great," SJ said. She'd had enough chamomile tea yesterday. Hughie had insisted it was more calming than coffee, which it undoubtedly was. But she felt very much in need of coffee right now. This was starting to feel a bit surreal.

"I didn't actually come round to ask if I could use your loo," she said, as Tanya filled up the kettle, her back to SJ.

"No, I know." Tanya said without turning round. "But I'm glad you came round."

That was a giant leap forward. "You are?"

"Yes." She dropped a teaspoon on the side and there was a world of pain in that little clatter. And suddenly SJ knew why her intuition had brought her here. And she knew what to do. She got up and went to stand beside Tanya and in the next moment they were hugging. A messy, awkward kind of hug at first where Tanya's nose bumped hers and then SJ trod on Tanya's toe and then finally they got it right and they just hugged. And SJ could feel that Tanya was trembling a bit and her shoulders were shaking and she was reminded of herself the previous day.

"I'm so sorry," she said. "That I hurt you. It was the very last thing in the world that I meant to do."

"No, SJ, it's me who should be sorry. I was so awful to you. I said the most horrible things."

"I knew you didn't mean them. It's okay." SJ's heart felt really big and full. This had so been the right thing to do. Why hadn't she done it before? Why had she not realised that a hug could sort out a million problems, smooth out the most painful of quarrels.

Tanya's cheekbones were wet when they drew apart. "Look at me," she said, wiping her face with the back of her fingers. "Crying all over you. What am I like? I've done enough crying this morning already."

"Oh my goodness. Why?" SJ was suddenly struck afresh by the fact that Bethany wasn't here. Where's Bethany? Is everything all right?"

"Michael's got her. He always has her when I've got a counselling session. And I always cry my eyes out when I have a session – what's that about?" She smiled as she caught SJ's astonishment. "Yes, that's a bit of a turn up, isn't it? Your totally together friend having therapy. Actually, I'm quite enjoying it. Although I haven't got a dishy counsellor like you had. I've got a woman called Brenda. She's very nice, though."

Tanya picked up the two mugs of coffee she had made and carried them over to the kitchen table. "We've got a lot of catching up to do," she said. "So I think I had better start at the beginning."

SJ nodded. There was something different about Tanya. She was just trying to put her finger on what it was when Tanya suddenly leapt to her feet. "I've forgotten something really important," she said, heading back across the kitchen to a cupboard. She came back carrying a packet of chocolate biscuits and a plate. "These are amazing," she said, ripping open the packet and scattering biscuits onto the plate. "Not just biscuits, but…"

SJ smiled. "Who says advertising doesn't work."

As Tanya pushed the plate across the table, SJ realised what it was that was different. Tanya wasn't wearing nail varnish, yet her nails looked perfect. Beautifully cut and filed in perfect semi circles with white half-moons.

"Have you been to the nail bar?" she asked.

"What? Ah – no," Tanya said, following her gaze. "I'm just taking better care of myself – but not in quite such a perfectionist way. I've realised I don't have to be perfect. That's Brenda's fault," she added. "But anyway. Where were we?"

"Why are you having counselling?"

"Because Michael – and you – well, you were both right. I did – do – have a form of post natal depression. Quite an extreme form, as it happens. I didn't think it was possible. I mean Bethany's three in August. But when I started talking to Brenda I realised that I haven't been right since Bethany was born. It was very…" she broke off.

"You don't need to explain," SJ said.

"Yes, I do. It's okay. I can. I've amazed myself lately over what I can talk about and, SJ, I owe you, of all people, an explanation."

There was steel in her green eyes and SJ realised she hadn't seen that either for a very long time.

That was the other thing that was different – the main thing. Tanya had a new found strength.

"When Michael and I lost Maddie, it broke my heart. Having a baby die inside you, SJ, is the worst thing. Especially so late in the pregnancy. I had to give birth to her, even though I knew – everyone in the delivery room knew – that she was already dead."

SJ nodded. She wanted to tell Tanya to stop – tell her that she didn't have to relive one of the worst times of her life, but she didn't because she could see in Tanya's face that this was what she wanted to say – that this was all part of the deal.

"You don't just lose your baby. You lose the entire future too. Because, of course, by that time you've got it all planned out. You've imagined their first day at school, their graduation ceremony, driving lessons, their first date. I used to have this little fantasy about going to Maddie's wedding. I know it's totally mad. You shouldn't do it. But we all do it, especially if you wait a long time – like Michael and I did – to have a child. It's part of being human, Brenda says."

"Brenda sounds very sensible."

"She is, SJ – she's about twenty-two stone and she has this mass of black hair and she has eleven kids. Eleven kids! Is that even possible?"

"No," SJ breathed. Even though it clearly was.

"Anyway, she's a great counsellor. Totally empathetic, massively perceptive and the most non-judgmental person I've ever met. Apart from you – possibly." Tanya smiled. "When I was pregnant with Bethany, I didn't dare to imagine

271

the future at all. I didn't dare to hope she might survive. I didn't even imagine me or Michael pushing her around the park in her pram. I was too scared."

"It's not surprising, honey."

"I know. But it meant that when she was born I was in total shock. I couldn't quite get my head around the fact that she'd arrived. And I also felt massively guilty. How come she had survived when Maddie hadn't? I was eaten up with guilt. I was too scared to enjoy her. I was convinced something bad was going to happen to her. Or to me. And that feeling got worse and worse and worse." She paused for breath. "Brenda says that I probably didn't grieve for Maddie properly when we lost her. I think she was right. I didn't. And, of course, when Bethany arrived all that unresolved grief came back." She paused once more for breath.

SJ put her hand out and touched Tanya's fingers. "And how do you feel now?"

"I'm getting there." Tanya picked up a chocolate biscuit and bit into it. "I'm sorry that I didn't phone you. I owe you an apology."

"You don't."

"Yes, I do, SJ. You told me the truth. Even though I didn't want to hear it. That's what best friends are supposed to do. And I chucked it all back in your face."

SJ didn't answer. She had not expected the morning to go like this – not in her wildest dreams. Hey, she wasn't dreaming, was she? She wasn't still in her bed, pondering about whether to use the last of her Oyster Card credit to visit Tanya?

"I'm just really, really glad you're okay," she said at last. "I've been worried about you. Does this mean that you and Michael...?" She didn't really want to mention Andy's name, so she broke off.

"Me and Michael are fine. He was never having an affair – of course he wasn't. And Andy, lovely man that he is, has forgiven me for my ranting and for all the nasty things I said. He's been round for dinner a few times. He's really nice. Pity he's gay." She narrowed her eyes thoughtfully. "He'd have suited you, SJ. Shall I get more coffee?"

SJ nodded. "And more biscuits," she called.

"You're stronger than me, SJ," Tanya said, as she tipped out the rest of the packet of biscuits. "You always have been. You faced up to your problems as soon as you realised you had them – you got things sorted – you got your life back on track. I know how hard that was for you, but you did it. And now look at you. You're happy today, aren't you? That's one of the reasons I hadn't phoned you yet. I feel as though you're streets ahead of me. I was trying to pluck up the courage to speak to you."

SJ gasped – always a bad move when eating biscuits. When she'd stopped coughing and could finally speak again, she said, "You wouldn't think that if you'd seen me yesterday afternoon. Yesterday afternoon, I was sitting in The Bentley Arms with a stonking great glass of Chardonnay in front of me. And the only reason I didn't drink it was because someone from AA walked in."

"No!" Tanya said, coming back to the table and putting her hands on the back of the chair she'd been sitting in. "What on earth happened?"

"It's quite a long story," SJ said. "Maybe I'd better start at the beginning."

Chapter Thirty

The first person SJ saw when she got to Barney Hall on Friday evening was Half Pint Hughie. He was sitting down talking to someone, but she couldn't see who because the place was unusually crowded.

She headed towards him and as she got close and could see around the surfeit of heads she saw that he was talking to Number Ten Tim. She hesitated, a little afraid they might be talking about her – and her nearly relapse. Even though logic told her they wouldn't be. Half Pint Hughie was not the gossiping type. She had got that about him too, when he'd spent the afternoon at her flat. Maybe she should catch up with him later. But he'd seen her now, so had Tim, and they were both standing up.

"SJ," Hughie smiled widely. "It's good to see you here, so it is."

"Good to see you too." She pecked him on the cheek.

Tim was smiling too. "Long time no see, sweetheart. I thought you'd disappeared." He stepped forward. "Don't I get one?"

He was talking about a kiss, she realised, after a second or so of confusion. As he leaned closer she could smell the lean, musky scent of him and she was transported back to Boscombe Beach and she felt suddenly shy as she kissed his smooth cheek. She had forgotten how gorgeous he was.

"I thought you'd disappeared too," she said, stepping back and just missing treading on Penny, who gave her an exasperated look.

"Work's mad. I've not been to many meetings. I'm glad I've caught up with you though. I've got a new phone. My old one gave up the ghost a while back and I lost all my numbers."

So that was why he hadn't been in touch. Well possibly why. He was smiling at her, his black eyes warm, his teeth very white.

"Could I have it again?"

"Have what?" He was having a curious effect on her.

"Your phone number?"

"Sure thing." She ruined the cool effect of 'sure thing' firstly by not being able to find her phone in her bag – she really needed to get a smaller one – and then by dropping it on the floor when she did finally locate it.

Both Tim and Hughie bent to pick it up. But Tim, being about thirty years younger and more agile, was quickest.

"Thanks," she said, her face flushing scarlet as he passed it over and their fingers touched. What is wrong with you, SJ? He must think you're completely nuts.

She was about to put it back in her bag, having by now completely forgotten why she'd got it out in the first place, when Tim said, "Would it be easier if I just gave you mine?"

"No, I'm there. Right, here we go." He stood very close to her while she read out her number, tapping it into his smartphone with long agile fingers. His fingernails were very pale in contrast to his skin. She watched him mesmerised. Why was she imagining how his fingers might feel if they were linked with hers? For heaven's sake, SJ. She hadn't met a man who'd had this effect on her since Kit.

At the thought of Kit her face sobered and Tim finished what he was doing and glanced at her at just the wrong moment.

"Is everything okay, SJ? You look a bit…"

"Yes, it's fine." She scuttled away from him before she could make any bigger fool of herself. Luckily the meeting was just about to start. People were taking their seats. She found a spare one right at the back and sat on it, her heart pounding madly. She was acting like a ridiculous teenager. She had to get a grip. Tim wasn't in the slightest bit interested in her. He was just being kind.

It was routine for people to swap phone numbers at AA; men to women, as well as men to men and women to women. She was probably one of dozens on his list. She stared at her hands and didn't glance up until someone came and sat beside her. But when she did look up, it was slap bang into Tim's eyes.

"Last seat," he said, with a wink. "Don't mind if I sit here, do you?"

She shook her head. Barney Hall was a bit of a crush tonight and it was hot too. The scents of people were all around: women's perfume; men's aftershave; sweat; cigarette smoke, and somewhere not too far from her the sickly smell of alcohol. Someone close by to them had been drinking recently. SJ felt a pang of sympathy. That could so easily have been her. Would she even have come to this meeting if she'd drunk that wine in the Bentley Arms? No, she wouldn't. She would have been too ashamed, too full of self-pity – too full of a thousand things. Would she have ever come to this meeting again?

The combination of her churning thoughts and the fact that Tim was sitting beside her meant that she barely heard a word of the share. She was very conscious of Tim's presence, his long denim-clad legs almost touching hers. It was odd seeing Tim in jeans and a blue cotton shirt, open at the neck. He usually came straight from work and was wearing a suit. The last time she'd seen him this casual they'd been at the beach. Just before Kit had died.

Bloody hell, she found that she was blinking away tears again. She might not have drunk anything but she was still a wreck emotionally. Thank heavens for Half Pint Hughie. Where was he? She was tempted to go and find him and give him a big hug.

As the meeting drew to a close and the pot was passed round the room for donations, Tim leaned in close to her. "SJ, have you got a minute or are you rushing off?"

"I'm not rushing off." Her mouth felt dry. What on earth could he want?

She followed him outside into the cooling evening. A crowd of smokers parted to let them through. Most of them were puffing on electronic cigarettes, although there were still a few old timers on roll ups. How times had changed. SJ was quite tempted to get an electronic cigarette – even though she had given up smoking ages ago. Just so she could join in. Apparently they had all sorts of different flavours: vanilla; Morello cherry; mint; rum – hmmm, funny how quickly her mind flicked back to alcohol. More evidence of her nuttiness, she acknowledged with a little sigh.

"I heard about Kit Oakley," Tim said when they were a little apart from the group. "I didn't know him personally, but I'm a mate of Ebby's and he told me what had happened. He mentioned you two used to be close – I hope you don't mind me asking, but I was…am…a bit worried about you."

SJ was about to protest that she was fine. But Hughie's voice popped into her head. 'We need to acknowledge that bad stuff happens too.'

"Yes, Kit and I were close once," she said quietly. "It was a huge shock when I saw him in such a state. I always thought he would be okay. I knew he was – you know – having problems but I didn't expect him to die. He was so strong. Mentally, I mean. He was brilliant when I gave up drinking."

"It can happen to the best of us," Tim said. "Just one mistake, one slip, one weak moment. Some people never come back from that." His eyes were very serious and she wondered if he knew about hers: sitting alone in a pub with a glass of temptation in her hand. Alco's voice telling her it would be okay. Already it seemed impossible. Light years away. But it wasn't. Maybe it never would be.

Thank heavens for Hughie.

There was a pause. She glanced longingly at the smokers. Maybe she should take up smoking again. Yes fine plan, SJ. After all, you've got plenty of money to burn, haven't you!

"He was alone, you know, Tim – that last night in hospital. It was just me and Ebby holding his hands. I don't even know if he could hear what we were saying."

"I'm sure he could." Tim touched her arm in a little gesture of camaraderie. "My ex – the one who was the lab technician – told me once that the hearing is the last sense to go. I'm sure Kit knew you were there with him. And I'm sure it gave him great comfort."

"Thank you," she said, struggling to swallow a huge lump that had risen in her throat.

"Hey – I didn't mean to make you cry."

"I'm not crying." She was, though. Crap – she should definitely be out of tears by now.

Tim was patting his jean pockets and frowning.

"Sorry, no tissues."

"I have an endless supply," SJ said, dipping back into her bag. Mostly screwed up ones. Damn. She blew her nose loudly. "I've sorted things out with Tanya, though," she said, anxious to prove she wasn't a complete saddo. "Remember the friend I told you about on the coach. I went to see her."

"Excellent." He smiled at her. "If ever you need a friend, SJ – you will phone me, won't you?"

A friend! Of course that's how he saw her. How else would he see her?

"Sure," she said, in her brightest voice. "I'll be straight on the phone."

He glanced at her, clearly puzzled, and then someone on the edge of the group of smokers waved at him.

"Tim, honey. There you are – I need your advice…"

It was a woman. Of course it was a woman. Tall, willowy, super glamorous – she looked a bit like a black Marilyn Monroe. SJ shot her a smile and tried not to feel snubbed when it wasn't returned.

Tim murmured his apologies before turning towards Marilyn, who put her hand on his arm and steered him away. SJ couldn't hear anything else of their conversation.

She was suddenly alone in the dusky air with a huge Tim shaped hole beside her.

Chapter Thirty-One

"I can't believe how close I came to blowing it, Dorothy. I can't believe I was going to throw away nearly five years of sobriety for a glass of Chardonnay."

"But you didn't," Dorothy said for what must have been the fifth or sixth time since they'd been talking. "So, stop beating yourself up, hen."

She broke off because her phone was ringing again. Glancing at SJ apologetically she said. "Sorry, I need to take this."

SJ nodded. Dorothy had only been home twenty-four hours, but clearly she wasn't the only person who was thrilled to have her back. The phone had already rung about fifty times.

She pulled her mobile out of her bag to check it while Dorothy said in a soft voice. "Could I phone you back in a wee while, I've got a friend here."

There was a text from Didi.

DIDI TO BASE – DAY TWENTY-ONE. GET ME.

ROGER THAT, SJ typed back, feeling a little thrill of pleasure. *GET YOU, INDEED*. Who'd have thought she'd have got so much satisfaction out of someone else's sobriety? She must actually be getting less selfish.

She was very glad Dorothy was back, though. It felt wonderful to be sitting in her comfortable burgundy lounge, drinking chamomile tea. Dorothy hadn't even unpacked properly yet. A couple of posh frocks hung on the back of the lounge door and there was a half open case by the television.

She should probably have given Dorothy a bit more time before turning up and pouring out her heart. Maybe she wasn't getting any less selfish, after all.

"Where were we?" Dorothy said, putting the phone back in its cradle. "I've turned that off now so we won't be disturbed."

"I was just telling you that I didn't drink that wine for all the wrong reasons," SJ said thoughtfully. "We're supposed to stay sober for ourselves, aren't we? That's what you've taught me anyway. It was only the thought of Didi that stopped me. I didn't care about staying sober for myself."

"Working the program is what keeps us sober," Dorothy said with a slightly exasperated sigh. "And sponsoring other people is part of the program. So I think we can safely say that you were working the program, could we not?"

She gave SJ one of her serene smiles.

SJ felt breathless. Until that moment she hadn't looked at it like that at all. "I suppose I was!" she said wonderingly. "Well, get me!"

"Now, in other news…" Dorothy said, raising her eyebrows in a 'thank-heavens-we've-got-that-sorted kind of look. "How is the rest of your life? When is your dad's biopsy?"

"Tomorrow," SJ said. "Monday is the consultant's surgery day. I'm not sure what time, but he has to go in first thing and sit in a queue. Well, not literally a queue, but apparently all the patients who are having surgery tomorrow morning go in at the same time and wait."

"Are you going over there with him?"

SJ shook her head. "Mum's taking him. And she's going to sit with him until he gets called in. Dad's not too keen on hospitals. He doesn't want us all over there, though. He doesn't want any fuss. And they won't have the results back for a week or so." She blinked a few times.

"At least he'll know then what the situation is," Dorothy said, leaning forward and touching her arm. "Which is a step forward, for you all."

"What if he's got cancer, Dorothy? I don't think I could cope."

"What if he hasn't? Why don't you stop second guessing it and wait and see? And you will cope – whatever the outcome. You're a lot stronger than you think."

"Am I?"

"Yes, you are." Dorothy had her no-nonsense voice on. "How about the job front? Have you had any luck with that?"

"No," SJ said. "I can't even get a waitressing job. Mind you, it's not helping that Miguel won't give me a reference."

"Hmmm," Dorothy said. "You're a wee bit over qualified to be a waitress, aren't you? Have you thought about going back into teaching?"

"Not really," SJ said with a sigh. "I think I left that job under a bit of a shadow too."

"Did they actually say that? I thought the college terminated your contract because they didn't have enough students that year."

"That's what they said. I didn't believe them, though. I think it had more to do with my drinking."

"It's worth a phone call though, surely?" Dorothy said. "You're a very talented teacher, SJ. You're inspirational. You know exactly how to get the best out of people." She paused. "Remember that guy who came to Poetry and a Pint for a while a couple of years ago – the one who had Tourette's?"

"How could I forget?" SJ said. "He was rather gorgeous, wasn't he? Despite all his problems."

"And you brought out the best in him. You made him shine, SJ. Did I ever tell you what his carer said to me one night after the session?"

"I don't think so, no."

"She said they'd tried joining all kinds of classes, but the only one he'd really felt comfortable in was yours. It was the only place he'd ever felt confident enough to share his poetry."

"His poetry was brilliant," SJ said. "Genius. Do you remember that amazing sonnet he wrote about the sea?"

"I do, hen. And if you hadn't made him feel comfortable no one would ever have heard it. You did that for him. You let him shine. Lots of people can teach, but not so many are able to inspire. It's quite a rare gift."

Her eyes were sparkling. SJ felt warmed. "Thanks," she said. "For being so lovely. You always say exactly the right things."

"I have my moments," Dorothy said. "But I mean it about the teaching. Will you get in touch with the college?"

"Well, as you're the second person who's mentioned it lately, I probably will."

"Ouch," Dorothy said. "So my advice isn't good enough to take on its own."

"I didn't mean that," SJ said in alarm.

"I'm teasing you, hen. So who was the other person?"

"Half Pint Hughie."

"Ah – yes, well he's a lot more sensible than most people give him credit for – but I expect you got that when he spent the afternoon at your flat. I'm going to make another drink. Would you like one?"

Dorothy got up, more slowly than she usually did and SJ looked at her in concern. "Are you okay?"

"I pulled a muscle in my back when I was learning to dance the tango."

"Dance the tango? Wow! You never said!"

"We've been talking about you." She headed for the kitchen. "I met a man too," she called back over her shoulder. "He doesn't live a million miles away. I think I might see him again."

SJ followed her. "How exciting. What's he like? What's his name? What does he do?"

"His name is Stewart Callego," Dorothy said. "He's very kind. He's sixty-two and he's a dance teacher and he's also a recovering alcoholic."

"A toy boy," SJ breathed. "Well, as long as you don't pull too many more muscles. Have you got any photos?"

"He emailed me some," Dorothy said. "I'll show you them in a minute. Now tell me some more about this sponsee of yours. How's she getting on?"

SJ told her as much as she could without breaking any confidences. And ended by saying. "I'm seeing her tomorrow. We're doing the second part of Step One."

"Good luck with that," Dorothy said in a voice that made SJ think she must have given away more about Didi than she'd intended.

287

Chapter Thirty-Two

'Step One – We admitted we were powerless over alcohol – that our lives had become unmanageable.'

"Yes, that's all very well. But what does it actually mean?" Didi asked.

They were sitting in Didi's kitchen, which SJ had decided was a lot easier, in the big scheme of things, than de-whiting her flat every five minutes. Not that she minded de-whiting her flat any more. She would happily have shrouded the whole place in orange throws if she'd thought it would help. But it was more practical to come here.

"I mean in real terms." Didi tapped her red fingernails against the black topped breakfast bar. "Tell me."

"It's simple," SJ said, even though nothing was actually simple where Didi was concerned, because she was the most analytical and possibly the most argumentative person in the universe.

"You admit that you are powerless over alcohol – agreed?"

"I suppose so."

"Good," SJ breathed a sigh of relief. Maybe this was going to be easier than she'd imagined. She was worried about Dad and what was happening at the hospital and she wasn't in the mood for an argumentative Didi as well.

"And you've decided that your life is unmanageable…"

"I've decided that my drinking is unmanageable," Didi corrected with an irritatingly superior smile. "The rest of my life is perfectly manageable."

"I thought we'd agreed that having to avoid all things white was a little bit unmanageable," SJ said patiently.

"I'm used to it."

"Yes, but that's not actually the point I'm making. The point I'm making is that it's not exactly manageable – and what about the gym?"

"What about the gym?" Didi looked annoyed but SJ was relentless.

"Normal people with manageable lives don't go to the gym for seven hour sessions."

"It was only six yesterday. And going to the gym is very good for you. Anyone will tell you that! In fact, you should go – I could get you a free trial offer if you like? I know them very well."

"I bet," SJ said under her breath. "I don't want to join a gym." She put up a hand to stop Didi interrupting. "Even though, yes, I agree that it's healthy. But you're not doing it for health reasons."

"Of course I am."

"You're not."

"Am."

"Not."

"Am."

"Didi, for goodness sake, this is getting us nowhere. I think you are going to the gym as an alternative to drinking."

"That is completely ridiculous. Going to the gym is healthy. Drinking is not healthy. How can it possibly be a substitute? And even if it was…" There was a glint of triumph in Didi's eyes. "At least it's a healthy substitute."

"Nothing is healthy if you're obsessive about it. Don't you remember our chat about alcoholics and obsessions?"

Didi folded her arms and opened her mouth.

"Anyway," SJ said, knowing she was about to be completely diverted from Step One, or any other sensible conversation they were supposed to be having, but unable to resist. "How do you manage with the white stuff at the gym? Haven't they got loads of white equipment?"

"I use a blindfold," Didi said, blinking slowly. "I have a selection."

SJ nearly fell off her stool. "You *are* kidding me. How do you know where you're going? Don't you get some funny looks? Actually, I suppose you wouldn't know if you did, would you?" She giggled at her own wit.

Didi was smiling like a cat.

"You are kidding me, aren't you?"

"I am. Entertaining idea, though. Although rather dangerous in practice I should think. Especially on the running machines. I wear tinted contact lenses, SJ. They make them for skiers – to cut out the glare of the snow. They're perfect."

"That's brilliant." SJ paused, her thoughts churning madly. "So why don't you wear them all the time – wouldn't that be easier than having to avoid white?"

"Not really. They make everything look a bit too dark, which is depressing. And they dry out my eyes if I wear them too much. They are very handy for emergencies, though."

"Right." SJ paused, wondering if she could ask Didi the other burning question she had, which was about how she got on with white-skinned naked men. This was absolutely none of her business. She knew that, but it had been bugging her for weeks.

"Yes?" Didi said, as if she was expecting SJ to ask something else.

Oh, what the heck. Why not? While they were in banter mode. "Do you use the tinted lenses when you're working then, or do all of your – um – clients have tans?"

Didi laughed in delight. "What a question! I'll tell you the answer to that if you tell me more about those dog whisperer classes you're allegedly doing."

"I'm not doing them," SJ said promptly. "The class doesn't even exist. I made it all up."

"You made up the fact that there was a dog whisperer class." Didi widened her eyes incredulously. "And you think that MY life is unmanageable. Why on earth did you do that?"

Oh crap, this was humiliating. "I made them up," she said slowly, "because…" Her mobile started to ring. Phew. Saved by the bell. She rummaged for it in case it was Mum – Dad may have been in for his surgery by now – and whisked it out.

"Sorry, gotta get this. Hi, Mum."

291

"Sarah-Jane, is that you?"

She was tempted to say, of course it's me, you just phoned me – but her mother sounded distraught. "What's happening? Is Dad okay?"

"No, no he's not." SJ sat up straighter on her stool. "He's really not. They did the biopsy and...and...and it isn't...it isn't very good..." Mum's voice broke and SJ felt a terrible fear spiking through her heart. "They've just had to rush him back into theatre." She began to sob. "Can you come, please, Sarah-Jane? I don't know what to do."

"Of course I'll come. Of course I will. Where are you? What ward is he on?"

She wrote down the details on a piece of pale blue note paper that Didi pushed across the breakfast bar towards her and then disconnected. The shaking that had started in her stomach spread through to her fingers and her hands trembled as she tried to pick up the piece of notepaper.

"It's my dad. Oh, Didi, it's my dad. I have to go."

"I'll drive you."

"But, Didi, you can't it's a hospit..."

"It's fine." Didi's voice was ice calm. "It's the quickest way. Just give me two minutes."

She disappeared from the kitchen. SJ stayed where she was on the stool. Her head felt oddly light. All her senses were on full alert. She could hear Didi's feet on the stairs, smell the white lily air freshener in the hall – odd that there had never been any white lilies, just their essence trapped in

292

an electronic freshener. She could feel the dampness of her own sweat in her hair. It was like being in a bubble of other-worldliness where everything had slowed up and the smallest of details seemed significant.

"Okay, are you ready?" Didi had reappeared in the doorway, dressed in her long, black leather coat.

SJ nodded. "I could get a taxi," she said, wiping her hands, which felt clammy, on her jeans and following Didi out of the front door.

"It would cost you a fortune. And you're broke, aren't you?"

"I meant – well…Maybe, I could borrow some money…"

"This is quicker." Didi pointed a remote at the electronic door of her garage, which opened to reveal a black Mercedes Sports.

"I'd pay it back." She began to fumble with the zip on her bag.

"You're in no fit state." Didi flicked SJ an irritated glance. "Stop arguing and get in."

The passenger seat was very close to the ground and quite an effort to slide into. SJ could feel her heart starting to race. She couldn't stop thinking of Mum's sobs and her father. If anything happened to her lovely dad.

"I'm sure he'll be fine," Didi said, giving her a quick glance as she reversed out of the drive. "He's in the right place."

She cut through the London traffic expertly. Never breaking the speed limit, but nipping down back streets SJ hadn't known existed.

Mind you, Didi did have the help of her in-car satnav, which, SJ realised with a distant, observer-like part of her mind, didn't order Didi around but said things like, *'take the next left, please.'* Had Didi had that made especially too? Was she so paranoid about being out of control that even her satnav was deferential?

Didi was a very good person to have about in a crisis. Very calm. Very composed. SJ was surprised on one level and not in the slightest surprised on another. Anyone who made as much money as Didi clearly did from her profession would have to instil the utmost confidence in her clients. The utmost trust.

Until that moment, SJ had never considered the question of whether she trusted Didi. She had known Didi trusted her. When they had met she had told Didi that honesty was vital. That trust was right up there at the top of the list when it came to Must Haves in Relationships. That if the sponsor-sponsee thing was going to work, there could be no lies.

Trust had been a deal breaker between her and Kit. And it had once been a deal breaker between her and Tanya. SJ was hell bent on making sure that it didn't bugger up any of her other relationships.

"Anything you tell me is in strictest confidence," she had told Didi. "And I'd like that to be reciprocal."

"Of course," Didi had said lazily. "Trust is very important in my profession too. If my clients didn't trust me completely they wouldn't return."

This hadn't been quite what SJ had meant, but she'd known it was all she was going to get.

Now, as she watched Didi's elegant fingers gripping the steering wheel, the gold sovereign ring she always wore glinting in the sunlight, her perfect nails gleaming – her perfect mask for the outside world in place, SJ realised that she did trust her.

Right now, there was no one else she'd rather have had beside her. It was a strange feeling. Didi had run her ragged in the few short weeks she had known her. She had been flaky, unreliable and utterly selfish. But she was none of those things now. It was quite humbling.

"Thank you so much," SJ said, as they drew into the hospital car park. The same hospital car park where she had sobbed in Ebby's arms only a month ago. Bad memory overlaid bad memory. As Didi drove around looking for a space SJ found it got harder and harder to breathe.

"Let me give you some money," she gasped, as Didi finally found a space.

She unzipped her bag and fumbled for her purse. Her fingers still weren't working very well. She must be in shock. How weird.

"Don't be ridiculous," Didi said, getting out of the driver's seat with effortless elegance and coming round to open SJ's door.

"I want to." As she scrambled to get out, SJ's bag tilted and most of its contents scattered over the tarmac and into the foot well of Didi's car.

She bent over to pick them up, but it was suddenly impossible to breathe. The harder she

295

tried to suck air into her lungs the less there seemed to be until she was gasping. And still there wasn't enough. Her heart was going at a thousand miles an hour and her surroundings had gone out of focus. The world was a blur of no breath and fear. No blood was left in her skin, yet she felt trapped in her own body. A dizzying sickness rose up fast.

"Take deep breaths," Didi's voice cut through the terror. "Nice slow ones. In...out, in...out, in...out. That's it. Nice and easy. There's nothing you can do while you're panicking. Nothing at all. In...out...in...out, in...out. That's it. That's very good."

She had never heard Didi go into full control mode before. Her accent was very cut glass, very authoritarian, very soothing. It felt odd, but desperately reassuring.

Until that moment she hadn't realised she was gripping on tight to the handle of the car door. It was the only solid thing in the world. That and Didi's voice, which was starting to calm her, starting to bring the rest of the world back into focus.

"In, out. In, out, that's it. Is it going off?"

SJ nodded. "A bit." She gulped, stared down at her fingers. The blood was flowing back into her white knuckles. She was starting to feel less sick. "What happened? What was that?"

"Panic attack. They're a lot more common than people think."

"I thought I was going to die."

"They're very frightening. But harmless. Although there is a physical reason apparently. They're brought on by shallow breathing so you end up with a build-up of carbon dioxide in the body."

"Right." SJ was close to tears.

"The best way to deal with them is to slow your breathing."

"You sound like you know all about them."

"I do." Didi smiled. "Are you feeling better?"

"Much." She started to retrieve her possessions from the foot well: a comb, her purse and her railcard that had fallen out of it. The only trouble was she kept dropping them again.

"No, you're not." Didi gave a little sigh. "Sit still for a moment."

"Sorry," SJ said.

"It's okay. You're upset. Understandably." Didi knelt on the tarmac, gathering items, her face in profile so it was impossible to tell what she was thinking. She handed a nail file, a pack of tissues and three pound coins to SJ. "I'll come in with you."

"You don't need to do that."

"I think I do." For a moment her eyes met SJ's. "You would do the same for me."

Chapter Thirty-Three

Didi took hold of her arm, as if she were a little infirm, and marched her through the glass double doors of the hospital and into reception. SJ gave up trying to stop her. She had started to feel strangely detached, as if all of the morning's events were happening to someone else and that she was a disconnected onlooker.

At the desk, she watched Didi ask the unsmiling woman on duty where Ward H4 was and then interrogate her for directions.

"Turn left past A&E, then first right, follow the signs for Oncology, past the pharmacy, keep going straight. It's a very long corridor. For Ward H4, go to the end and turn left."

Didi was still gripping her arm. But it was only as they set off that SJ realised that Didi was holding on so tightly because it was the only way she could cope. Not that you could tell any of this from her face, which was a study in blankness.

It was how she had coped when she was small, SJ remembered. They'd talked about it once, although she doubted Didi could remember the conversation because she'd been out of her head on vodka at the time.

"I used to pretend I was Rapunzel," Didi had said. "And that I was being held prisoner in a tower by a wicked wizard. The room where Dad used to take me was in the attic conversion in our house so it wasn't such a massive jump. Except for a table with the sheet there was no furniture. And there were no windows, just one skylight way up high.

"I used to lie on that table looking up at that square of blue," Didi had continued, her eyes dreamy. "Sometimes a bird would fly past and I would pretend it was a prince's messenger, sent to find me. I would pretend that one day a prince would follow. He would come riding up on his jet black charger. He would slay the wicked wizard with one blow from his sword. Then he would scoop me up, and take me off to his red and black castle where we would live out the rest of our lives in separate rooms."

A macabre twist on the classic fairy tale, SJ had thought, wanting to weep for the child Didi had once been.

"I was glad really, when it didn't happen," Didi had said at the end of her story. "Because Daddy would have been slain and I loved my daddy."

Beside her now, Didi's movements had become mechanical. She was putting one foot in front of the other by sheer force of will. They'd reached the long corridor. It was very bright. Windows dotted along one wall let in the sun and highlighted its whiteness. A trolley, being pushed by a porter, was heading towards them at speed.

As it passed them SJ felt Didi flinch. Her gaze was fixed on the unconscious woman who was wearing a regulation, blue cotton gown, one of its tie-up tapes dangling over the edge of the trolley. Her hips were barely covered by a white blanket.

"Didi, are you okay?"

For a second Didi didn't seem to hear her and SJ knew she was in a place far away. A make believe hospital with a make believe patient and a make believe dad. The kind of make believe that no child should ever have to bear: that no adult should ever have to remember. "Didi," she said urgently. "Are you okay? Talk to me."

"I'm fine." Didi's voice was ghost-like. Fragile as dust. A little girl's voice in a little girl's past.

SJ gave herself a shake. The disconnected feeling was starting to fade and she felt more normal. Didi had got her here. Now it was her turn to help Didi. Her turn to haul Didi back from unseen terrors that were no more real, no more dangerous than her panic attack had been, although she knew without a shadow of doubt that they were equally terrifying.

How the hell did she do that?

"Didi, listen to me. Hey. Come back to me." She waved a hand in front of Didi's face. Her eyes were glassy.

If it had been a film, SJ would have slapped her face. Wasn't that supposed to shock people back into reality? She was pretty sure that slapping people's faces was much more effective at adding tension to television dramas than having any real actual practical value.

"I made up the dog whisperer classes," she said, "Because I'd already made a complete and utter fool of myself answering the phone. I was trying to be cool by saying yep and I said yip instead. That's just typical of me. I'm an utter plonker. If I can muck something up, I will."

She knew she was gabbling, but Didi was at least now listening. Her eyes flickered. She looked like she was coming out of a trance.

"Did I ever tell you I was totally in awe of you when we first met? Do you remember the woman in the lime green coat? I thought she was you. I went up behind her and I said what an amazing coat she was wearing because I wanted to say something nice. I thought she – you – might be scared."

"I was scared." Didi's voice was still a thread but at least she was here. She was talking. They were in a bright, white hospital and not the dark old past.

"It takes a lot of courage going to your first meeting, not knowing what you're going to find."

"I wasn't brave," Didi said. "I was drunk. I had a half bottle of voddie in my bag."

"I know. Well not about the voddie, obviously, but I knew you'd been drinking."

"Yes." Didi gave a half smile. "You're the most intuitive person I've ever met." Now she met SJ's eyes. "And the bravest. And the kindest… And you have no idea how much you've helped me."

SJ stared at her in amazement. They had come to a halt by a grey painted door that led off to a ward. Didi seemed more comfortable out of the white corridor. She was starting to get some colour back in her cheeks.

"I've never had a real friend," Didi said, clasping and unclasping her fingers, which were linked in front of her. "I didn't mix very well when I was small. And when I grew up there were

301

just people I got drunk with. I never let any of them get close. I've never had a friend like you, SJ. Someone who didn't want anything back, I mean. Someone who just wanted to help because they cared." A tear rolled down her cheek and SJ rummaged in her bag for her pack of tissues.

Didi took them and wiped her face. "I wasn't exactly grateful either, was I? I led you on a right old merry dance. I've let you down, over and over again. I was so up myself. I let you think I was an actor, back then, didn't I? Someone important."

SJ smiled. "I thought you were on television." She remembered the silly fantasy she'd had about Didi telling Ant and Dec she had saved her life and the stirring music and the applause – the shallow glittering nonsense of it all.

Another tear ran down Didi's face. SJ realised it was the first time she had ever seen her cry, and she ached.

"You didn't deserve what happened to you," she said fiercely. "You deserved to have loving parents who protected you and kept you safe. But your father doesn't have to control your life for another minute. Another second. I promise you, Didi. We can't change our pasts. But we can change what happens today. With the right support, we can do things we wouldn't have dreamed were possible on our own."

"I believe you." Didi dabbed at her nose and put the rest of SJ's tissues in her bag. There was trust in her eyes and something else – hope. SJ had never seen such hope in another human being's eyes.

She swallowed. Standing here now in a hospital corridor beside this beautiful, fragile woman – hearing her talk about friendship and unconditional love – had touched her beyond belief. The reality of what she felt, right now in this moment. The joy of knowing she'd helped another human being – really, really helped them – well, it eclipsed the Ant and Dec fantasy utterly.

It was such an intense moment that SJ almost forgot why they were here. It was Didi who broke it.

"We should find your mum," she said quietly. "Shall I come with you or would you rather I slipped away? I could wait in the car park – if you need a lift back, I mean."

And then the question was suddenly rhetorical because SJ could see her mother hurrying up the corridor towards them. She was wearing her best navy blue coat, but she had done the buttons up wrong so it hung lopsided. She would never have done such a thing if she was in her right mind.

"Sarah-Jane. Oh my goodness. Thank heavens." She looked dazed.

SJ hugged her. "Mum, this is my friend, Didi. She gave me a lift."

"Hello, love." Mum was polite, even in her distress. "That's kind of you, thank you." She turned back to SJ. "It's okay, I mean it's not okay. But it's not as bad as I thought. I think I may have got you here under false pretences."

"You're not making any sense."

"No. Sorry. I'm not." Mum took a shuddering breath. "When they did the biopsy they also took out the lump thing, you know that they found, and they're pretty sure it's harmless. It's not a tumour – I don't know how they can tell, but Mrs Khan said it's not the right kind, although they'll send it away to be sure." She dabbed at her eyes.

"Maybe you should sit down." SJ looked around for a chair, but it was Didi who fetched a grey plastic chair from a pile at the entrance to the ward. She put it down against the wall and SJ's mother sat in it with relief.

"Thank you, dear. Your dad was in the recovery room but then he starting bleeding – you know from the surgery. They had to rush him back into theatre to stop it. That's when I phoned you. But it's all right. He's going to be fine. I just spoke to the surgeon. He's absolutely fine." She took another deep breath. "Listen to me! I'm all of a dither."

"You've had a shock," SJ said. "I'm really glad you called me. Where's Dad now?"

"He's in the recovery room again. It'll be a little while before he's well enough to go back on the ward. We can see him later."

"Have you eaten anything?" Didi said. She had her authoritative voice on again. "I think I saw a canteen near the foyer, where we came in."

She was shifting from foot to foot. She may have got used to the idea of being inside a hospital but she was still pretty edgy, SJ realised.

"Let's all go," she said. "And then you can get back, Didi, if you need to. I'm sure you're pretty busy."

"I am." Didi shot her a look of gratitude. "Thank you."

In the canteen, which had pale green tables and chairs and a slate grey floor (SJ was nearly as attuned to colours today as Didi was) SJ found her mother a place to sit and then walked with Didi towards the door. "Thank you so much," she said softly. "For coming here."

"Tinted lenses," Didi said with a streak of her old flippancy, "are a wonderful invention."

"So's courage," SJ said and something flickered in Didi's face.

"That question you asked me earlier," she said with a slight lift of one eyebrow. "About human skin?"

"Yes?" SJ was agog, only partially aware of the smattering of people around them, the clattering of cutlery, the hissing of a coffee machine on the counter.

"Well, generally speaking, it's more pink than white. I don't mind pink." Didi smirked, then paused as if she wanted to say something else, but couldn't quite find the words.

"What?" SJ prompted, hoping for something salacious.

"Regarding Step One." Didi flushed. "Maybe my life is a tiny bit unmanageable, after all."

Chapter Thirty-Four

Epping Forest was at its most beautiful in July, SJ thought, as she and Didi followed Tanya and Bethany down a sandy path, which led between an avenue of old trees. On either side of them ferns spread across the forest floor in a vibrant, foot-high green carpet, and the air smelled of hot earth and summer. Tanya was carrying a picnic basket, one of the old fashioned types made of wicker with leather straps around it.

Didi was pushing the buggy, which was packed with another two carrier bags of provisions and SJ was carrying a giant tartan throw, which Tanya kept especially for picnics. They had enough food to feed an army, probably. Tanya always went overboard on food.

Ahead of them, Bethany zigzagged across the path with her arms outstretched, making aeroplane noises.

"I don't know where she gets the energy," SJ said. "How far are we going anyway?" Picturesque as it was, walking was not her favourite pastime unless you had a dog – which they didn't. And she was also starving, having missed breakfast. One bit of the forest looked the same as any other bit as far as she could see.

"Not far," Tanya said, flicking a glance back over her shoulder. "There's a little stream just up here. It's the most peaceful place on earth."

"Sounds fabulous," Didi said, adding more quietly to SJ, "And no doubt beset with flies."

SJ smiled. She'd been a bit worried about today. She'd been worried that Tanya and Didi might not hit it off. The first time they'd met the circumstances had been – well – extreme wouldn't have been overstating it to be honest.

The first time they had met had been after that afternoon at the hospital. Once SJ had seen with her own eyes that Dad really was okay, and she'd spoken to his consultant and left Mum with Alison and Clive, she had phoned Didi and discovered that she hadn't gone home at all but was still sitting in the hospital car park.

"I thought you might need a lift back," Didi had said in explanation, but her voice hadn't been quite steady and when SJ had sunk into the passenger seat beside her she had seen that Didi's face was wet with tears.

"Okay, so I couldn't see straight to drive," she said. "What of it?"

"Come back to mine," SJ had said. "I've got some cold chicken in the fridge." Didi had nodded and gripped the steering wheel hard to stop her fingers trembling and SJ had thought that sometimes you needed to forget about nightmares and Rapunzel locked up in in towers and just focus on the basics, things like getting through the rush hour traffic and having a plate of cold chicken and a friend hovering in the background until you were steady enough to face life again.

They had talked all night and Didi had done a lot more crying and SJ had thought that maybe that always needed to happen. The crying before the healing – as though tears were the physical medium through which pain left the body. In the same way that blood carried oxygen to the heart and lungs via your arteries, the pain in your soul had to be carried out of your body via your tears.

Instinct told SJ that it was important to let out the dark past, before you had room in you for the new and brighter now. Or maybe that was utter tosh. Once again, she had wished Kit was around with his dry, quiet wisdom. Kit would have known exactly what to do with Didi that day.

The one thing SJ was 100 per cent sure of was that tears pressed down inside would fester and become poison. So it was better to get them out. With this in mind, she had supplied Didi with endless tea and tissues and she had hugged her and she had listened to the things Didi had never shared with another living soul.

Things that had made SJ feel physically sick. Things that had taken Didi an ocean of vodka to blot out and at the end of it Didi had been paler – which had struck SJ as ironic – and less imperious. She had been a softer shadow of the spiky, diamond bright woman she had been before.

"I feel like I've lost a part of myself," she had told SJ. "Even though it was a part that was crippling me inside I don't feel as though I'm the same person I was yesterday. That doesn't make any sense."

"It might," SJ said. "When you've had a few days to process it." She hadn't known how she knew this but she had felt the truth of it in her own heart.

Tanya had turned up, unexpectedly, the following morning. Tanya, who had never been short on compassion, but had always been fiercely private, had seen at once that Didi had needed a friend. She had told Didi how she had lost her first little girl. How she'd been obliged to give birth to her dead baby – how she had buried the pain so deep that it had come out as a kind of madness. She had told her story with such courage and humility that SJ had felt awed. And at the end of it she had given Didi Brenda's phone number.

"She's the best counsellor in the world – apart from SJ's Kit," she had said softly. "I'm sure she could help you with your past too, Didi, why don't you call her?"

To SJ's relief Didi had nodded and tucked the card into her bag.

That day had been just over a month ago. That day had been all darkness and hurt. Today was all summer and light – a picnic in the forest with Bethany being an aeroplane, and warmth filtering its way down through the canopy of leaves and touching all of them with optimism.

Tanya had suggested it. She had asked if Didi wanted to come along.

"The more the merrier," she said. "Does she like kids?"

"I'm sure she does," SJ had said, thinking of Didi's impatience, her imperiousness, her slightly cruel streak. The chances of Didi – even the new softer Didi – liking kids seemed pretty remote.

Oh well, she could probably cope for a couple of hours. Bethany was good company – rowdy as a

309

puppy, she wasn't in the slightest bit like her mother – the word tomboy might have been designed for Bethany.

SJ was so wrapped up in her thoughts that she didn't notice they'd even left the main path and were going deeper into the forest until Tanya said, "Here we are. Ta Da – what do you think, guys? Magical isn't it?"

SJ stopped and glanced around. They were in a clearing which sloped down to a stream, well more of a brook really, where the water was clear and sparkling. An old stone bridge, covered in moss and ivy arched across it.

"Put the blanket here," Tanya instructed, setting down the picnic basket on the ground. "It's flat enough for us all to sit. No one ever bothers to walk this far. So we should have the place to ourselves."

Didi had abandoned the buggy and had got out her phone to take a photo.

Bethany was looking at the exposed roots of a tree which fanned out across the forest floor a short distance from where SJ had put the blanket. It looked like a great green hand with mossy knuckles. Bethany's eyes widened in fascination. "Look, Mummy – hands."

Didi glanced at her and then to SJ's surprise she went across and hunkered down to the little girl's level.

"All trees have hands," she said, lowering her voice conspiratorially. "They need them because at night time the trees come alive and they hold hands while they dance."

Bethany looked at her with great suspicion. "No, they don't."

"They do," Didi said, stretching out her red tipped fingers to stroke the root. "They get into a great big circle and they all hold hands and they dance with each other until it gets light. Then they stop moving before the humans get up and see them."

Bethany giggled and stroked the root next to her foot. "It's hot," she exclaimed.

"Dancing makes you hot," Didi said, raising one eyebrow.

Bethany looked at her, considering. "Can you show me how the trees dance?"

"If you like," Didi said, standing up and holding out her hands.

Bethany took them.

"Like this," Didi said, jiggling a little on the spot and then kicking out a booted foot behind her.

They began to dance in a tight little circle. Didi leaned back, laughing, her black bob flying out behind her. Even when she was messing about she had a cool grace, SJ thought. Every movement poised and beautiful, as if she followed some ancient rhythm in her head. Bethany screeched in delight as she let Didi swing her into the air, trusting, so trusting that she wouldn't be dropped, her face screwed up in excitement. "We're doing the tree dance, Mummy," she shouted. "Look. Look!"

"So I see," Tanya said, laughing.

SJ decided she had slipped into an alternative universe. Never in her wildest dreams had she

311

expected Didi to get so effortlessly on to Bethany's wavelength. Didi – whose own childhood had never really got off the ground. Or maybe that was exactly why she could do it. SJ decided to stop analysing it.

"What did you say Didi did for a living?" Tanya asked as she began to unpack scotch eggs and cheese and a very long French stick and a little pack of butter from the picnic basket. "She isn't a teaching assistant, is she?"

"Um no," SJ said, relieved that Didi and Bethany were heading back.

"Can I help?" Didi asked. "Shall I do the drinks?"

"I want to learn the tree dance," Tanya said.

Didi winked. "You can't learn anything on an empty stomach."

After they'd stuffed themselves with the sandwiches they'd made that morning – Didi and Bethany filled theirs with crisps and had a competition to see who could make the loudest crunch – Bethany and Tanya took off their socks and went paddling in the stream.

Didi and SJ stood on the bridge and watched.

"So who would you rather kiss? Christian Bale or Matt Damon?" Didi asked as they stood at the bridge with their arms resting on the warm stone.

"Christian Bale," SJ said without hesitation. "You?"

"I'd kiss Matt Damon," Tanya called up to them. "How about you, Didi?"

"Neither." Didi looked thoughtful. "Benedict Cumberbatch," she said after a slight pause. "He's the only actor I've ever really fancied."

SJ smiled. She wasn't surprised somehow.

"So if we were to go closer to home," Didi said idly. "Who do you fancy?"

"No one," SJ said. "That's sad, isn't it? I haven't fancied anyone for ages."

"How about Number Ten Tim?" Didi's eyes were guileless. "I thought I noticed a frisson between you two in the meeting last week."

"Everyone fancies Tim," SJ said and then paused because Didi was smiling. One of her rare sweet smiles.

"I don't. Although he is fit – I'll give you that. But actually I meant that I think he quite likes you."

"I don't think he does."

Didi picked something up from the forest floor. "Have you ever played pooh sticks?" She twirled a dark twig in her fingers.

"Of course," SJ said. "You throw them in the water and the first one under the bridge wins the race."

"These are match-making pooh sticks." Didi said. "In my right hand is Tim and in my left hand is you." She twirled a shorter lighter coloured twig in her left hand and winked. "Now watch closely." She leaned over the bridge. "If they come out side by side then you'll be together, but if they come out separately you won't."

"I already know the answer to that one," SJ said, her heart beating faster despite herself, as Didi tossed the twigs into the water.

A heartbeat of a pause. "They've both disappeared," she said in disappointment.

"No – they haven't. Look." Didi bent over the water just as the two twigs emerged – so close they were touching.

"How did you do that?" SJ stared at her in disbelief.

"I didn't. Madam Fate did." Didi looked very pleased with herself. "Looks like you two are very well matched. Watch this space."

"I won't hold my breath," SJ said, feeling her heart singing a little. Not because of Tim or the prospect of going out with him, but because today was infused with magic.

Much later when they walked back to the car, having done more paddling, more tree dancing, and quite a bit more eating, Didi said to Tanya. "Thanks for putting me in touch with Brenda."

"Did you phone her?"

"Mmm. I went to see her."

"It might take some time."

"Yes," Didi said, watching Bethany walking in front of them, her hands stuffed in the pockets of her dungarees. "SJ, do you think that if you miss your childhood you can ever get it back?"

"I think you can get joy back," SJ said. "Whatever age you are."

Chapter Thirty-Five

One and a half months later.

Things, for which I am eternally grateful!

1. Dad does not have cancer.

2. Dad does not have constipation any more (which, according to Dad is actually nearly as good as not having cancer).

3. I have the best 'best friend' in the world (when she's not having a mad Post Natal Depression moment, but thankfully they're now few and far between).

4. I have the best sponsee in the world (tinted lenses rock!).

5. I have a new contract with the college. Yesss! Result. Dorothy was right.

6. I am going to be teaching English Lit full time. And I will be earning more money than I've earned for years. (Ever to be honest).

7. Tim is taking me out – okay not taking me out exactly – we're going blackberry picking, but it's just the two of us – so it's kind of a date.

8. ...

SJ studied her list. She didn't know whether to fill in number 8 or not. It was the thing she was most grateful for in the world. For without it, none of the others would be possible. But she didn't want to tempt fate. Technically speaking, she couldn't say that she was grateful for it until tomorrow. Because technically speaking, it wasn't hers until tomorrow.

She glanced at the time and closed her iPad. Then she nipped into the bedroom and had another look in the mirror. Were her best skinny jeans and her pink top suitable attire for blackberry picking?

The top was a bit on the tight side, to be honest. It made her breasts look larger than usual – did she want her breasts to look larger than usual? Or was that too much of a 'check me out, I'm desperate' look?

Was Tim a leg man or a boob man? Was that whole thing about men being one or the other complete tosh? Because obviously women had both, didn't they? And hopefully both were quite nice. Although in her case her breasts were probably better because her legs were a bit wobbly. Well, her thighs were – she'd found a tiny bit of cellulite the other day.

'SJ, you are not going to be taking your jeans off so it doesn't matter.' That was her sensible voice. 'And you are not going to be wearing shorts.' It wasn't that hot. Maybe it was too hot for the pink top, though.

She tugged it off, messed up her hair in the process, which she'd teased into quite a good French plait earlier, and put on a more staid black tee shirt. Now she looked washed out. Bugger. What else was in her wardrobe? Nothing. So much nothing that there was hardly enough room to push the hangers apart. She must have a 'wardrobe clear out day'.

Ha. What was that? A lovely little pink and grey top that she'd bought at a Next sale earlier in the year. She pinged it off the hanger. It was a bit creased. But that probably wouldn't show once it was on.

Hmmm, not bad. Pink and grey suited her dark hair. It had got long lately, partly because she hadn't been able to afford to go to the salon for ages. Hence she'd plaited it, but now it was mussed up. Irritated, she unplaited it. There was just time to redo it before Tim arrived.

The intercom buzzed. No there wasn't. Crap. SJ pressed the front door release so he could get in. It didn't matter. It wasn't a date. It's just blackberry picking. SJ bet he hadn't gone to all this trouble. She bet he'd just thrown on a pair of jeans and a white tee shirt. He often wore white tee shirts. She bet he looked absolutely fab.

"SJ, good to see you." She was right. He did. Gosh, he was tall. The top of his head was almost grazing the top of her door frame. He bent to kiss her cheek. "You ready for the off?"

"Almost. Sorry about the mess..." She gestured through the open doorway towards her immaculate lounge, which she'd tidied in preparation for his visit. The Hoover was now tucked behind the door because she hadn't had time to put it away.

She'd envisioned they might sit in there and have a pre-blackberry-picking chat. Possibly even coffee. But Tim made no move to sit down. He rubbed his hands together. "I've been looking forward to this. Blackberry and apple crumble is my all-time favourite thing in the world."

"Mine too," she said. "Thanks for asking me."

"Happy to have you along. Of course you do realise that I wouldn't ask just anyone to come blackberry picking at the best spot in the world," he quipped. "For a start the location is a closely guarded secret."

"I'm honoured," SJ said, picking up her bag. "Will I have to be blindfolded for the journey?"

"Maybe for the last part," he said, with a suggestive lift of his eyebrows. Or maybe she'd imagined the suggestive bit. She'd been spending way too much time with Didi lately. "Shall we get going then?" he said.

Once they got downstairs she realised why he hadn't been too anxious to hang around. His shiny red sports car, which was even posher than Didi's, was already surrounded by a semi-circle of teenagers.

One of them spat on the ground, close to the back.

"Cool wheels, mate," another one shouted.

"Ta," Tim said, clicking off the central locking but also coming round to open the door for SJ. The semi-circle widened to let him pass.

"Hi, SJ," said one of the girls and SJ recognised her as someone she'd taken to a meeting a couple of weeks earlier.

"Hi, Siobhan, how's it going?"

"Not bad." Siobhan held up her right hand. "Five days. Five fecking days. Never thought I'd do that."

"That's brilliant." SJ gave her a thumbs up sign.

"Well done," Tim said, giving her a wink.

"Respect, Siobhan," shouted the guy who had spat. "Respect."

"They look a bit intimidating, but they're okay mostly," SJ said as they glided away from the estate. "Were you worried about your car?"

"Not really." He glanced at her. "It's just a car. I really was just anxious to get going. They've forecast rain later. And it's an hour or so's drive if there's traffic."

It was, in fact, only about forty-five minutes later that they drew up in the lane on the outskirts of Epping Forest. Not a million miles away from their picnic spot, SJ mused, feeling warmed by the memory.

"My gran used to bring me and my brother here when we were kids," Tim said as he parked beside the five bar gate and they got out of the car. "We used to come here because it was such an out of the way spot. Hardly anyone knew about it and you always got such a bumper crop. You couldn't even see some of the bushes because they were so full of blackberries." He reached into the back and retrieved a plastic tub – the kind that's once held ice cream. "We shall need this."

"You're really building it up," SJ said, following him towards the gate. "What if it's not the same any more?"

319

"It will be." He gestured her ahead of him and closed the gate behind him. His black eyes flashed in the sunlight. "There aren't many things in life you can rely on, SJ, granted. But brambles are definitely one of them."

"Someone may have got here before us."

"Nah, they won't." He was very sure of himself. She liked that in a person – a bright unshakable confidence that had nothing to do with arrogance, but everything to do with feeling comfortable with who you were.

"I have fantastic memories of my childhood," Tim continued. "When I'm in Number Ten I'm going to make it compulsory that all kids get taken blackberry picking in September."

"How about strawberry picking in summer. And apple picking and raspberry picking and gooseberry picking...?"

"Those too." He paused, waiting for her to catch up with him over the uneven bumpy farm track. "And I'll make conker tournaments compulsory too – none of these namby-pamby Health and Safety regulations about how hard you can hit your mate's conker. It's good for kids to be outside."

"I agree." She smiled at him. "I have some brilliant memories of being at the seaside when we were kids. Me and my sister, Alison, had some excellent fights at the beach."

"Yeah. Me and Stephen, too..." He hesitated and she could have kicked herself.

"Was Stephen your brother...? Sorry..."

"SJ, it's okay. It's life, isn't it? It's full of change. People come and people go. We never know how long they're going to be around. Not really."

"I guess we don't." She thought briefly of Kit. It was getting easier to accept that he'd gone. But she would never regret that he'd been in her life. And Tim was right. You never knew how long anyone was going to stay.

Maybe she and Tim would only ever have this one day. In which case she should probably stop thinking about the past and make the most of it.

For a few moments they strolled in silence along the rutted track, which led between fields of gold stubble where the harvest had already been gathered in. It was very peaceful.

"I should blindfold you for the last part of the journey," Tim said, suddenly halting beside an overgrown gate that led off the main track. "So you can't sneak down here and steal the supplies when I'm not looking."

She giggled. "Got one with you, have you?"

He frowned. "What? Ah – a blindfold. Don't need one." In an instant he was beside her. "All I need to do is to cover your eyes, like this."

He demonstrated, gently cupping her eyes with his big hands. Caught off guard, SJ felt a quiver of lust. Crap, she kept forgetting how much she fancied him.

"Just kidding," he took his hands away. There was a sharp brightness in his eyes. He knew exactly what effect he was having on her, the bugger. Did that mean he felt the chemistry too? But then if he did it would mean he was teasing her – and he wasn't the teasing type. Not in a bad way anyway. Maybe he didn't know what effect he was having on her. Maybe she was kidding herself. Maybe the whole chemistry thing was in her head. She'd always had an overactive imagination.

He climbed over the gate and when he was on the other side he held out his hand to help her down.

SJ took it, even though she didn't need any help. Neither did she let go when she was standing beside him. He didn't comment. Still hand in hand, they began to stroll along the narrow grassy track, which was bordered by barbed wire fences and just wide enough for two people to walk side by side.

Did you hold hands with someone who was just a friend? She supposed it was possible. Had she and Tanya ever done it? Nope. She and Didi? Not really – even in the hospital, when they'd both been scared out of their wits, they'd been arm clutching, not hand holding. Arm clutching was for fear – hand holding was for romance.

"Is this another thing you're going to make compulsory when you're in Number Ten?" she asked, lifting up their joined hands.

"Walking in the country – yes," he said, deliberately misunderstanding. "Yes, I think I might."

"How about kissing?" She felt dizzy with her own daring.

"Definitely kissing." He gave her a quick sideways look. "That's if both parties are consenting adults."

"Oh definitely."

"Oh definitely you're consenting – or oh definitely you think it's a good idea."

She waited a beat to tease him, then said, "Both, Tim."

He halted abruptly. "I really did bring you out here to pick blackberries."

"I really did accept your invitation so we could pick blackberries."

There was that smile in his eyes again – the one that she was beginning to fathom meant, *I might seem to be pretty confident with the opposite sex, but actually I'm just as insecure as the next guy.*

He had turned slightly towards her – they were barely touching yet she could feel him. The warmth and the heat of him.

He dipped his head. "We should pick blackberries."

"We really should."

Their lips met. A 'hello you' sort of kiss. A 'hello you' sort of moment. It was lovely. Peaceful, exciting, filled with the promise of more to come. As they drew apart, he stroked her cheek with his cupped hand. The most tender, the most gentle of touches. So much softness in his eyes. SJ never wanted to look away.

"We should pick blackberries before it starts to rain." His voice was a little husky.

SJ looked up into the cloud dotted sky. The sun was just traversing a wide swathe of blue. It would be ages before it disappeared again. "Absolutely," she said.

For a moment they still didn't move. SJ could feel her heart beating very fast. They were in such an out of the way place. Who was likely to come by? No one probably. What if they were to just…? Now she knew that she was not imagining the chemistry. Stop it, SJ. (Bloody sensible voice again.)

If they were going to take this a stage further than friendship, they were definitely not going to do it in a field. A quick fumble in a field. Oh, classy. Very classy. Shut up sensible voice.

"Blackberries," she gasped.

"Blackberries," Tim agreed, grabbing her hand again and picking up the plastic tub from the ground. When had he put that down? "They're around the next corner."

Indeed they were. The lane opened out into a clearing – a little patch of heathland that was circled with blackberry bushes. And oh my, Tim was right. SJ had never seen so many blackberry bushes in one place. Or so many blackberries on one bush.

Tim led her over to the first bush in the clearing, let go of her hand and gave a little bow, as if he had just performed some conjuring trick. Which she supposed in a way he had.

"There must be pounds and pounds and pounds of them." They were so perfectly ripe that the patchy grass was dark with them too.

"Better get picking." He slid out a second plastic tub that must have been tucked inside the first and handed it to her.

They stayed by the first bush. There were so many blackberries that they didn't need to separate. They could probably fill up both tubs from just this one bush. Tim naturally gravitated towards the top of the bramble – he could get the ones out of her reach – and SJ began picking from the middle.

They came away easily in her hands, some a little squashy because they were overripe. "How come there are so many?"

"It's been a perfect summer for them. Plenty of sunshine, just enough rain."

She was a hundred times more aware of him than she had been before they had kissed: a shivery electric chemistry, but somehow there was a peace there too. Not just because of the soft air on her face, the grass beneath her feet, the scent of the countryside, but because he was peaceful. Tim was peaceful. How had she ever thought that he wasn't?

She remembered the first time she'd taken Didi to a meeting. The way her heart had sunk as she'd noticed him heading towards them. She hadn't wanted him to come over. She'd felt super pressured. Perhaps you were in denial, her sensible voice pointed out. Perhaps you knew you fancied him, even then, and you didn't want him coming over because you knew you'd fade into the shadows beside the ultra-glamorous Didi. Had it really been that simple? Maybe it had.

"Penny for them, SJ?" he said.

She wasn't telling him that. One of her latest 'become a better person' strategies was to think before she opened her mouth.

"I, er, was thinking that blackberries are like people," she said, without having the slightest idea of where she was going with that.

"How so?" He stopped picking. He looked intrigued. She was on the spot now.

"Um – well, I guess it's because they are all living side by side with each other but not quite touching. They're all connected but not actually joined." She was warming to her theme now. "And, of course, they're all growing on the same bramble – the bramble being our planet."

Blimey, SJ, that was pretty impressive 'on your feet' thinking, if she did say so herself.

Tim looked pretty impressed too. Or did he just look puzzled?

She was so caught up in her metaphor that she stopped concentrating on what she was doing and snagged her fingers on a thorn.

"Ouch."

Tim frowned. "You okay?"

"I'll live."

"And sometimes our planet throws something at us that's painful," Tim took up the metaphor with gracious ease. "And sometimes it gives us sweetness." He popped the latest blackberry he'd picked into his mouth. "Wowsers that was a good one."

"And some of the blackberries are very extrovert and 'out there'. They know they are beautiful and perfect. 'Look at me,' they shout, 'pick me, pick me.'" SJ reached for a particularly large one in front of her and popped it into her mouth. "Yum – that was a good one too."

"And sometimes they are more introvert and hidden," Tim said, holding back a leaf to reveal a hidden blackberry. "But they are just as beautiful and perfect." He plucked it from the bramble and held it out towards her lips.

She opened her mouth. "Is it purple?" She stuck out her tongue.

"Yep." He placed the blackberry on her tongue with unhurried precision.

She caught his finger in her mouth, closed her lips around the tip of it and sucked gently. He didn't pull away.

Oh my God they should stop this.

"Blackberries," Tim said in a voice that sounded right on the furthest edge of self-control.

"Blackberries." She let him withdraw his finger.

His face was a breath away from hers.

"It might rain," she murmured. Making love in the rain sounded quite romantic.

"Yup."

Had she said that last bit out loud? She glanced at him. He had turned back to the blackberry bush, his face in profile. Maybe not then. Phew!

They resumed their picking. For a while they worked in the silence of the countryside, which was never completely silent: the call of a cuckoo; the distant sound of a plane; and closer by, the rustle of a breeze through the leaves that touched SJ's hair. She was glad she hadn't put it back into a plait. It felt free. She felt free. She hadn't felt this free for years.

Soon both tubs were full, even though they'd only got as far as the second bush. There was a cloud shadow in the clearing – a flicker of light and shade – the smell of rain on the air.

"I know an excellent place we can have lunch."

"Did I tell you it's my birthday tomorrow?" They spoke at the same time and he was the first to speak again. "Which birthday?"

"The important one. My sobriety birthday. Tomorrow, God willing. I will be five years sober."

"That's fantastic. What are you going to do? You must celebrate. Mark the occasion. Have a party."

"A party?" SJ frowned, remembering her dwindling resources. "I like your thinking, but…"

"No buts. It doesn't have to be anything big. I'll help you organise it."

"Now there's an offer I can't refuse." She smiled at him and he touched her face again.

"I was hoping I could come up with quite a few offers you won't want to refuse, SJ."

Chapter Thirty-Six

"So, that's the man you've been keeping under wraps." Alison winked at SJ as she gestured across the room with a perfectly manicured hand. "Well, well, who'd have thought it? Mind you, you always did have a soft spot for older men, didn't you, Sis?"

SJ followed her gaze, saw that she was looking at Half Pint Hughie, and smiled. "Appearances can be deceptive," she said. "That man is one of the kindest, sweetest, most unselfish human beings on the planet."

"He hasn't got any teeth though, has he?" Alison's voice was all honeyed lemons.

"Don't knock it till you've tried it." SJ smiled at Hughie, who was now looking their way. He must have sensed that he was being talked about – or possibly he'd heard that he was being talked about – SJ's lounge wasn't that big, and Alison did have quite a loud voice.

"Let me introduce you," SJ said, beckoning him over. "Hughie, I'd like you to meet my sister, Alison."

"Charmed, I'm sure." Arriving at Alison's side, Hughie leaned in for a kiss, lips puckered, and Alison leaned backwards to avoid him.

SJ suppressed a smile. Even her sister couldn't spoil today. She'd actually thought twice about inviting her. But then she'd relented. After all, she had invited her parents, and Kevin and Sophie. It would have seemed mean not to have invited Alison.

It had taken a while for Mum and Dad to get the significance of the event. "But it's not your birthday," Mum had said, pursing her lips. "So I don't understand how you can say it is."

"It's my sobriety birthday," SJ said. "Which is much more important than my bellybutton birthday. I am five years sober today."

"Bloodeh hell, that's an achievement, love," Dad had said, and had then promptly ruined his apparent understanding of the situation by adding, "Are we to bring a bottle?"

Right at this moment he was sitting in her armchair in the corner of the room chatting to Tim. They were having a whale of a time putting the country to rights. Dad had plenty of ideas for what he'd do when he was in Number Ten too, and Tim seemed to agree with most of them.

Kevin, bless him, was doing his best to chat up Didi, who'd assured SJ when she'd arrived that she'd got her tinted lenses in, which was just as well because Kevin was wearing a blinding white tee shirt beneath his black leather bomber jacket. Every so often, Didi leaned back a little, clearly pained by its brilliance, despite the lenses.

Tanya was chatting to Penny in the hall. Last time SJ had passed them she'd heard the phrase 'dog whisperer classes'. They'd both jumped guiltily when she'd glanced in their direction. But her heart had been so full of bonhomie that she hadn't cared if they were taking the piss. A heart full of bonhomie, a room full of laughter, and there wasn't an alcoholic drink in the place. How cool was that!

Her mantelpiece was crammed with cards. Most of them said things like *Happy Birthday. Five Today*. Even Alison's card had a yellow smiley badge with *Five Today*, attached to the front.

Ebby and Dorothy and Mum and Sophie were on the settee and Dorothy's new man, Stewart, the dance instructor, who'd turned out to be a right old charmer, was perched on the end. Every so often he and Dorothy exchanged glances. They were clearly smitten with each other.

Sixteen of the people she loved most in the world, all crushed into her tiny flat. Who'd have thought that would be possible? Five years of being happy and sad, of laughing and crying, without the aid of an alcoholic drink, who'd have thought that would be possible either?

SJ looked around the room. Someone was missing. Who was it?

Didi had vanished, she realised. Oh gosh, had she had enough already? Had she had to escape? She'd told SJ she might slip away early. Michael was missing too – with Bethany. Maybe he'd taken her to the loo.

But even as she was thinking this there was a bit of a commotion from the direction of the kitchen – a commotion that sounded as though it was heading towards the door of the lounge. There was a sudden hush as an imposing figure appeared in the doorway.

Didi, SJ realised, glancing across – her eyes widening as she saw what Didi was carrying. The most enormous cake she'd ever seen. The most enormous snowy white cake, topped with five blazing candles. She held it aloft – so that it was just inches from her face.

Only SJ knew what anguish that must be causing her. But her face was a mask of perfect calm, her eyes expressionless.

"Happy Birthday to you." It was Bethany's clear high voice, egged on by her father's, that started the age old tune. Then they were all joining in, their voices rising in a raggedy refrain that grew stronger and more beautiful as the song went on. A song that made SJ's heart swell with love for them all.

By the time they got to the final *Happy Birthday to you*, SJ could feel tears on her face. But for once they were the right kind of tears. And she didn't even bother to wipe them away until she'd blown out the candles and rescued Didi from the huge white cake.

"Speech," someone called. "Speech, speech." Until everyone was joining in. SJ put up her hands. "Okay," she said. "Okay. I'll keep it short. I'm sure you all want a piece of cake."

There were murmurs of agreement.

"And all I really want to say is thank you. Thank you all for coming. Thank you for the presents and the cards – there was really no need. But most of all, I want to thank you for the last five years. You have all been a part of my journey. If it wasn't for you guys, I wouldn't be here. If it wasn't for some of you, I may not even be alive." She met Half Pint Hughie's eyes as she spoke and he blinked in acknowledgment.

He had never told anyone about that day in the Bentley Arms. But she had. She had confessed all in a meeting a couple of Fridays later in the hope that it might help someone else.

Just after the meeting a girl had come up and thanked her. "I'd already decided this was to be my last meeting," she'd said. "I'd decided I was going to go straight out of here and get a four pack. Thank you, SJ. I'm not going to do that now."

It was what it was all about, she thought. Not doing things alone – sharing how it was for you. Sharing honestly, unreservedly. No pretence. No lies.

"I've learned a lot about love in these past five years," SJ went on, wishing her voice didn't feel so croaky. "The kind that's unconditional I mean. Not the romantic sort."

Her gaze touched Tim's as she said this and he winked. "Not that I've anything against the romantic sort," she said and Tim mouthed the word, "Phew!"

"But right now I'd like you to raise your glasses with me for a toast." Everyone started hunting around for their glasses of coke and lemonade and in Mum and Dad's case, tea. She should really have warned them she was going to do this. The noise levels and the faffing rose higher and higher and SJ thought she would never get them back.

It was Didi who came to the rescue. She banged the side of her glass with the blade of the knife they had brought in to cut the cake.

"Could you all be upstanding for SJ's toast," she said, and after a bit of grumbling and fidgeting and scrambling they all got to their feet. Not one single person ignored Didi's authority. The room was quieter, even than it had been before.

"To unconditional love," SJ said, raising her glass high.

"To unconditional love," they roared back.

Acknowledgements

Without you guys this book would be much less rich. Thank you so much for your invaluable help and advice.

Angela Westwell, Becky Bagnell, Clarice Clique, David and Cathy Kendrick, Dunford Novelists, Ian Burton, Jan Wright, Jonathan Evans, Paul and Lorna Stafford, Peter Jones, Sarah Palmer, The staff at Poole Hospital, The Wednesday night class.

Thank you all.

Ice And A Slice

The third full-length novel from
Della Galton

Ice And A Slice

Life should be idyllic, and it pretty much is for Sarah-Jane. Marriage to Tom is wonderful, even if he is hardly ever home. And lots of people have catastrophic fall-outs with their sister, don't they? They're bound to make it up some day. Just not right now, OK! And as for her drinking, yes it's true, she occasionally has one glass of wine too many, but everyone does that. It's hardly a massive problem, is it? Her best friend, Tanya, has much worse problems. Sarah-Jane's determined to help her out with them – just as soon as she's convinced Kit, the very nice man at the addiction clinic, that she's perfectly fine.

She is perfectly fine, isn't she?

Praise for Della's novels

"Della's writing is stylish, moving, original and fun : a wonderfully satisfying journey to a destination you can eagerly anticipate without ever guessing."

Liz Smith, Fiction Editor, My Weekly

Visit amazon to
buy the book
and find out more Della's fiction at
DellaGalton.co.uk

Printed in Great Britain
by Amazon